TRUCKER

A GOOD GUYS NOVEL

JAMIE SCHLOSSER

Trucker
Copyright © 2016 Jamie Schlosser
All rights Reserved.

ISBN-13: 978-1535204958
ISBN-10: 1535204958

Cover Design: Oh So Novel
Formatting: Champagne Book Design
Editing: Wordsmith Proofreading Services

DEDICATION

To all the romance addicts out there who love to read about a
good guy—this one is for you!

Angel

I know what you're whispering in the car as you pass me by.

Hitchhiker.

When you see me walking along the side of the road with my thumb out, you'll probably keep driving without giving me a second glance. You probably think I'm foolish. Naïve.

You might assume I've made some bad decisions.

You might think I'm too young to be on my own.

You might be right.

Travis

I love my job, but driving an eighteen-wheeler comes with a certain stereotype. When you hear I'm a trucker, a specific image might come to mind. Uneducated. Dirty. Perverted. Rough around the edges and a little bit dangerous.

But the truth is, I'm not any of those things. In fact, I'm pretty far from it.

You'd be surprised to find out I'm one of the good guys.

PROLOGUE

One Month Earlier

Angel

My aunt's fingers felt cool and smooth as I held her hand in mine. I softly hummed 'Don't Worry Baby' by the Beach Boys as I filed her nails until the edges were rounded and smooth. Claire never wore nail polish. She said she couldn't stand the smell. I wasn't sure if the hospital would have allowed it anyway.

I glanced up at her closed eyes, silently willing them to open, even though I knew—*I knew*—it wasn't going to happen. The steady rise and fall of her chest generated by the machines was a cruel illusion.

I squinted my eyes against the harsh lighting of the sterile room and continued shaping her fingernails while medical terms like 'irreparable brain damage' floated around in my mind.

Brain dead.

That's what the doctors told me.

But I still had a little bit of hope. Miracles happened every day.

After I finished her manicure, I planned to read to her. I'd snagged a gossip magazine from the waiting room, and although it wasn't the best option, it was better than nothing.

Putting down the nail file, I decided to try reading, hoping the sound of my voice might cause some improvement. I picked viii | JAMIE SCHLOSSER

it up and cleared my throat.

"Okay, uhh…" I flipped through the first few pages, passing perfume ads until I came to the first article. "Who wore it best at the VMAs?" I announced the headline.

Well.

She couldn't actually see the dresses, so I skipped ahead a few more pages. "Celebs dish their secrets to achieving—" *multiple orgasms*. I didn't finish the sentence out loud.

I'm not even touching that one.

Then again, if anything could snap Claire out of it, surely it would be the opportunity to torture me with more awkward sex talks.

I closed the magazine, then opened it to a random page somewhere in the middle. "Um… Something about a Kardashian, blah blah blah…"

Oh my God. I really suck at this.

I was willing to bet most of the stuff in there wasn't even true anyway.

Setting the useless gossip aside, I decided I would just bring a book from home next time. Probably *Anne of Green Gables*. My heart warmed at the memories of all the times we'd read it together.

"Claire, please," I pleaded quietly as I grabbed her hand. "Please wake up. You're all I have left."

Was it possible to guilt-trip someone out of a coma? It was worth a shot.

Needing something to do, I went back to filing her already perfectly shaped fingernails.

The door to the room swung open, and Claire's doctor walked in with a nurse following close behind. I squeezed her hand one last time before turning away from the bed.

Their somber expressions had me giving them my full attention.

The doctor was a tall, thin man with wire-rimmed glasses. His salt and pepper hair indicated he was probably in his late forties. He quickly checked over the machines and tubes surrounding my aunt before turning to me.

I felt numb as he told me the stipulations of Claire's will—she didn't want to be kept alive under these circumstances, and she was an organ donor.

"Time is of the essence," the doctor said as he explained what would happen over the next several hours. Claire's healthy organs would be harvested, saving the lives of the lucky recipients. There was no emotion in his voice, no sympathy behind his eyes. He might as well have been telling me what he had for lunch earlier that day.

After the doctor left, the nurse gently patted my arm and I barely registered the words she said. She kept saying things like 'give you a few minutes to say goodbye' and 'social services' and 'foster care'.

"Hon, do you understand what I'm saying?" she asked, but I couldn't respond. "I'll go see if the grief counselor is available."

With hurried footsteps, she left the room. I stared down at the little wooden nail file I was still gripping in my hand as I tried to process the fact that the only person I had was gone.

CHAPTER 1

Present Day

Travis

Stereotype. That thing people did when they made assumptions about the kind of person I was, just because I drove a semi.

When they heard the term 'trucker', they had a certain image in mind—usually one that included a beer gut and a bad case of BO.

Rough around the edges and a little bit dangerous. Uneducated. Perverted.

Much to their surprise, I didn't fit into the mold. In fact, I was far from it. My sexual experience—or lack thereof—was probably the biggest shock of all.

So, how did a guy end up still a virgin at twenty-one?

The short answer was a combination of plain bad luck and standards.

And bad dates. Lots of them. Much like the one I was on right now.

Kendra's grating laughter cut through the air as she drunkenly babbled to herself in the passenger seat of my pickup truck. I'd stopped trying to make sense of what she was saying an hour ago.

When I'd agreed to go out with her, I didn't realize her idea of a good time was main-lining tequila.

Don't get me wrong, I liked to party when the time called for it.

But not on a first date. I could give her the benefit of the doubt—maybe she was just nervous. But it didn't change the fact that I knew there wouldn't be a second date in the future.

The incoherent noises Kendra was making suddenly stopped as she clamped a hand over her mouth.

"I think I'm gonna be sick," she muffled against her palm.

Now *that* I could understand.

I slammed on the brakes to pull over and hoped she could hold it in long enough to make it outside. I followed behind her as she stumbled out of my truck, and I caught her around the waist to keep her from falling into the ditch.

Wrinkling my nose in disgust, I looked away as she started to heave.

My mind decided to take a trip down memory lane to escape the predicament I was currently in the middle of.

I'd had my fair share of disastrous dates, and obviously tonight was no exception.

When I was fifteen, my buddy Colton and I had a double date with a couple of girls from two towns over. Colton had just gotten his license and we thought we were hot shit for getting dates with girls who weren't from our high school.

To top it off, Amanda and Amber were twins. *Twins.*

When we got to their house they showed us to their room and said they were going to the kitchen to get some snacks. Told us to make ourselves at home. Being the nosy pricks that we were, we decided to snoop around.

On opposite sides of the room were matching twin beds with three shelves of collectables on the wall in between. Amanda and Amber seemed to have an unhealthy obsession with unicorns. Glass figurines and snow globes made up most of the collection.

On the other side of the room was a TV. We found an old kickboxing workout DVD and decided to put it on. Mimicking the kicks and punches in such a small space was a bad idea. Because we were rambunctious ass-hats, things quickly got out of control.

Colton sent a high kick to my chest and I fell backwards against the wall, causing all three shelves to collapse. Unicorn horns, broken glass, water, and glitter covered the floor.

It was a unicorn massacre.

Colton and I did the only thing we saw as an option at the time—we ran.

I realized how shitty it was to break all their stuff and leave without even saying goodbye. I still felt bad about it to this day. We ignored angry texts for at least two weeks. Getting text-tag-teamed by twins was brutal. I liked to think that was punishment enough.

When I was sixteen, I got the courage to ask Jenny Jenkins out to a movie. She was cute, smart, and willing to go out with me—all good things.

I arrived at her house on time, just three minutes shy of 7 P.M. Jenny must've been excited because she came out to meet me in front of her house. She said she needed to get her purse from inside and gestured for me to follow.

What happened next was like watching a train wreck in slow motion.

On her way up the steps, Jenny tripped and face planted on the porch. Hard. Between garbled sobs and lots of blood coming out of her mouth, she told me she bit her tongue and to call her mom.

What followed was the shortest, most awkward phone conversation of my life.

We made our way inside to the kitchen, where she grabbed a towel and some ice. I tried my best to comfort her, but she was hysterical.

Her mom showed up a few minutes later and glared at me as if I had personally tried to rip out her daughter's tongue. Jenny managed a "sorry" and something about the hospital and so I left, dateless.

When I tried to talk to her at school on Monday, her face turned bright red and she mumbled something about needing stitches and another "sorry" before making an excuse about getting to class. She was obviously mortified, and the whole situation was so awkward we ended up avoiding each other for the remainder of our high school days.

The summer before my senior year, I got a job with Colton's dad, Hank. He owned Hank's Auto Shop and I loved it.

Around the same time, I started dating Ashley Peterson, one of the hottest girls in my class. We went to homecoming together, had a couple dates, passed notes to each other in the hallway between classes, and spent a few evenings fooling around in the bed of my truck. For a couple months, I thought I was the luckiest guy in the world.

But while I'd been busy working, Ashley had been hooking up with the quarterback.

I was pulled from my thoughts by the sound of retching, and I cringed as I realized Kendra had vomited on my shoes while I was holding her hair back.

I could kill Colton for setting me up with his girlfriend's best friend. But really, it was my own fault for agreeing to go out with her. Even before the date, I knew I didn't have romantic feelings for her.

She was attractive, with dark, shoulder-length hair and brown eyes. With the new summer tan she was sporting, she had a bit of an exotic look going on.

Unfortunately, the girl didn't have much going on upstairs,

and there were times when I'd seen her be a pretty big bitch to Colton's girlfriend, Tara, even though they were supposed to be friends.

Tonight, Kendra had insisted on going to Buck's Tavern where she was a bartender. Being friends with everyone meant free drinks, though I stopped after two beers. The amount of tequila she was able to put away might have been impressive if she could've kept it down.

After leaving the tavern, Kendra begged me to take her for a drive in my '72 Chevy pickup truck.

City folks might not see how driving around aimlessly in the middle of nowhere could be fun, but when you live in a small town, it's necessary to get creative when it comes to entertainment. Country cruising was one of our favorite pastimes.

And now, we were pulled over on the side of a country road while Kendra emptied the contents of her stomach onto my new Redwing boots.

The icing on the cake? It was fifty-cent taco night at Buck's.

At least she didn't puke in my truck.

"I think I'm done now," she half-sobbed.

"I'll take you home," I said, patting her back.

"Nooooo," she moaned. "My parents can't see me like this."

Shit. I forgot she still lived with her parents.

I led her back to my pickup truck and helped her into the passenger seat. "You can stay at my place. I'll take the couch," I said as I buckled her seatbelt.

"You don't have to sleep on the couch," she slurred. "We can share the bed. I can take care of your little problem…"

"My problem?"

She giggled. "Yeah, you know, your V-card." She giggled again.

Damn Colton and his big mouth. My virgin status wasn't a secret, but I didn't go shouting it from the rooftops either. I bet he told Tara and Tara told Kendra.

I made my way around to the driver's side and got in.

"Kendra, I don't think you're in any state to be offering. You've had a lot to drink." I made the excuse, but didn't bother to tell her I wouldn't take her up on it sober either. Ever.

I didn't think she'd appreciate that and I didn't want to piss her off.

"God, you're such a tease!" she screeched.

So much for not pissing her off.

"Besides," I went on, "I don't see it as a problem. I've gone this long. When I'm finally with someone," I paused, knowing I was going to sound like a complete pussy. "I want it to mean something."

I heard quiet snoring and looked over to find Kendra passed out, her head leaning against the window.

I wasn't surprised by her offer. I wasn't conceited, but I knew girls thought I was good-looking. After joining a gym a couple years ago, my once-lanky six-foot frame was now filled out from weight-lifting. I noticed—and appreciated—the appraising looks girls sent my way.

Kendra hadn't exactly been shy about her attraction to me, either. Throughout our date, she had repeatedly complimented me on my dimples. Repeatedly. Plus, I wasn't oblivious to 'fuck-me' eyes and she eye-fucked the fuck out of me all night long.

When we got back to my apartment I tried to wake her up, but she swayed on her feet so badly that I had to carry her. Grunting, I fumbled with the keys while trying not to drop the dead-weight body in my arms.

By the time we made it to the bedroom, she seemed to perk up a bit. "Ooooh, you have a big bed. This is going to be fun." She giggled.

"I'll give you a minute to change," I said, ignoring her comment as I got a T-shirt and gym shorts for her to wear. Thinking it was better to be safe than sorry, I grabbed the trash can from the bathroom and held it up for her to see before setting it beside the bed. "In case you get sick again."

She just giggled and kicked off her shoes.

I left the room to grab her a bottle of water and a couple Advil. I had a feeling she would need it in the morning.

By the time I got back, Kendra was passed out face down on the bed with her legs dangling halfway off. Her skirt was caught around her ankles and it looked like she had unsnapped her bra but couldn't get it all the way off her arms.

Letting out a deep sigh, I took a second to shoot Colton a text.

Me: You're a fucking dick. Never again.

After getting a couple blankets from the closet, I moved Kendra's legs onto the bed and covered her with one.

I took the other blanket out to the living room and settled in on the couch. I'd slept in less comfortable places.

I was just glad the date from hell was finally over.

CHAPTER 2

Angel

I was officially a runaway.

At first, the idea of being on my own was intriguing. The freedom. The independence. The adventure.

The reality, however, wasn't living up to the hype. The uncertainty. The hunger. The smelly bus rides.

Before Claire passed away, I'd lived with her for five happy years. Abandoned by my mom at seven and orphaned by my dad at twelve, she didn't even hesitate to take me in. Claire was my dad's sister, and we'd always been close since she didn't have any kids of her own.

It wasn't my dad's fault, the way he died. There were risks that came with being a police officer—risks I'd often worried about every time he left for a shift. I'd imagined bank robberies or drug busts gone wrong. My worries never involved him getting shot during a routine traffic stop.

Although Claire wasn't much of a parent, she was my friend. My best friend. No one could've predicted she would have a massive stroke at the age of forty-three. She was active, ate the right foods, and she had a Zen-like quality about her. She was the picture of mental and physical health. Her death was so unexpected and, honestly, I still hadn't come to terms with it.

With just one month until I graduated high school, my

life was uprooted. They said I was lucky they found a foster home willing to take me in. Unfortunately, the family lived forty-five minutes away and I had to finish my senior year in an unfamiliar school with a bunch of strangers.

One month in foster care, and I decided I'd had enough. In the beginning, I'd been worried about what I would encounter there. I'd heard the horror stories of abuse and neglect in foster homes before.

But the family I got placed with wasn't that bad. Actually, they were pretty nice, although they seemed overwhelmed by the kids. I was one of five in the home, the youngest being seven, and the oldest being myself, at seventeen. While I was grateful for a place to live and food to eat, it was always crowded and I had zero privacy.

And although I was constantly surrounded by people, I'd never felt more alone.

I was lonely. Painfully lonely.

It was a sense of longing I felt deep inside. I ached for a place to belong. A place to call home.

I'd planned on staying with the family until I aged out, but with only two weeks until my eighteenth birthday, I didn't see the point in sticking around.

I had big plans, and my dreams weren't going to pursue themselves.

On the last day of school, instead of stuffing my backpack full of books, I'd packed the essentials—several changes of clothes, a toothbrush, some travel-size toiletries, and some pictures I couldn't bear to part with. Dressed in skinny jeans and my favorite Beach Boys T-shirt (in honor of Claire), I left the foster home and didn't look back.

When I was a kid, I read a short story about a very resourceful homeless woman. She washed herself in gas station bathrooms and collected free make-up and perfume samples from department stores. She walked through the grocery store filling her cart with items she didn't intend to buy while eating a banana and grapes, looking like a leisurely shopper. Then she would suddenly realize she 'forgot' something in her car or have an emergency and would have to abandon her cart—without paying for what she'd already eaten.

For the past three days, that's basically what I'd been doing. I hadn't actually stolen anything yet, but I needed to make it across the country while spending as little as possible.

While getting to California was the ultimate goal, being homeless was not. From what I'd heard, living expenses weren't cheap.

After emptying my savings account, I had roughly $1,700. My short stint as a waitress and all those summers of dog-walking and pet-sitting were finally paying off.

The first night on my own was spent on a bus, which took me from Portland, Maine to Philadelphia. The twelve-hour ride was long, but I slept for a good part of it.

The next night I found a cheap motel where the guy working the desk didn't care that I wasn't eighteen. He barely glanced up at me from the newspaper he was reading as I handed him cash and he tossed me a room key, no questions asked. It was a seedy motel and I was sure questionable things went on there, things I didn't want to know anything about. I knew I was spending my money faster than I should, but I'd desperately wanted a bed and a hot shower.

After taking another bus to Columbus, Ohio, I toyed with the idea of hitchhiking. It was the most obvious solution if I wanted to save my dwindling funds.

Letting out a sigh, I stopped walking along the busy street to take an old postcard out of my back pocket. It was one of my most prized possessions.

Vehicles whizzed by as I studied the tattered piece of

paper. The edges were worn and the corners curled from the thousands of times I'd looked at it. It was from the San Diego Zoo and it had a picture of otters on the front.

There was no message on the back. No well wishes or words of love. Only my mom's name was written there in faded ink—*Deeana*.

I shoved it back into my pocket as I resumed walking while contemplating my next step.

As I approached a Holiday Inn, my nerves set in because of what I was about to do. I wasn't good at lying. In fact, I was just about the worst liar ever. Always had been.

I tried to mentally psyche myself up. I just had to walk in and pretend like I belonged there. My growling stomach reminded me of why I had to do this. I hadn't had much food in the last few days. Granola bars only went so far.

Walking through the automatic sliding doors, I tried my best to seem nonchalant. The desk clerk was on the phone and didn't even notice me as I made my way straight to the elevator. I went up to the second floor and searched for a room with a 'Do Not Disturb' sign on the door.

Ah, room 221.

Next, I took a peek around the corner to find the maid making her rounds with the cleaning cart.

Bingo.

"Excuse me." I approached the woman. "My parents and I are in room 221 and they want to sleep in, but wanted me to see if I could get some more shampoo and stuff?"

"Sure, honey. What do you need?" she asked in a thick accent. Her curly brown hair, streaked with gray, was pulled into a neat bun at the back of her head. She was probably in her fifties and she had kind, brown eyes.

I felt bad for lying to her. When she looked at me, she probably saw an innocent girl, not a sneaky, lying thief.

"Um, three of everything?"

She gathered the shampoo, conditioner, soap, and lotion, and handed them to me with a bright smile. "There you go."

"Thank you so much," I said with a relieved sigh.

The amount she gave me would get me through the next couple of weeks.

Going back to the elevator, I took it down to the lobby where the smell of the continental breakfast made my mouth water.

I looked like any other hotel guest coming down for a late breakfast. I reassured myself no one had any reason to suspect me of deceit, but that didn't stop me from being paranoid about it.

Keeping my head down, I went straight for the bagels. After piling on some bacon, scrambled eggs, and a banana, I sat down to enjoy my meal.

As I looked around, I noticed I was the only person sitting alone. The table next to me was a family of four, and the two children were bickering over who got to have the last mini cereal box of Apple Jacks. Being an only child definitely had its perks, but when I was a kid I would've given my right arm for a sibling.

Too afraid someone might realize I wasn't a hotel guest, I finished my food quickly. Before leaving, I grabbed a couple more bagels and an apple and stuffed them in my backpack.

I walked away from the hotel with a sour feeling in my stomach, and I recognized it for what it was—guilt.

I had lied. I took something that wasn't mine and I felt bad about it. I'd never stolen anything before, at least, not on purpose. One time, I forgot to tell the cashier at Walmart about the case of water on the bottom of my cart, so technically, I stole that.

But this was different. What I did at the hotel felt wrong.

It solidified my resolve to hitchhike. If I wasn't spending money on bus fare, I could afford a little food here and there. Forcing the guilt to the back of my mind, I thought about my next step—find somewhere to wash up.

I saw several options as I walked down the street, away from the hotel. There were some fast food restaurants and a large convenience store, but I knew the bathrooms would most likely have several stalls and a lot of people going in and out. Not the best idea since I was going to be washing my hair in the sink.

Grimacing, I ran my fingers through my hair, which was wild from sleeping on a bus all night. The long blonde strands were also getting oily. I wasn't one of those people who could skip a shower and get away with it. With quick work of my fingers, I put it in a braid to tame it down.

I'd been walking for at least an hour when I saw a truck stop. It was so generic-looking. There wasn't even a name— the faded yellow overhead sign just simply said 'Truck Stop'. The store was small, and I could see it had the kind of bathrooms around the back where you needed a key to get in.

Perfect.

While I was in the store, I decided to splurge on a protein bar and a bottle of water. I was going to need the energy with all this walking.

The cashier was a man, probably in his thirties. His curly brown hair was grown out to his shoulders and with the tie-dye shirt stretched out over his large stomach, he totally had the hippie vibe going on.

He looked incredibly bored as he rang up my items and told me the total. I couldn't help wondering if I would end up in a job like this when I made it to California. With only a high school education, it's not like I'd have many choices.

After I paid and got the bathroom key, I went around to

the back of the building. I was ready for my shower. I just hoped they had one of those automatic hand dryers.

~

It didn't have a dryer.

The sink was tiny. Soap got in my eyes. The floor got soaked. I slipped and almost fell on my ass. I ran out of paper towels.

As I did my best to wring the excess water out of my hair, I felt like maybe my naivety was catching up with me. Honestly, I had absolutely no idea what I was doing.

I realized now I didn't really put much planning into the plan. I didn't have much real-world experience. I'd never even been camping before.

And now I thought I could just travel across the country spending little to no money? Did I really think I could pull this off? Claire would have said I was 'winging it' or 'Flying by the seat of my pants'.

Not exactly the best motto for success.

Panic clawed at me when I considered the possibility that I'd made a big mistake. A mistake so big I wouldn't be able to dig myself out of the mess I'd created. A mistake that left me feeling even more lost than I did right now.

The fluorescent lights flickered overhead as I gazed at the forlorn expression reflecting back at me in the small, square mirror.

Taking a deep breath, I shook the negative thoughts from my mind. I refused to let the fear and doubt creep in.

Besides, it was too late to turn back now.

CHAPTER 3

Travis

The sound of 'On the Road Again' by Willie Nelson started blaring from my phone just as I got into the driver's seat of the semi.

"What's up, Hank?" I answered without even needing to look at the caller ID.

"Travis, what's your twenty?"

I chuckled because he'd really taken a liking to trucker lingo. "Just filled up outside of Columbus. Made the delivery. I'm taking a lunch break, then I'll be back on the road."

"Copy that," he said as if we were really talking over a CB radio. "You dropping the trailer off in Mount Vernon on your way back?"

"Yep," I confirmed. "I'll spend the night at a rest stop and go by there first thing in the morning."

"Ten-four. See ya back in Tolson." He ended the conversation and hung up.

Tolson, Illinois. Population 320.

It couldn't keep a grocery store in business, but for some reason the tiny town could support two taverns. And the taverns didn't just do well, they thrived. The good people of Tolson were social butterflies. Any day of the week (except for Sunday, of course) you could go into either tavern and find familiar faces, a cold drink, and good food.

Over the years, many other businesses had tried to make a go of it and failed. Hair salons, convenience stores, even a gas station.

A few years ago, Hank's Auto Shop was struggling, offering only mechanic services, so he decided to add a truck testing station as well.

That's where my love for the truck-driving industry began.

The rumble of the engine. The hiss of the brakes. I loved the power behind a semi. Loved the idea of long hauls on the open road.

After high school, Colton and I both attended the community college automotive program to become certified mechanics. It seemed like the most logical step since we planned to stay on at the shop. Plus, I didn't have the money to go to a four-year college.

Sure, I could've applied for financial aid, saddled myself with student loans, and spent four years getting a degree I didn't even want. But I knew that wasn't for me.

A year ago, Hank had the idea to buy a rig and start a transportation company. The shop still wasn't bringing in enough money and he needed to expand his business if he wanted to keep it going.

I'll never forget how excited I was when Hank told Colton and me we needed to get our CDL so we could start truck-driving.

Hank & Sons Transport was born. *Sons.*

I wasn't too much of a man to admit that my eyes got misty when he announced the name. He wasn't my dad, but he was the closest thing I had to it.

The business was genius. We were basically a moving company, but we didn't have to pack and unpack people's crap. I simply dropped the trailer off at the client's house for a day or two while they loaded it up with their belongings. Then,

I hooked it back up to the semi and delivered it to the new location.

The thing about moving? Most people had a lot of stuff. And not everyone felt comfortable behind the wheel of a giant U-Haul.

I enjoyed driving across the country, so I usually took the long-distance hauls while Colton did most of the local business.

We didn't normally have deliveries back to back, but the business was growing quickly. Hank had even mentioned getting a second rig in the future and I thought it was a great idea.

Slipping my phone back into my pocket, I locked up the cab and went inside the truck stop to pay for the fuel and get something to eat.

While I was perusing the chips, a girl in the aisle over caught my eye. I was tall enough to see over the median but she hadn't noticed me. She held up two different protein bars and seemed to be having one hell of an inner debate about which one to pick.

It was cute. *She* was cute.

Actually, cute wasn't a strong enough word to describe her. She was downright *angelic.*

Her long blonde hair was pulled into a messy side-braid and several strands had escaped to frame her heart-shaped face. She had big, crystal blue eyes and her cheeks were slightly rounded, reminding me of the angels I'd seen in a famous painting once. It didn't look like she had any makeup on, but a girl like her didn't need it.

She finally made her selection, and walked away, ending my trance.

In the far back of the small convenience store, the refrigerator held a limited selection of pre-packaged deli sandwiches. With a sigh, I settled for a turkey and cheese, then grabbed a bottle of water.

The protein bar girl ended up in front of me in line. She was a tiny thing. Maybe 5'3". Although she was thin, she had curves in all the right places. She was wearing a white, off the shoulder tee, and jean shorts. I would've had a good view of her rounded ass if her backpack hadn't been in the way.

Damn. The backpack probably meant she was still in high school, which meant I shouldn't even be looking at her like that.

It didn't matter anyway. I wasn't from around here and I'd never see her again.

~

I was sitting behind the wheel, finishing my lunch, when I heard my phone ping with an incoming text.

> **Colton: When do you grab ass tomorrow?**
> **Me: wtf?**
> **Colton: Dammit. Ducking autocorrect.**
> **Colton: Fuck**
> **Colton: What time do you get back tomorrow?**

He had no idea I was cracking up at his expense.

> **Me: Probably mid morning. Definitely by noon. What's up?**
> **Colton: You and me. Buck's. Tomorrow night.**
> **Me: Fuck you, dude. I'm avoiding that place for a while and you know it.**

There was no way I was ready for a run-in with Kendra. Her texts requesting a second date had been relentless.

Colton: Fine. Brick House then.
Me: Fine.

The Brick House was a bar in another small town about five miles away from Tolson. With a DJ, dancing, and drink specials, it was a hot spot on Friday night. I never danced but it was amusing to watching Colton try.

Just as I pulled my hat low over my eyes and sat back in the seat for a fifteen-minute snooze, I saw the same girl from inside the truck stop come out of the bathroom at the back of the building.

She'd been in there a long time and she had different clothes on. Now she was wearing jeans and a light blue tank top. And her hair wasn't in a braid anymore—it was lying around her shoulders in long, wet waves.

What the hell did she do in there, fall in?

After my post-lunch nap, I drove away from the truck stop with thoughts of how to effectively thwart Kendra's efforts to pursue a relationship. I didn't want to hurt her feelings, but avoiding her wouldn't work forever.

Unfortunately, dating options in our age group were scarce in Tolson.

After graduation, everyone scattered. Most couldn't wait to get away from the small town, wanting to spread their wings and learn about the world.

Find out what else is out there.

But I was happy to stay put. I didn't need to go anywhere else to know I was already home.

I'd only been driving for about a mile when I saw someone walking along the side of the road in the distance.

As I got closer I saw the backpack and blonde hair. She turned toward my semi before sticking her thumb out.

"Shit," I whispered, recognizing her right away. Even from a distance, I could see the hopeful expression on her face, and I felt something twist in my chest.

What the hell did she think she was doing? Hitchhiking was dangerous.

For a split second, I thought about not stopping. I could just keep on driving and forget I ever saw her.

But just as fast, all the possible scenarios played out in my mind. All the things that could happen to her. All the sick, depraved people who could be the ones to pull over and lure her into their vehicle with the promise of a safe ride.

I'd never picked up a hitchhiker before.

Had never planned on it.

But there was no way I could leave this girl out there on her own.

CHAPTER 4

Angel

The June heat beat down on my shoulders as I walked along the side of the side of the two-lane highway. Every time a vehicle passed by I stuck my thumb out, but no one even tapped their brakes.

I couldn't blame them for not stopping. I wouldn't pick up a hitchhiker either.

My backpack was starting to feel heavier by the minute and I was becoming very aware that my Converse shoes weren't meant for long-distance hikes. The only sounds to keep me company were the chirping birds, the whooshing of cars passing me by, and the noise of my own footsteps. The side of the road was filled with gravel that crunched under my Chucks with every stride.

Crunch.

Crunch

Crunch.

The scenery left something to be desired. Tall trees lined each side of the highway and that was pretty much it. Then again, most places couldn't compare to Maine. I thought of the lighthouses along the rocky coast and how beautiful the trees were in the fall.

I wondered if I'd ever go back. I hoped so. Before I left, I spread Claire's ashes by our favorite lighthouse. She hadn't specified where she wanted her ashes to go, but I knew it was the right spot.

I'd been walking for about twenty minutes when a giant semi started to slow and pulled over about thirty feet ahead of me.

The brakes hissed as it came to a complete stop, and the constant roar of the engine was loud as I approached the intimidating vehicle.

My heart slammed in my chest as I quickly walked to the passenger side while silently praying in my head.

Please don't be a pervert.

Please don't be a pervert.

The outside of the truck was bright red and the logo on the side said Hank & Sons Transport in bold black and white letters. Taking a deep breath, I opened the door and ungracefully clamored up into the seat—not an easy feat for someone my size.

I turned to thank my rescuer and froze. My eyes went wide as I took in the man before me.

I was face to face with the most gorgeous guy I'd ever seen. I wasn't sure if I was going pale or blushing, because I felt hot and cold all at once. Every single cell in my body was going haywire and I suddenly felt like I couldn't breathe.

Thick eyelashes framed hazel eyes. Or were they green? I couldn't be sure because the brim of his ball cap shadowed his eyes. Although his hat covered his head, I could see light brown hair that was short on the sides. He had a day or two of scruff on his face and it added to his sexiness. His nose was straight and masculine, yet somehow *cute* at the same time.

It made him look younger. Boyish.

Honestly, I'd expected it to smell in here. Like gasoline, cigarettes, and man-stench. It didn't. Not even a little. The scent was masculine and clean. Maybe soap or deodorant? It didn't smell strong enough to be cologne.

I heard him clear his throat, and that time I did blush because I realized I'd just been staring. Just *staring* at him.

Oh my God. How embarrassing.

He smiled, and my heart did a thumpity-thump. *Dimples.* "Where are you headed?"

"How far are you going?" I asked, coming to my senses.

"Last stop is Tolson, Illinois."

"That works, if you don't mind." I'd never heard of Tolson but he was headed in the direction I wanted to go, which was good enough for me. "Thank you. I really appreciate it."

He nodded and put the truck into gear as I fumbled with the seat belt.

After a minute of awkward silence, he spoke, "So, what's your name?"

"Angel Thomas," I replied, and he snorted. Maybe it was more of a scoff, but it was obvious he thought I was lying. "What, you don't believe me? I'm serious. Here, I'll even show you my ID."

As I started to rummage around in my backpack, it occurred to me that it might be common for hitchhikers to lie about their name. And now that I thought about it, maybe I should have, too.

"No. No, it's fine," he said. "It's not that I don't believe you, it's just…" He trailed off.

"It's just what?"

"Nothing." He shook his head. "You just look like an Angel."

CHAPTER 5

Travis

Her name was Angel.

I laughed because of my previous thought when I saw her at the truck stop. Then I felt my face go hot as I realized how my statement came out.

"Sorry." I laughed. "That just sounded like a really bad pick-up line. I meant the name suits you. It's a good name. I mean, you look like your name would be Angel," I tried to clarify.

Fuck. I was rambling. One minute around this girl and I turned into a bumbling idiot.

Really smooth.

However, I didn't miss the way her gaze lingered on me when she first got in. The way her eyes widened and her lips parted. Maybe the instant attraction I was feeling wasn't completely one-sided.

"What's yours?" she asked, and I looked over to see her trying to hide a grin. Hopefully, that meant she didn't think I was a creep. Or maybe she was just trying not to laugh at me.

"Travis Hawkins," I told her.

"Well, Travis," she said, turning her body towards me. "You're certainly not what I was expecting."

She was direct. I liked that.

"Let me guess," I started. "You thought I'd be an old hairy

dude with a beer gut and tattoos. Maybe a mullet?"

She laughed, and I really liked the sound. I wanted to make her do it again.

"Something like that, yeah," she admitted, having the decency to look sheepish from her assumption.

When I made the impulsive decision to pick her up, I hadn't thought about what it would be like to sit this close to her. To share the same air.

She was two feet away but I could smell her. Vanilla and honey. It made me want to lick the skin on her neck and bury my face in her hair. She had a full, pink mouth and her bottom lip was slightly bigger than the top. I had the sudden urge to bite it.

Shit, maybe I really was a creep. I didn't even know how old she was.

"How old are you?" I decided to get the question out of the way. "You look a little young to be on your own."

"I'm not a kid," she said a bit defensively. "I graduated high school and I'll be eighteen on June 15th. Seriously, do you want to see my ID? It even has my correct weight on it." She huffed. "That's a big deal. I totally should have fibbed a bit and subtracted ten pounds."

"I believe you." I held up a hand in surrender. "Okay, so you're almost eighteen." Thank God. She wasn't *that* much younger than me.

"Speaking of age, are you sure you're old enough to be driving this thing?" She narrowed her eyes at me and waved her hand around the cab.

I had to laugh. She was the most animated person I'd ever met. When she talked, she used wild hand gestures, and at least six different expressions could cross her face in a single sentence.

"I'm twenty-one, so yes, I'm old enough. I've got my CDL

in my wallet if you want to see it." I smirked. "But my wallet is in my back pocket and you'll have to fish it out for me, seeing as how my hands are occupied." I wiggled my fingers without taking my hands off the wheel.

I couldn't help but flirt with her a little. And the pink blush that spread across her cheeks? Fucking adorable.

"I'll just have to take your word for it," she muttered and shifted to look out the window. I could see her smiling in the reflection of the glass.

With her head turned, I got a good look at her profile and couldn't help thinking that she was perfect.

Long eyelashes swept away from the biggest blue eyes I'd ever seen, and her nose was slightly turned up at the end. The tank top she had on was form-fitting and I could clearly see the swells of her perky breasts.

I felt my dick twitch in my pants and I mentally chastised myself for being such a pervert. All she wanted was a ride, not to be eye-fucked by a stranger.

"So," Angel turned back to me abruptly. "Since we're going to be traveling together, we should get to know each other a little. I feel it's only fair that I tell you my negative qualities first."

Is this girl for real?

I'd expected small talk about the scenery or the weather. I was a complete stranger and she was trusting me to know things about her. Personal things. Hell, she'd already told me her full name and her birthday.

"You know, you really shouldn't be hitchhiking," I interrupted her. "There are a lot of crazies out there who would love to take advantage of a vulnerable girl."

"Which brings me to character flaw number one." She held up a finger. "I'm a terrible judge of character. I just think everyone is great until they show me they're not." She shrugged.

I had to grit my teeth to keep myself from lecturing her about the dangers of being so trusting. I wasn't kidding when I told her people would take advantage of her. She was far too young and innocent to be out there alone. My fists tightened on the steering wheel when I thought about what could've happened to her if she'd been picked up by someone else, and I knew I'd made the right decision.

There was a reason truckers had a stereotype. A lot of them were family men—good men—just trying to make a living, counting the days until they got back home to their loved ones.

And some of them were, well, not. Just like any other group of people in life, there were a few bad apples. Rough, dangerous men. Predators.

They were the ones who picked up the hookers who hung around the truck stops, not caring about how young they were or what brought them to that life. One glimpse of Angel, and they would see her as an easy target.

"Character flaw number two." She held up two fingers. "If I have something to say, I say it. It's just a good thing I'm actually a nice person because if I wasn't, I might really hurt someone's feelings. I have a bad habit of over-sharing." She cringed. "Which is pretty much what I'm doing right now."

"That's not a bad thing. Being honest. Straightforward. I like that," I told her. "So what's next? Lay it on me."

Her lips pressed together while she thought about it. "Well, I'm really bad at multi-tasking. As in, I can't do it. It's why I was a terrible waitress. I mean, really, the *worst*." Her animated ways were in full force as her hands slashed through the air and she successfully mimed dropping a tray.

I couldn't control my laughter. She was so entertaining. I'd never had anyone tell me so much about themselves within five minutes of meeting them.

"So, what about you?" she asked, turning the tables. "Negative qualities first."

I made a humming sound and paused to think. "I sing in the shower."

Now it was her turn to laugh. "How is that a bad thing?"

I self-consciously scratched my jaw. "I guess if you heard it, you'd understand why."

CHAPTER 6

Angel

And now I was thinking about him in the shower. Not in an innocent way either. No, I was imagining the whole shebang. His hands soaping up his body, water running down bare skin all the way down to his... What was wrong with me? I was being so inappropriate.

Maybe it wasn't so much about what was wrong with me, but what was *right* with him.

Travis was hot. Really hot. And I wondered why he was here, behind the wheel of a semi, instead of modeling somewhere.

It wasn't just about physical attraction, though. He had a lightness to him. He exuded happiness. When he laughed, it was unrestrained. Big belly laughs. And he was the first person to make me smile—really smile—in over a month. My own laughter sounded foreign to my ears.

Maybe he affected me this way because he was older. He wasn't a *boy*.

The boys at my old high school were rowdy and immature. I'd had a brief relationship with one guy at the end of my junior year.

After dating for two months, word got back to me that he had been bragging to all the guys in the locker room that we'd had sex.

Not just any sex—anal sex.

Only, he worded it much more *crudely* than that. It was disgusting. It was disrespectful. And most importantly, it was a big fat lie. The truth was we'd barely made it past second base.

I broke up with him—very publicly in the lunch room—and swore off dating until college.

That was one reason I hadn't been terribly opposed to switching schools after my aunt's death. When you're forever dubbed "butt-sex girl", moving on doesn't seem like such a bad idea.

Yawning, I suddenly realized how tired I was. The past few days of traveling were catching up with me.

"Why don't you take a nap or something?" Travis suggested. "You look exhausted and we'll be on the road for hours."

It wasn't a bad idea. I suddenly felt the fatigue weighing down on me and my knees were starting to ache from all the walking.

"Yeah, maybe just for a little while," I agreed as I laid my head against the passenger door.

I thought about thanking him again, letting him know how grateful I was for the ride, but my eyes were already closing.

∾

When I woke up, I was momentarily disoriented because it was dark outside.

"Hey," a voice said beside me, and I jumped.

It took a second for the events of the day to come back to me. The awful truck stop bath. Hitchhiking. Travis.

I looked outside and realized we were parked at a rest stop.

"Hey," I said, rubbing my eyes. "I didn't mean to sleep so

long. Where are we?"

"Near Mount Vernon, Illinois. I got dinner for us about an hour ago but I didn't want to wake you up." He pointed at the fast food sack between us. "I didn't know what you like. I hope you're not a vegetarian."

"Nope, I'll pretty much eat anything except for sushi," I said, already digging through the bag. "Because sushi is disgusting. I know, I know. Everyone is supposed to love sushi. It's like New York City or wine or The Beatles," I rambled on. "Everyone says they love it because everyone else says you're supposed to."

My mini-rant ended when I took a very unladylike bite of the cheeseburger and moaned. It didn't even matter that it wasn't warm anymore. Delicious.

"You don't like those things?" He chuckled.

I made a face when I remembered the sip of Merlot Claire let me try at dinner once. "I've only tried wine one time. I expected it to taste like grape juice. It didn't." I shuddered. "And I don't dislike The Beatles. Love them, actually. But I bet if I didn't, you'd give me a funny look," I accused. "And I've never been to New York City, so the verdict is still out on that one."

Seeming amused, Travis sat back in his seat and allowed me to finish my food in silence.

"Thank you, Travis," I said, balling up the wrapper and placing it back in the sack. "You didn't have to get me dinner."

"I ordered off the dollar menu," he informed me. "It's not a big deal."

He handed me a napkin and coughed to cover his laugh when he pointed at the giant glob of ketchup I had on my face. Grimacing, I wiped at my cheek. I couldn't seem to stop embarrassing myself around this guy.

"So, listen," Travis started, sounding hesitant. "I should've told you earlier that I have to make another drop off in the morning… Which means we'll need to find somewhere to stay the night. Usually I just stay at a rest stop because I have a sleeper cab," he explained, nodding his head toward the back of the semi where there was a beige curtain hanging over the small doorway. "But that sleeping situation isn't ideal for two people. We should get you a motel room. My treat."

I was already shaking my head before he could finish. "That's not necessary, really. You can still take the sleeper bed. I'll just sleep right here." I wiggled my butt in the seat, demonstrating how comfortable I was. Travis started to protest so I continued. "Seriously. I slept here just fine all day. I don't want to be in the way any more than I already am."

"You're not in the way. It's not safe for you to sleep up here, even with the doors locked. I wouldn't feel right about it," he explained, his voice gruff.

"And I don't feel right about making you get a motel room."

We entered some sort of stare-down, both of us trying to assert our stubbornness. I wasn't willing to use my own money for a motel and I wouldn't let him pay for it either. That wasn't his responsibility and he was being silly. There was no reason for him to change his original plan.

"Fine," he conceded. "A compromise then. You take the bed. I'll sleep up here."

"No way." I shook my head. "I'm not going to kick you out of your own bed. And you've been driving all day."

"Take it or leave it. Otherwise, I'm driving straight to the nearest motel and getting you a room." His tone left no room for argument as he leaned back in the seat and crossed his arms over his chest.

I narrowed my eyes at him and huffed out a breath of defeat. "Okay."

Travis's face broke out into a huge grin, showcasing

straight white teeth. You'd have thought the guy won the freaking lottery. "Dang, that was easier than I thought," he gloated.

His smug facial expression made my lips involuntarily curl up in a smile and he grinned back at me. A fluttery feeling spread through my chest as an awkward silence followed our little argument.

Our eyes were still locked, but it felt different now. The seconds ticked by and suddenly, the air felt charged. It was as if we didn't want to look away but neither of us knew what to say either.

We'd been staring at each other for far too long for it to be completely innocent.

Travis's eyes roamed my face before they flicked down to my mouth, and I automatically licked my lips. Which, in return, made me look at his lips. They looked soft, yet firm, and they parted as though he was going to say something, but he didn't.

More seconds passed. I felt my breathing pick up as I wondered if he was thinking about kissing me, which was crazy because I just met the guy.

Being the moment-ruiner that I am, I blurted out the least sexy thing possible. "I really have to pee."

CHAPTER 7

Travis

After using the restroom and having way too much fun with the vending machines, Angel and I made our way back out to the truck, our arms full of snacks and soda.

I'd changed into black track pants and white T-shirt to sleep in and Angel was now wearing black leggings and another off the shoulder shirt, this time a sky blue that brought out her eyes.

Before getting back into the driver's side, I assisted her up into the passenger seat, unintentionally admiring the way the tight material of the leggings stretched over her shape.

"I can do it myself, you know," she said, her tone exasperated.

"Oh, I know you can. Maybe I just like the view," I teased and winked at her, causing her cheeks to turn pink. Making this girl blush was quickly becoming my new favorite hobby.

After getting settled down behind the wheel, I turned to her. I wanted to know more about her, and I had no idea how long I'd have before she was gone. She could take off tomorrow and I'd never see her again.

"So, I'm dying to know what your end game is," I told her as we munched on Twix bars.

"My end game?" she asked.

"Yeah. Where are you going? And why do you think

hitchhiking is a good idea?" I tried not to sound like I was scolding her, but I couldn't keep the edge out of my voice.

She sighed. "It's a long story. I'll try to give you the Cliff's Notes version."

She went on to tell me about her dad's passing when she was twelve, her aunt's unexpected death, and her short time in the foster home. She sounded detached from it all, and I could tell she was trying to keep the emotion out of her voice.

The feeling of empathy that flowed through me was overwhelming. I knew what loss felt like. I knew what it was like to grow up with a single parent. But I still had my mom, Colton, and Hank. I had a home.

Hell, even any one of my neighbors would give me the shirt off their back. That's just how it was in Tolson. There was always a friendly face around the corner.

Angel didn't have anyone.

She told me she'd saved up some money and planned to find a job and a place to live in California. My chest tightened when I thought about her all alone in the world. I felt an overpowering urge to protect her, and I didn't even know why.

"Why California?" I asked.

Angel reached into her back pocket and took out a shredded postcard—or what used to be a postcard. It looked like it'd seen better days.

"My mom sent this to me when I was ten. She knew I loved otters the best." She showed me the picture on the front where two otters were floating in the water while holding hands. "I feel like she wanted me to know where she was."

"How do you know she's still there?" I reasoned. The postcard was sent almost eight years ago. Her mom could be anywhere by now.

Angel looked at me with a sad smile. "They tried to locate her after Claire died. Turns out, she's in a California state prison on a drug charge. She's up for parole in a couple months. I thought maybe..." She paused. "Maybe I should be there when she gets out. We could start over, you know? She'll need a place to stay and we could get to know each other again." She let out a deep sigh. "I know it might sound silly, but it wouldn't even matter that she left, as long as we could start over now."

"That doesn't sound silly at all," I said. "But there's gotta be a better way for you to do this. What you've been doing is too dangerous."

Her eyes swung my way with a look that told me she knew I was right. Before she could respond, I made a decision that would change my life forever.

"Stay with me when we get back to Tolson," I offered. "While you were sleeping I looked at my schedule, and I have a delivery to make in three weeks. Guess where it is." I raised my eyebrows at her.

"California?" Her lips tipped up.

"Yep," I popped the 'P' and drummed my hands on the steering wheel. "I'll take you there myself."

CHAPTER 8

Angel

I asked Travis to give me the night to think about his extremely generous offer, and he showed me to the back compartment of his truck. The tight space included a small bed which was more of a cot, but I wasn't going to complain. It looked like heaven.

After we said goodnight, I thought about the look on his face when he asked me to stay with him. It was as if he was genuinely concerned about my well-being, but I wasn't sure why he cared.

I really needed to weigh my options here.

If I accepted his offer, I'd be taking the risk that he could be a serial killer, which would be the worst-case scenario. However, I really didn't get the 'stranger danger' vibe from him. I mean, he bought me dinner and insisted on giving me the bed because it was safer than sleeping up front.

The other drawback was that I hated the idea of mooching off of him for the next few weeks. But maybe I could pay him back somehow after I got a job.

Then again, being around Travis for that much time could be difficult. I'd known him for less than a day and I already had this weird insta-crush on him. We'd basically be living together; he didn't need some random teenage girl mooning over him, following him around everywhere.

All the reasons I should say no shouted at me: Possible serial killer. Money-sucking mooch. Constant goo-goo eyes.

But what was my other option? I knew what I'd been doing was dangerous.

With the pros and cons swirling around in my mind, I told myself not to decide until the morning. I'd made enough life-altering decisions in the past several days. After shutting down my thoughts about the near future, I turned to other worries.

I missed Claire. A strong feeling of homesickness washed over me. I missed my home. Not just the place, but the *feeling* of home.

I don't know why my mind chose this moment to have the mental breakdown it so rightly deserved. Maybe it was because I had never really had a chance to grieve. Things had changed so quickly after Claire's stroke that I just had to focus on the next step, taking life one day at a time. I was forced to concentrate on one thing—moving forward.

The reason didn't really matter. All I knew was that the floodgates were opening and there was nothing I could do to stop it.

Sobs wracked my body and I tried to muffle the sounds in the pillow. I wrapped my arms around myself and curled into a ball, hoping I didn't wake Travis.

I was an ugly crier. Squeaky voice, puffy eyes, red nose, and the snot—oh, the snot.

"Angel…?" I heard Travis whisper before I felt strong arms close around my body.

He was hugging me. This gorgeous stranger was *hugging* me. I couldn't remember the last time I'd had a decent hug.

Physical affection wasn't something we did in my family. Usually, my first reaction to receiving a hug was to force myself not to recoil, awkwardly pat the person's back, and wait it out until the hugger was satisfied with said hug.

This should have felt awkward, but it didn't. Much to my surprise, my natural response was to wrap my arms around his neck and bury my face in his chest while I cried.

He didn't say anything. He didn't tell me everything would be okay, and I appreciated that. Empty promises wouldn't do me any good. He just rubbed my back and held onto me until I had no more tears left.

After the worst of my breakdown subsided, I became very aware of the close proximity of our bodies and the wetness I'd left on his T-shirt.

Cue the embarrassment.

I shifted away from him and tried to wipe my face.

"S-sorry I woke you up," I squeaked. I cleared my throat and gestured toward his chest. "And I'm sorry about all the tears and snot on your shirt."

And what did Travis do? He barked out a laugh then took off his shirt.

He took off his shirt.

"I wasn't asleep. And it's not a problem. Do you feel better now?" he asked, his face going serious.

"Yeah, kinda. I guess I needed that," I said, feeling grateful for his kindness, but also very distracted by his bare upper body.

The guy was ripped. His chest and arms were defined, and I counted his abs—*two, four, six*—yes, definitely six. No visible tattoos. Just smooth, tan skin. My eyes wandered down to the V-shaped muscles on his hips. A trail of light brown hair ran down from his belly button into the waistband of his pants.

Blushing furiously, I forced my eyes back up. He was no longer wearing a hat, and I noticed his hair was actually quite long on top. Messy brown strands fell onto his forehead, ending just above his eyes. I couldn't stop myself from reaching up and running my fingers through it.

"Your hair is a lot longer than I thought it would be," I said, transfixed by the softness.

When Travis tried to talk, his voice came out huskily and he cleared his throat. "The lady at the Quick Clip said it was the popular style now."

"I like it." I nodded, running my fingers over the longer hair on the top of his head and down the back where it was shorter.

Suddenly, I realized how close our faces were.

Inwardly berating myself for being so bold, I retracted my hand from his hair. I couldn't interpret the expression on his face, and it occurred to me that I might have made him uncomfortable.

"Let me get a new shirt," he said abruptly, and disappeared into the front of the truck.

His sudden departure was a reality check. He came back here to comfort me and I basically molested him. *Great.*

CHAPTER 9

Travis

S hit. Shit. *Shit*. I tried to take a minute to calm my body down while I looked for a clean T-shirt in my bag. Loose track pants were terrible for hiding a raging hard-on.

When I'd heard Angel crying, I couldn't stop myself from going to her. My intentions of comforting her had been completely honorable. And when she wrapped her arms around me, it felt like my heart cracked in my chest.

I wanted to make her feel better, but I didn't know how. Not knowing what else to do, I just held onto her and let her cry.

When I'd taken off my shirt, I didn't even think about what her reaction would be. It was an innocent move. But when her eyes raked over my body I'd felt my dick start to stiffen, and I had to bite back a moan when she ran her delicate fingers through my hair.

It felt so good to have her hands on me.

If I'd questioned whether or not she was attracted to me, I definitely had my answer now. I couldn't explain it, this connection between us, but I knew she felt it, too.

After pulling on a faded navy-blue tank top, I sat back down next to Angel. She looked apprehensive about what to do next, so I lifted my arm up in invitation. Her features relaxed in relief and she curled into my side.

"Do you want to talk about it?" I knew she might still be upset, and I was willing to listen.

"Not really." She looked up at me with red-rimmed eyes. "Thanks, though."

"When I was a kid, my mom would tell me stories when I was sad. I could just talk for a while if you want," I suggested. Maybe she just needed a distraction.

I felt her nod against my chest, so I kept talking. "You and I actually have a lot in common," I told her. "My mom is an alcoholic. I mean, it's not the same as having a problem with drugs, but it's still an addiction. She's been sober seven months now. She didn't always have trouble with alcohol, though. My dad died in a car accident when I was four. After that… She just couldn't cope. Her drinking never stopped her from being a kick-ass mom." I huffed out a laugh. "I guess you could say she was a high-functioning alcoholic. She made it to all my baseball games. Had dinner on the table every night. She's a great mom and I'm proud of her."

"I'm sorry," Angel interjected. "About your dad, I mean."

"I don't remember much about him." I tried to recall the few memories I had of my dad. "He used to let me sit behind him on the top of the couch and comb his hair. He'd hold up a cup of water so I could dip the comb in it to get his hair wet. He let me put it in all kinds of styles. Mohawk, Elvis hair…"

"It sounds like he was a fun dad," she said, her voice sounding sleepy. Her arm snaked around my stomach and I put my hand over hers to keep it there. I liked the way her arm felt around me.

"He was. But I've got Hank now."

"Hank and Sons," she repeated the company name. "Did your mom remarry?"

"No. Hank and I aren't related, but he's like a dad to me. When I was seven, Hank and his son, Colton, moved in three houses down from me. Colton and I were the same age," I explained. "'The first day we met we got into a scuffle over some game… Something to do with marbles…" I chuckled at the memory. "I gave him a black eye and he gave me a bloody nose. Hank put us in one of his big shirts—*together*—and called it our 'get along' shirt. We thought it was bullshit at the time but we've been inseparable ever since. We're actually roommates, so if you decide to stay with me for the next few weeks you'll get to meet him…"

I left that last part hanging in the air, wanting her to tell me she would stay, but I was met with silence. I looked down to find her eyes closed, her deep, even breaths fanning across my chest.

I sat with her for a few minutes, enjoying the way her body felt against mine. Very slowly, I tried to extract myself from under her arm but she tightened her hold on me.

Okay, well, I didn't try *that* hard.

Staying here for a few more minutes wouldn't be the worst thing in the world. As I held her, I tried to think of a way to convince her not to leave tomorrow.

CHAPTER 10

Angel

For the second time in twenty-four hours, I woke up completely disoriented. For some reason, I couldn't move. I tried to look around and realized I was trapped between a wall and a body.

Not just any body. Travis's body.

We were facing each other, our legs and arms intertwined. My head was tucked into the place where his shoulder met his neck. I inhaled and noted that he still smelled so good.

Was it aftershave? Body wash? Just *him*?

I thought back to the night before, and the last thing I remember was being next to Travis while he sat sideways on the cot. His voice had been so soothing. We must have fallen asleep and somehow ended up like this.

I'd never woken up next to someone this way before. Sure, I'd had slumber parties with friends when I was younger. But this wasn't a slumber party. Travis and I didn't paint each other's nails and gossip about hot guys.

He was the hot guy.

Light was coming in from outside and I wondered what time it was. I squirmed a little while trying to decide what to do next. Should I let him sleep?

My movement must have woken him, because I felt him stir a little before he spoke.

"Hi," I heard him say, his voice rough from sleep, and I looked up at his face.

Since he didn't have a hat on, I could see his eyes clearly in the daylight. They were hazel, but definitely more on the green side. His eyelashes were something to be jealous of. Dark, long, and thick. It was a look I'd tried to achieve with makeup many times, but could never get quite right.

"Hi," I parroted.

"I didn't mean to fall asleep back here with you," he said. "Sorry."

The smirk on his face made me doubt the sincerity of his apology.

"That's okay." I tried to shrug but couldn't under the weight of his arm that was draped over me. He didn't move it. In fact, he seemed completely fine with how close we were, as if it wasn't weird to wake up next to a girl he barely knew.

Then the thought hit me. Did he do this a lot? Pick up random girls?

Oh my God, he could have a girlfriend. He could have several girlfriends back home. I mean, why wouldn't he? He was extremely good-looking.

My lips pressed together and my brows furrowed at the thought of Travis going home to another girl tonight. Maybe he had someone missing him, waiting for him. If that was the case, it would make staying with him torture. I wasn't sure I could watch him be with someone else for three weeks.

"Hey, where'd you go just now?" He interrupted my thoughts, and smoothed his fingers over the worry wrinkle between my eyebrows.

"I was just wondering if you have a girlfriend," I blurted out. Immediately, I felt embarrassed. I wasn't entitled to the details of his private life. I needed to just stop talking. "Because if you did, this would be really inappropriate."

He threw his head back and laughed. "No, I don't have a girlfriend. And yes, this would be highly inappropriate if I did."

Travis reached out and ran his fingers through my hair. The action had no practical purpose behind it. He wasn't doing it to get hair out of my face or to tuck it behind my ear.

No, he was touching my hair because he *wanted* to.

And I didn't want him to stop.

Goosebumps broke out on my arms and I sighed at the feeling of his fingers scraping over my scalp.

An uneasy feeling came over me when I thought about saying goodbye to him today. I didn't know what this was, but I didn't want it to end yet.

With our eyes connected, my blue to his green, I made my decision.

CHAPTER 11

Travis

S mooth, silky strands slipped through my fingers when Angel said the words I'd been dying to hear.

"Well, that's a relief." She paused. "Because I'm going to take you up on your offer. So that means I'll be hanging around for a while… And it would have been really awkward explaining that to a girlfriend."

"Really?" My hand stopped moving through her hair and I felt my face stretch out into a huge grin. I probably looked like a kid on Christmas. "You're seriously going to stay with me?"

Her smile matched mine. "Yep."

I couldn't help it—I wrapped my arms around her.

"Oh my," she said. "You really are a hugger, huh?"

"Not usually," I said, my voice muffled in her hair. "Are you telling me you don't like hugs?" I asked, not loosening my arms at all. If anything, I squeezed a little tighter.

"Not usually," she grunted, because I was squeezing so tight she was having trouble breathing. "But for some reason I don't mind when they're from you." She wrapped her free arm around my back and laid the side of her head on my chest.

She liked hugs *from me.*

We didn't have time to talk about her confession because my phone started ringing from the front seat.

Hank's ringtone.

Reluctantly, I let go of Angel to retrieve my phone and I sat down in the driver's seat.

"Hey, Hank," I greeted. "I'm up."

"Just givin' you a wake-up call, son," he chuckled.

"I know, I know. I'll be dropping the trailer off within an hour and I should be back around noon. Will you be at the shop?"

Hank almost always called me bright and early when I was on the road. He knew I had a tendency to oversleep. I wasn't normally a morning person, but I was extra chipper today— because of a certain someone—and it didn't take long for him to notice.

"Yep, I'll be here." His tone turned suspicious. "What's goin' on?"

"I just, ah," I looked over at Angel. "I got someone I want you to meet."

"Ah, hell, Travis," he said. "What did you do?"

Hank was a smart guy. He knew how life on the road worked for some people and I knew what he was thinking. He was wrong.

"It's not what you're thinking," I promised.

He sighed. "Alright. I'll see ya here at the shop later."

"Ten-four," I said, and I could hear him snickering at my trucker lingo as he hung up.

I put my phone aside and looked over to find Angel threading her fingers through her hair, swiftly putting it into another messy side-braid. I fucking loved her hair like that.

"Alright, Angel." I reached over and gave her braid a little tug. "It's time for you to see how this impressive piece of machinery works."

After we left the rest stop, we went by a fast food place for some breakfast and coffee. We briefly argued over the fact that I insisted on paying again, but she gave in when I told her I would keep track of the amount I spent so she could pay me back once she got a steady income.

Did I have any intention of actually keeping her money? Hell no. But I didn't tell her that.

She made a face when she found out I drink my coffee black, and I learned that Angel doesn't drink coffee but it's her favorite ice cream flavor.

The residence where I was taking the trailer wasn't far from where we stopped, so the ride was quick, and Angel looked excited when I explained the process of detaching the trailer from the truck.

"So, you just leave the trailer at their house?" she asked.

"Yep. Colton comes back in two days to hook it back up, then he'll bring it up to Champaign to where they're moving." I told her about how Hank & Sons got started, how our company worked, and how I liked the longer hauls, while Colton did most of the deliveries closer to home.

"That's so neat, how you guys started this business," she praised, looking genuinely impressed. "What do you do between deliveries? Or do you have them all the time?"

"The transport business isn't always consistent, so I still work at the auto shop between hauls. My next trip is in a couple weeks," I said, realizing Angel would still be around. I could have her stay at my apartment during the trip, but I'd be gone for at least three days. "Would you want to ride along with me?" I asked her, hopeful.

I don't know why I was afraid she'd say no. I guess I just really liked the idea of her being on the road with me.

"Yes!" She bounced excitedly in her seat. "Where are you going?"

"Denver, Colorado. When I drop the trailer off, the clients have a six-hour window to get their things unloaded, so I usually sight-see or do touristy stuff for the day. That's one of the reasons I like long road trips. It's like getting paid to take a mini-vacation."

"Can we go snowboarding?" she asked, still jumping in her seat. Biting my lip, I held back a groan because the movement was causing her tits to bounce up and down. I tried to avert my eyes but it was a struggle. "I've never been snowboarding before," she continued, oblivious to my ogling.

"We can do anything you want," I told her, and I meant it.

I had a feeling she would get her way with me a lot.

CHAPTER 12

Angel

I followed behind Travis while he prepared the trailer to be detached from the truck. There was a lot of unhooking, unplugging, and hissing sounds.

"You gotta release the fifth wheel pin—that's this part right here," he explained as he pulled on a metal bar under the trailer.

He said a few more truck terms I'd never heard before, and I tried not to let my eyes glaze over. It's not that it wasn't interesting, because it was. But he may as well have been speaking another language.

The most interesting part was watching him, watching his body as he moved around the semi. He definitely knew what he was doing. It looked like he'd done it a hundred times, and I guess he probably had.

A couple times he bent over and his white T-shirt rode up exposing tan skin and two dimples in the muscles of his lower back. The jeans he'd changed into were worn and they fit snugly to his backside.

He has such a nice butt.

I blushed because I'd been openly checking him out, but luckily he was too busy concentrating on the truck to notice.

Travis pushed some buttons inside the cab and two thick metal legs descended to the ground where he'd placed square wooden platforms. He explained that the legs would support the end of the trailer once it was fully detached.

After he seemed satisfied with all the tinkering he'd done, he hopped back into the driver's seat and shot me a sexy half-smile while I stood a good distance away to watch.

The engine rumbled as he drove forward and just like that, the huge semi looked... Tiny.

Well, it was still a big vehicle, but it was tiny in comparison to what it used to look like with the trailer on the back end. It was unbelievable.

I stood next to the truck while Travis had the clients sign a form saying he had delivered the trailer, and I heard him tell them Colton would pick it back up in two days and bring it to their new location no later than 4PM that same day. I was impressed with how professional he was.

After that, we were back on the road headed to Travis's hometown. When I agreed to stay with him for a while, one thing I hadn't considered was the fact that I was probably going to meet his family and friends.

Suddenly, I was nervous. Really nervous.

How could I explain how Travis and I met?

Oh, I was just hitchhiking across the country because I'm a homeless runaway...

It was that moment when I realized how screwed up my life truly was. I was a mess.

Travis had it all figured out. He had a home, a stable job, and family that loved him.

The crush I had on him suddenly seemed ridiculous. Did I really think I had a chance with him?

How could I be so silly? There was no way he needed someone like me barreling into his life, stirring things up, then leaving.

Just as I thought about backing out of our deal, I felt

something slide across my palm. I looked down into my lap to find Travis's fingers intertwined with mine. His hands were calloused and rough. A working man's hands. Tingles raced up the skin on my arm as I felt his thumb gently rub back and forth across my knuckles.

He gave me a reassuring squeeze before putting two hands back on the wheel. "It's gonna be okay," he promised.

It was as though he could read my mind, and his words were reassuring. How was it possible for him to instantly make me feel better?

Maybe it wasn't normal to feel so safe with someone I just met. Maybe there was something wrong with me. But maybe I just didn't care.

"Do you have any good friends back in Maine?" Travis asked once we got out on to the highway.

"I had a few friends at my old school, but we lost touch when I moved away. The foster family I lived with had a no social media rule. I had to deactivate my accounts and they took my cell phone." I shrugged because it really wasn't that big of a deal since I didn't have a lot of people to call anyway. "Plus, we were all graduating and a lot of people planned to go to college out of state. They had their big plans and now I have mine."

"You didn't want to go to college? I'm not judging, by the way," Travis added.

"I'd gotten accepted to the University of Maine, but that was before…"

He nodded in understanding. "And now you're here."

"Yep. Now I'm here." I shrugged.

The next couple of hours went faster than I thought they

would. Travis let me have complete control over the radio, telling me he liked everything except for death metal. I decided on an oldies station, but neither of us seemed to pay attention to the music.

To pass the time, we played Twenty Questions—celebrity edition. Eight questions later, I correctly guessed his pick was Tom Hanks, while it took him twelve questions to figure out I was thinking of Lady Gaga. Travis retold the story of how he and Colton met, since I'd fallen asleep in the middle of it the night before, and he fondly described the town of Tolson. When he talked about his home, small town pride was evident in his voice.

Before I knew it, we were driving down Main Street of the smallest town I'd ever seen. The strip of houses was only about a half a mile long with a few businesses in between, including Hank's Auto Shop. Across from the shop there were two taverns, a small bank, and an even smaller post office.

As Travis pulled the semi up next to the side of the white brick building, the gravel of the parking lot crunched under the tires and the apprehension I'd been feeling earlier returned with full force.

For a second, I honestly thought about making a run for it. Looking around, I saw nothing but a couple side streets and a lot of cornfields. We were literally in the middle of nowhere, so, unfortunately, making a run for it was out of the question.

Travis killed the engine then turned to me. "Let's go meet Hank." He smiled, seemingly oblivious to my inner panic attack.

Before we got out of the truck, he grabbed his bag and I did the same because he told me we'd be leaving the semi at the shop. As we were walking, he lifted my backpack off my shoulder and carried both bags in one hand.

Show off.

I scoffed. "I can carry that, you know."

He shrugged. "It looked heavy."

Two garage doors were at the front of the building, one of which was open. Travis sauntered into the shop while twirling the keys around his finger.

"Yo, Hank!" he bellowed, and I had no choice but to follow behind.

As we walked through, I saw a blue sedan with the hood propped up. The scent of tire rubber and motor oil permeated the air with the typical auto shop smell. An older man came out of a small office on the right and stopped in front of us, glancing back and forth between Travis and me.

"This is Angel," Travis introduced me, and I gave an awkward wave.

"Hi, there. I'm Hank Evans." He smiled. "Welcome to my shop. I'd shake your hand, but mine are a little dirty right now." He held his hands out and I could see that they were dark with motor oil and grease.

"Angel Thomas," I responded, wishing I could read his mind. He was looking at me as though he was trying to solve a puzzle.

Another guy, close to Travis's age, came from the back of the garage. There was no doubt in my mind this was Hank's son. Both men were wearing gray coverall uniforms with 'Hank's Auto Shop' embroidered over the left breast pocket, but the similarities didn't end there.

While Hank had hair that was mostly gray, Colton's was a dirty blond and both men had it buzzed short. They also had the same color eyes—a blue so light it almost looked silver. As I studied them, I noticed they also had the same build. Hank and his son were an inch or two shorter than Travis, but their shoulders were broader.

I wondered if all the men of this town were good-looking.

Is there something in the water?

"Look what the cat dragged in," the guy clapped Travis on the back. "And who do we have here?" he asked while giving me the same inquisitive look as Hank.

Both men had their heads cocked slightly to the right as they eyed me curiously. It would have been comical if I hadn't been so nervous.

"You must be Colton," I said, and I suddenly had to fight off a grin because I was picturing a younger version of him and Travis stuck in a shirt together.

"Colton, this is Angel," Travis said. "Angel, this is Colton. Best friend. Roommate. Pain in my ass," he said as he roughly hooked his arm around his friend's neck.

Colton guffawed. "I'm the pain in the ass? Tell her about the time you threw guinea pig poop in my mouth." He reached up and knocked Travis's hat off before attempting to get the upper hand on their impromptu wrestling match.

"You deserved it," Travis grunted as they started grappling in earnest.

"Alright," Hank interrupted their good-natured ribbing. "That's enough, boys." He turned to me. "So, Angel, where are you from?"

"Maine." I knew the questions were coming. My plan was to keep my answers short, if possible.

"And what brings you to these parts?" he asked.

"I was just… traveling. And Travis gave me a ride. I'm on my way to California," I answered vaguely.

"When you say 'traveling' you mean hitchhiking?" Hank crossed his arms over his chest and gave me a very effective 'dad' look.

I sighed. "You're not going to let me get away with the

shortened version of this, are you?"

He chuckled. "Not a chance."

I took a deep breath, preparing to give my entire life story to someone who was not only a complete stranger, but also a father figure to the guy I was crushing on.

Thankfully, Travis came to my rescue again.

CHAPTER 13

Travis

"**Y**eah, she was hitchhiking, but it was the only time she's ever done it. She wants to find her mom in California and doesn't have much money to get there," I cut in before Angel could ramble on about sushi and The Beatles for ten minutes.

Not that I minded her rambling. Actually, I thought it was pretty cute, but I could tell she was uncomfortable. Angel shot me a grateful look and mouthed a 'thank you' for taking over the conversation.

Technically she was a runaway, but we left that part out as we told Hank how I picked her up on the side of the road in Ohio.

"Do you have any idea how dangerous hitchhiking is? Especially for a young woman." Hank's eyes burned into Angel as he gave her his most stern voice. He wasn't usually a serious guy, but he had the ability to make a person feel two inches tall if he wanted to.

Angel swallowed hard. "Yes. It's the only time I've ever done it and I know it was risky. I'm just glad it was Travis who pulled over for me."

"That's why she's going to stay in Tolson for a few weeks," I chimed in. "And I'll drive her to California when I have the Sacramento delivery."

"I think that's a good idea," Hank said before turning his serious voice on me. "And you. You know better. I set rules for you boys when we made this business."

"I know you did. And I broke that rule, but I'm not sorry. I couldn't just leave her there," I said as I looked him in the eye.

'No hitchhikers' had been one of the first rules he made, and at the time that had been a given. Picking up a random person off the side of the road had never been something I thought I'd do.

I knew Hank still saw me as a kid and he was just looking out for me. But I couldn't be sorry about this. If I hadn't been at the right place at the right time… I didn't even want to think of where Angel could be right now. Her eyes darted back and forth between Hank and me while a silent communication passed between us. I could see he understood what I meant. Then I saw the wheels turning in his head and a slow smile spread across his face.

Ah, shit. He could tell I had feelings for her.

"Alright then," he said, still grinning like an idiot. "I'll see you on Monday, Travis. It was great to meet you, Angel."

On that note, Hank walked back to his office while whistling a random tune, and I realized Colton was still hanging around. He'd been pretending to fiddle with a carburetor while eavesdropping.

Nosy prick.

"So, I guess that means you're coming with us to The Brick House tonight?" he asked Angel.

"The what?" She looked confused.

"Dinner, dancing, drinks…" Colton explained.

"Oh, well, I'm not old enough to drink." She nervously toyed with the end of her braid. "Is it a bar?"

"It's a family restaurant," he informed her. "And it also happens to be a bar. They don't usually let people under the age of twenty-one in after nine, but if you come before then, they won't kick you out."

"I don't want to be party pooper. Maybe you guys should go without me. Plus, I don't really have anything to wear…" She looked at me for help. People had a hard time saying no to Colton. The guy was so damn friendly, not to mention persistent. "And I don't dance," she added.

"Hey, that's perfect actually." He gave me a pointed look. "Because Travis doesn't dance either."

"Can I think about it?" she replied.

"Nope," he said and walked away while yelling over his shoulder. "See you tonight!"

I laughed and grabbed our bags. "I'll show you to my place. It's not far."

I led her out of the open garage and took a left down Main Street.

Illinois weather was always unpredictable and inconsistent, especially when the seasons changed. The whole month of June could alternate between hot and humid one day to rainy and cold the next. Today, however, was perfect, with clear blue skies and temps in the mid-eighties.

We passed an empty storefront that had been unoccupied for two years, since the salon didn't work out. I gave Angel a brief history lesson about the different businesses that didn't last.

Just on the other side of the vacant windows, there was a building that used to be somewhat of a warehouse. Someone bought it and turned it into four two-bedroom apartment units. One of them was mine.

"Wow." Angel laughed when we came to a stop at my door. "You said it wasn't far, but I didn't think you meant a block." She looked back down the street, noticing how close I lived to the shop.

"It's convenient, to say the least," I said as I turned the key in the lock and motioned for her go in ahead of me.

Once we got inside I showed her the galley kitchen and the small dining area off to the right.

As if seeing it for the very first time, I looked around and realized she might not be very impressed. I'd never been self-conscious about my place before, but I knew it wasn't extravagant.

The man who remodeled the place did a great job, but didn't use fancy materials. The kitchen had white appliances, oak colored cabinets, and gray laminate counter tops. Throughout the entire apartment, the floor was a peel-and-stick vinyl that resembled wood flooring and the walls were painted a basic off-white.

Frowning, I looked at the eating space, which was just an old card table and three chairs.

In true Angel fashion, she pointed out the obvious. "What happened to the fourth chair?"

I chuckled. "There wasn't one. We bought the set from a yard sale down the street when we moved in. That was three years ago." I self-consciously raked my hand through my hair, realizing I'd left my hat back at the shop when Colton knocked it off. "I guess it's probably time for an upgrade."

"Don't be silly!" Angel exclaimed. "It gives the space character."

She turned around and took in the living room, which was literally two steps away. My apartment had an open floor plan, but the space was small.

"The living room," I said pointlessly, making a sweeping motion with my arm.

Colton and I spent a decent amount of money on the beige microfiber living room set. An armchair sat adjacent to a large couch that lined the back wall of the living room. The coffee table sat on top of a large white shag rug and our 46" flat screen TV was mounted to the wall opposite the couch.

"It's really nice." She turned in a full circle and smiled.

I could tell she was being honest. She really did think it was nice. I guess I could add 'low-maintenance' to the growing list of things I already liked about her.

"Thanks. Colt and I like it."

"You know what I'd really love?" She looked up at me with those big eyes. "A shower."

Angel then proceeded to explain her unfortunate attempt at bathing in the restroom at the truck stop. By the time she finished the story I was laughing so hard I could barely breathe. I flopped down on the couch and she sat next to me.

"That's why you looked like a drowned rat when you came out." I sucked in a breath, trying to get my laughter under control.

"You saw me?" Angel gasped. "You were there?"

Although she glared at me, the corners of her lips twitched. I thought it was cute she was pretending to be offended. She knew that shit was hilarious.

I nodded. "Yeah, I recognized you. That's why I pulled over."

Her eyes softened, and her voice came out quietly. "I'm really glad you did."

"So am I. If I hadn't, you could be sopping wet on a bathroom floor somewhere," I teased.

She shuddered and shook her head. "I'll never do that again."

"You won't have to, even when we go on trips. The truck stop we were at was small and outdated but most of them have showers now, especially the big chain stores," I told her. "Some of them are really nice and truckers usually get free shower coupons when we buy fuel. It can get a little expensive for other people, though. Sometimes six to twelve dollars per shower…"

I trailed off because my attention was drawn to her mouth. She was biting her lower lip and looking at me like she wanted to say something. Or *do* something.

Fascinated, I watched all the thoughts play out across her features. I could clearly see her contemplating her next move. She was so transparent. I could get lost in all her different expressions.

Taking me by surprise, Angel lunged forward and hugged me around the neck.

"Thank you," she whispered, but she didn't let go.

I knew what she meant. This wasn't a simple thank you for the trip we were going to take or the hot shower she was going to get. She was grateful for *everything*.

At first glance, someone could assume Angel was spoiled rotten. That she'd lived a life of privilege. But they'd be wrong. She was one of the most sincere, humble people I'd ever met.

She was sitting on her knees next to me on the couch and her arms were still wrapped around me as I returned the embrace. I felt her breasts press up against me and they rubbed up and down slightly with each breath she took.

I thought about how easy it would be to hook my hand under her thigh and bring her leg around my waist so she was straddling me. And I wanted that. Wanted her legs wrapped around me.

My skin tingled everywhere she touched me and I wondered if she felt it, too.

She pulled back until our faces were so close I could feel her breath against my cheek. Her eyes were wide and searching as she looked at me, and I could tell she didn't know what to do next.

But I knew.

I slowly brought my lips to hers and gave her a gentle kiss.

Keeping my eyes open, I watched her reaction. Her eyes lids dropped and she softly returned the chaste action, her lips automatically responding to mine.

Then I did what I'd wanted to do since the first time I saw her. I drew her pouty bottom lip into my mouth and bit down a little. Angel gasped, and I released it. But I wasn't done yet. And the look in her eyes said she wasn't either.

This time when we kissed, she parted her lips and I slipped my tongue inside her mouth.

When her soft tongue met mine, the kiss turned heated. Her hands left my neck to thread her fingers through my hair. Our mouths melded together as we desperately nipped and stroked each other in perfect rhythm. She sucked my tongue into her mouth and I groaned.

Bringing my hands to her waist, I dragged her onto my lap, placing her thighs on either side of mine. My hands slid down from her waist to grip her hips, while my mouth traveled to her neck. I gently sucked the place under her ear and she whimpered.

Sexiest fucking sound I'd ever heard.

Returning my lips to hers, I didn't hold back. I sucked her bottom lip into my mouth. Hard.

Whether it was intentional or not, her hips bucked forward over mine and I hissed when her hot center rubbed over my throbbing, hard-as-hell cock.

We both went completely still, panting into each other's mouths. Her fingers were tangled in my hair and my hands still gripped her hips.

I think we both realized at the same time we needed to slow down.

The kiss had been so unexpectedly explosive, and the attraction was intense—so far beyond anything I'd ever experienced before. I think we were both surprised by the impact of the moment because the look of shock on her face mirrored mine.

The hammering in my chest was so loud, I was sure she could hear it.

Who knew a kiss could be so powerful?

CHAPTER 14

Angel

I was completely out of control.

My mind told me one thing—*Don't dry-hump him on the couch, Angel*—and then I did the exact opposite.

Travis's hands left my hips and came up to cradle my face, but he didn't kiss me again.

He gently ran the tip of his nose down the slope of mine.

Such a simple gesture.

It was sweet and intimate and it made butterflies erupt in my stomach. It was, hands down, the most romantic thing anyone had ever done.

"You better go take that shower," he whispered against my lips. "Feel free to use as much hot water as you want." He released my face and leaned back. "Because I'll definitely need a cold shower after this."

I giggled. Well, I attempted to giggle but I was so wound up from the sexual tension it came out sounding more like a squawk.

After awkwardly climbing off his lap, Travis showed me to the bathroom and got me a towel from the hall closet.

The bathroom was small, but surprisingly clean for a bachelor pad.

Feeling giddy, I stepped into the stand-up shower. I took my time getting clean, enjoying the hot spray and making the effort to shave. If we were going out tonight, I would probably wear a dress—the only dress I had in my backpack. I almost hadn't packed it, thinking I wouldn't have a reason to wear it. Now I was really glad I did.

I changed back into my leggings and a clean tank top, realizing I needed to do laundry soon.

After coming out of the bathroom, Travis finished the tour of the apartment.

Leading me down a small hallway, he pointed to Colton's door before showing me to his room, which had one of the most comfortable beds I'd ever seen. A fluffy, dark blue comforter was spread neatly over the mattress and several white pillows were piled at the head of the bed.

"You can have the bed and I'll take the couch," he said.

"Seriously?" I leveled him with a look and raised my eyebrows. "We spent last night on your tiny sleeper bed. This bed is huge." I pointed to the king size monstrosity that took up most of the room. "There's no reason why we can't share. I'm not making you sleep on a couch for the next three weeks."

He looked torn and roughly ran a hand through his hair. "We can see how it goes."

I held my hands up. "I promise not to accost you while you're sleep. We can even put up a pillow wall between us," I suggested.

"It's not you I'm worried about," he grumbled quietly. "Hey, do you need a hair dryer?" he asked, effectively changing the subject. "Girls like those, right? Colton's girlfriend left one here if you want to use it."

"Seriously? Yes!" I practically screeched, and Travis winced from how loud it was. We both laughed, and I shrugged sheepishly. "My hair can be really hard to manage if I don't dry it straight." I waved my hand towards the wide, natural waves.

Not knowing what else to do with it, I'd haphazardly thrown my hair back into a braid after the shower. But now, the rogue strands were barely contained, giving me a bit of finger-in-light-socket look.

Travis told me the dryer was under the bathroom sink, and said he'd be in the kitchen trying to figure out if they had any food. Apparently, Colton wasn't much of a grocery shopper.

While I was drying my hair, my mind wandered to what happened on the couch earlier. Just thinking about it made me throb between my thighs and I could feel a slickness beneath my damp panties.

I looked at my reflection as I ran the brush through my hair, which was now sleek and free of my usual messy waves. My cheeks were flushed and my lips were still a bit swollen from the make-out session.

Tilting my head to the side, I ran the tips of my fingers over the spot on my neck where Travis's mouth had latched on. There was no mark left behind, no evidence of where his lips had been. But I could still *feel* it.

Actually, I felt hot and tingly all over. Even my fingertips buzzed with excitement. All I could think about was how much I wanted to do it again, but I wasn't sure jumping on the guy was the best idea. Travis had looked just as taken aback by the encounter as I felt.

After I was done in the bathroom, Travis decided to take his turn in the shower.

I was in his bedroom sorting through my dirty laundry when I heard yelling. Or what I thought was yelling. At first I was alarmed, then I realized what the sound was.

Is that singing?

Travis wasn't kidding about singing in the shower. Or

how bad it was.

It was terrible. Like a stampede of pissed-off elephants kind of terrible.

Holding a hand to my stomach, I doubled over from laughing so hard. His voice carried loudly above the sound of the running water, totally off-key. It was so bad I couldn't even make out what song he was singing.

Or attempting to sing.

It was pure, uninhibited hollering.

As I listened—because I had no choice to do otherwise—I made out a couple of words. At some point, he shouted 'highway' and 'drive', but it still didn't clue me in on the song.

I was still wiping tears from the corners of my eyes when Travis came out and my laughter died in my throat.

He was wearing a towel. Only a towel.

Drops of water still trailed down his chest and stomach. One drop was caught on his right nipple and my face grew hot at the thought of licking it off.

His face was clean-shaven now. Not only did it make him look younger, but it made his dimples pop more when he smiled.

And he was probably smiling because he caught me checking him out.

I realized I was staring but I couldn't stop. Travis slowly walked towards me until I could feel the heat coming off of his body. He brought his finger up to my face and for a second I thought he was going to kiss me.

When he pushed up on my chin, I realized he wasn't going to kiss me—he was closing my jaw for me *because I was just gaping at him*. I hadn't even realized my mouth was open.

I was one step away from drooling. *Awesome.*

Totally embarrassed, I glanced up to see him smirking at me and all I could do was shrug.

Terrible singing forgotten, I shuffled around him so he could get to his room to put some clothes on.

The rest of the afternoon was fairly uneventful. Travis and I watched some bad reality shows and after showing me what little food they had, he said we would need to go grocery shopping tomorrow. The contents of their fridge was seriously lacking. There was an old pizza box, a jar of pickles, bottled water, and beer. That was it.

I didn't put on makeup often because I'd never been very skilled at it. The mascara wand and I had a tumultuous history and I valued my eyesight.

Tonight, however, was sort of a special occasion. I hadn't been out with friends in forever. Distracted by funeral arrangements and grief, I'd even missed my senior prom.

Travis and Colton were new friends, but they were just about the best friends I had right now.

Sad? Yeah, sort of. But I was too excited to care.

Being very careful not to poke myself in the eye during the process, I applied foundation, blush, eyeliner and mascara, then finished off my look with some pink lip gloss.

Next I put on my sundress, which had a retro-style feel to it. It was navy blue with tiny white polka-dots and had a halter top that tied around my neck. The fabric was lightweight cotton and it was perfect for warmer days.

The flowy skirt fell to mid-thigh and I completed my summer look with white sequined flip-flops. My only other option were my Converse sneakers and I knew they wouldn't look right with a dress.

When I glanced in the mirror, I was pleased to notice my breasts look fuller from the shape of the sweetheart neckline. I even had some cleavage going on.

I wasn't a fashion guru, but I was satisfied with my look. Simple. Pretty.

After running the brush through my hair one more time, I came out of the bathroom and found Travis watching a baseball game on TV in the living room. His eyes flitted up to me and his jaw went slack.

CHAPTER 15

Travis

Angel was trying to kill me.

When she came into the living room in that dress, I had to clench my fists to fight off the urge to run my hand up the smooth skin on her thigh. My fingers itched to run through her hair, which looked even longer now that it was straight. The shiny blonde strands almost reached her waist.

She had makeup on, but somehow it made her look more innocent, with her eyes looking bigger, her cheeks pink, her lips plump and shiny. It looked like she'd even swiped a bit of blush onto the tip of her perfect nose.

And that dress... That fucking dress. She looked like a modern-day pin-up girl.

She was every fantasy I'd ever had, come to life.

After fidgeting for a couple seconds, she took a seat on the couch and tucked her feet underneath her thighs. She sent me a shy smile and I regretted choosing to sit in the chair instead of on the couch, where I could've been next to her.

It was a good thing Colton chose that moment to come home because I had no idea what to say. She'd rendered me speechless.

"Hey, roomie," he said to Angel when he saw her. He ruffled her hair as he walked by to the kitchen.

She made an exasperated sound as she tried to comb it back down with her fingers.

"Hi," she grumbled, but I could tell she wasn't mad because she was fighting a grin.

"You look beautiful," he said to her.

"Thank you," she beamed at him, and I felt a bolt of irrational jealousy.

I was suddenly pissed at myself for not telling her first. Actually, I didn't say *anything* to her. I just leered at her like a jackass.

"I'll be right back," I told Angel as I followed Colton into his room and shut the door behind me.

He just crossed his arms over his chest, raised his eyebrows, and waited for me to say what he already knew was coming.

I sighed heavily and hung my head. "I'm so fucking screwed, man."

"I know." He smiled. He was actually enjoying this. For the first time ever, he was seeing me twisted up over a girl. A girl I barely knew, at that.

"It's been less than two days, Colt. And I already like her. A lot," I admitted.

I filled him in on all the details of how she ended up coming back with me, most of which he overheard in the shop. Then I told him the things I didn't tell Hank—that she was a runaway. How we ended up falling asleep in the sleeper cab together, how we almost kissed in the truck, and how we did kiss here at the apartment.

"It's about time you found someone who can drive you crazy. And it's no wonder. She's hot. Seems really nice, too."

The look on my face must have clued him in on the uncharacteristic jealousy I was experiencing, and he held his hands up. "Damn, dude. I'm not gonna hit on your girl.

Besides, I'm already taken. You know I'm a one-woman kinda guy."

I shook my head at how ridiculous I was being. "I know. Sorry."

"I see the way she looks at you," he said, ignoring my irrational moment. "It's pretty obvious she feels it, too. Why don't you just go for it?"

"Go for what?" I asked.

If he was suggesting I just try to bang her before she left, there was a chance I might deck him. Angel deserved better. The thought of anyone trying to take advantage of her situation made my blood boil.

But I should've known better. Colton knew me better than that and he proved as much when he spoke next. "If you want to be with her, really be with her, then do it. Get to know her. Take her on dates and stuff."

"She's only here for three weeks," I pointed out.

"So? That's enough time for you to figure out if there's something real there."

"And if there is? Then what? I'll be here, and she'll be two thousand miles away."

Colton shrugged. "Figure that out when the time comes. If you want it bad enough, you can make it work. This could be the best thing that ever happened to you," he spouted optimistically. "And if isn't, then hey, she'll be two thousand miles away." He grinned.

He had a point.

"You know, you're a smart guy sometimes," I told him before I turned to the door. "And sorry for almost punching you in the face."

"You didn't almost punch me in the face," he said, confused.

"But I thought about it." I grinned.

Colton chuckled. "Wouldn't be the first time it happened."

True. I could count on one finger how many times we'd come to blows, and it was the same story I'd told Angel about the first time Colton and I met.

The talk helped to shed some light on my predicament. He was right. Angel and I had three weeks together, and I decided I wanted to make the most of it.

Angel and I left for The Brick House before Colton, and I told him we'd snag a table before it got too busy.

As I opened the passenger door to my 1972 Chevy to let Angel in, she shot me a look. I laughed because I could tell what she was thinking and she didn't even have to say it.

"I know, I know. You can get in by yourself. I just really want to impress you right now." I winked, and she laughed.

Once I got into my side, I turned the key in the ignition, loving the familiar rumbling purr of the engine.

"Well, I love your truck. Is it vintage?" She rubbed the tan leather seats with her hands. "I really don't know anything about trucks but it looks old."

I grinned. "Yeah, you could say it's old. I restored it myself the first year I was working at the shop. Someone sold it to Hank as a junker for three hundred dollars. I'll never forget when Hank handed me the keys and told me it was an early graduation present. You can imagine my surprise when I tried to start it up and nothing happened." I chuckled at the memory. "The engine had to be rebuilt and the transmission was shot. I had a lot of fun fixing it up, though. It's a gas-guzzler, but I don't drive it much." I lovingly rubbed the dashboard.

Even though it had a few rust spots, I'd left the outside of the truck alone. It was painted an aqua blue, and there was no way the exact same color could be replicated. Besides, I liked the imperfections.

"You've got a really good thing here, you know that? Colton and Hank… I don't know if I've ever had friends like that." She paused and glanced my way. "If I'm being completely honest, I'm a little jealous."

"You don't have to be." I frowned. I didn't want her to feel like an outsider while she was here. "Colton and Hank are like a couple of ticks. They'll accept you as their own and you'll see what I mean. Once they latch on, it's hard to get rid of them," I joked. "Just wait 'til you meet my mom."

"Your mom?" she asked, her tone incredulous.

"Yeah, tomorrow night," I said. "I have dinner with her every Saturday."

"Travis, you don't have to let me tag along to everything you do. I know you have a life here and I don't want to impose."

"Believe me, she'll love you," I assured her.

In all honesty, my mom would probably be planning our wedding before the evening was over. I'd never introduced a girl to her before. To say she was going to be excited was an understatement.

Pulling up to The Brick House, I could see the Friday night crowd was already in full swing. I parked my truck and told Angel to stay in her seat so I could open her door.

As I helped her out of the truck, I laced my fingers with hers.

"You really don't have to do that, you know. Not only can I get into a truck by myself, I can get out, too." She smiled cheekily.

"I know," I told her. "But I want to do things right tonight."

"Is this a date?" she asked candidly, her head cocked to the side.

"Yes," I said without hesitation.

"Oh." Her face showed she was a little shocked by my answer. The smile on her lips also told me she was happy about it.

"Is that okay with you?" I asked as I squeezed her hand and led her toward the building.

"Yes," she said without hesitation, and I laughed.

The Brick House looked exactly as the name said. From the outside, it looked like a normal rectangular ranch-style home with a natural brick exterior. It had a metal roof and the shutters were painted a bright bubblegum pink.

The inside, however, was set up like a sports bar. As soon as I opened the door, sounds of voices, raucous laughter, and music carried out.

The open space was basically one giant room. A long bar jutted out on the left side, and on the far-right end of the large dining area there was a dance floor which was empty at the moment. In between, there were dozens of tables scattered over the floor. Most of them were filled with people, but I saw an open booth in the back close to the dance floor.

On the way to our table, I guided Angel with my hand on the small of her back and politely said hello every time someone greeted me. As always, there were a lot of familiar faces here tonight.

"Wow, you know everyone," Angel said.

I shrugged. "Small town."

Our waitress, Tammy, came over with our menus. Colton used to have the biggest thing for her in back in the day, but she was crazy in love with her high school sweetheart. She ended up marrying him a couple years ago.

Just like me, Tammy was a small-town lifer. Born here. Raised here. Would probably die here.

"Hey, Travis. Good to see ya. Who's this?" she asked, raising her eyebrows at Angel.

"This is Angel. Angel, this is Tammy. We went to high school together." I was able to put my arm around her shoulders because I had her take the seat next to me in the booth.

"This might be the first time I've ever seen Travis here with a date," she said to Angel. "I could tell you some stories about this guy."

"That won't be necessary," I cut in with a smile.

"So lame," Tammy sighed, and Angel laughed.

"You may as well leave a third menu. Colt should be here any minute."

"Sure thing." She nodded and took our drink orders—beer on tap for me and an ice water for Angel.

Angel perused the menu, but I didn't need to because I already knew what I was getting.

"What's good here?" she asked while looking at the sandwich section.

"I always get the loaded nachos."

She hummed. "That actually sounds really good."

"We can just share if you want. It's huge."

"Okay," she smiled and set her menu aside.

"You know, you really do look beautiful," I told her as I ran my hand through her hair. "I should've told you back at my place, but Colton kinda beat me to it."

"You didn't really have to say anything." Her lips curled up at the corners. "Remember how I looked at you when you came out of the shower?" she asked, and I was surprised she was calling herself out like that. "Well, that's what you looked like. I think I might have even seen some drool."

"What can I say? You're worth drooling over," I said honestly, and she blushed.

Colton slid into the booth across from us. "Alright, what did I miss?"

"We already ordered. Tammy's our waitress tonight." I

smirked at him.

He put a hand over his chest like he was wounded. Even though he'd moved on from that long-ago crush, I still liked to remind him of the rejection from time to time.

"She wanted to tell me stories about Travis, but he wouldn't let her." Angel mock pouted.

"Oh, don't you worry about that. I've got plenty to tell," Colton offered, and I shot him a glare.

Thankfully, our food and drinks showed up, interrupting any embarrassing tales from my childhood.

When Angel took her first bite of the nachos, she closed her eyes and moaned. I felt another little stab of jealousy because I hadn't made her make that sound.

I shook my head because I was being ridiculous. Was I seriously jealous of tortilla chips?

Watching Angel eat was its own form of entertainment. She wasn't shy about how much she ate—which I loved—and more often than not, food ended up somewhere on her face because she was messy as hell. She also talked with her mouth full.

It was endearing. It was adorable. And it made me want to kiss the fuck out of her.

After Colton ordered, he talked about what went down at the shop the past couple days—mostly oil changes and tire rotations, which was the norm.

As he spoke, I had my arm lazily slung around Angel and I liked being able to graze my thumb over the smooth skin of her shoulder. I didn't miss the way her breathing hitched every time I touched a sensitive spot by her neck.

Throughout dinner, Colton and I asked Angel questions about Maine and what it was like, because neither of us had ever been there.

"The lighthouses are gorgeous. A lot of people go there

for sight-seeing in the fall because the colors are just amazing. It always smells like the ocean…" She trailed off and looked a little homesick.

"Bet you've never seen so many cornfields before," I joked, trying to keep the mood light. "That's about all the sights you're gonna get around here."

Her faraway look cleared and she laughed lightly. "You're right about that. You basically live in the middle of a giant cornfield."

As we finished our food, the atmosphere in The Brick House slowly changed from a family-friendly restaurant to a night club. The lights dimmed and the music got louder, making it more difficult to have conversations.

The DJ started getting set up a little after 9 p.m. and for the first time ever, I actually thought dancing didn't seem like such a bad idea. If anything, it was a reason to have Angel close to me, to have my hands on her.

One of the reasons the Friday night DJ was so popular was because he played a little bit of everything, from oldies to country to current pop music.

It was tradition for him to kick off the night with a line dance. When 'Electric Slide' pumped through the speakers, Colton let out a loud hoot before excusing himself to the dance floor.

"Watch this," I said to Angel and I pointed at Colton.

Angel and I started cracking up as he attempted to follow along with the moves. He was two steps behind everyone else and almost tripped over his own feet a couple times. At one point, he just started doing some random jig that resembled River Dancing.

"Is he always this bad?" Angel laughed as she gestured towards his jerky movements, which made him look like me might be having a seizure.

"Only for line dances. Doesn't keep him from doing it, though."

"Well, good for him. But you won't see me out there," she replied.

I was never one to back down from a challenge. Angel didn't realize she'd just made it my mission to get her to dance with me.

When 'Earth Angel' came on, I laughed out loud because it was too perfect. It was also incredibly cheesy. I slid out of the booth and held my hand out to Angel.

"Come on," I said.

"I thought you didn't dance," she said as she reluctantly stood up.

"I don't usually, but we're dancing to this."

She rolled her eyes and followed me to the dance floor.

I took both of her hands and brought them up around my neck, then let my hands trail down to her waist.

As the song went on, we gravitated toward each other while we swayed to the music.

By the end, there wasn't any room left between our bodies and I touched my forehead to hers. Her fingernails lightly scratched the short hair on the back of my head and it made my skin tingle.

I wanted to pull her further against me, but it wasn't possible. Our bodies were already plastered together. Any closer, and we'd be giving these people one hell of a show.

It felt like Angel and I were in our own bubble on the dance floor. It was so easy to tune out the rest of the world. All the people, all the noise. Everything else fell away as I held her in my arms.

Billy Currington's 'Must Be Doing Something Right' came on next, and I sent a silent thanks to the DJ for playing another slow song. I wasn't ready to let her go yet.

Our faces were so close together that I could feel each puff of her breath against my lips. Just as I was about to close the distance, I felt a hand on my shoulder.

Colton stood beside me, and he had an apologetic look on his face.

"I'm sorry, dude. Check your texts," he said cryptically, before walking away.

Without letting go of Angel—who looked just as confused as I felt—I took my phone out of my pocket.

Colton: Alert. Alert. Tara and Kendra are on their way here.
Colton: I repeat. Kendra Mc-Pukes-A-Lot is coming
Colton: Check your ducking phone
Colton: Fuck

Fucking great. Just as I slipped my phone back into my pocket, I felt a hand on my other shoulder.

It wasn't Colton this time.

"Hey, Travis," Kendra purred as she rubbed my shoulder. "I was hoping I would see you here."

I felt Angel stiffen in my arms. Her hands fell away from my neck and she tried to step back, but I held onto her.

"Hi, Kendra," I greeted her. I decided I might as well get the awkward introduction out of the way. "This is Angel. Angel, this is Kendra, Tara's best friend."

Hurt flashed through Kendra's eyes and I felt bad. My intention wasn't to hurt her, but she needed to know there wasn't going to be a romantic relationship between us.

My momentary guilt didn't last long though, because her glare turned hard and I could see the hurt turn to anger. I'd seen Kendra have a pretty nasty attitude in the past, but it had never been directed at me before.

"I see you're dancing tonight," she observed as her eyes briefly flitted to Angel. "You gonna save one for me?"

I sighed, and suddenly wished I'd been more straightforward with her earlier in the week instead of avoiding her. I knew that was going to come back to bite me in the ass.

"Hey, give me sec, okay?" I asked Angel. "I'll meet you back at the table."

She nodded. "Sure."

She didn't look sure.

Before walking away, she paused. "It was nice to meet you, Kendra."

She was so fucking sweet. Even with some strange girl staring daggers at her, Angel did the right thing. It wasn't lost on me that Kendra didn't return the sentiment.

The smug look on Kendra's face gave way to disbelief when she realized I wasn't going to dance with her. I walked off with her to an area where she could hear me better.

Because I needed her to hear me loud and clear.

"What the fuck, Travis?" she screeched.

"Listen," I started. "There isn't going to be another date for us. I should've been honest with you about that, and I'm sorry."

"Is it because of *her*?" I realized the shrieking might be something she did often.

"No," I told her honestly. I'd already known there was no future with Kendra even before I met Angel. Hell, I hadn't wanted to go on the date with her in the first place. "I just don't have those kinds of feelings for you. I'm sorry if I misled you," I said, trying to let her down gently.

"What kind of name is Angel anyway?" she sneered. "Where the hell did she come from? Is she even old enough to be in here?"

Her rapid-fire questions about Angel pissed me off. If

Kendra was thinking about trying to get her kicked out of here, we were going to have a serious problem.

"Angel isn't your concern. Neither am I. You and I had one date, but that's where it ends." My tone was hard, and she blanched.

Kendra's eyes narrowed into slits and I was afraid she was going to cause a scene. Instead, she huffed and stomped away.

I hoped that was the end of it, but I should've known getting rid of Kendra wouldn't be that easy.

CHAPTER 16

Angel

When Travis asked me to go back to our table, I thought maybe he was actually going to dance with that girl. A sigh of relief left me when I realized that wasn't the case.

But now I was stuck in some kind of limbo, standing between the dance floor and our table, because Colton and a blonde (who I assumed was his girlfriend) were having an argument in the booth.

I glanced over to where Travis was standing with Kendra, and he seemed to be in the middle of a heated discussion as well.

Since I didn't have anywhere to go I tried to act nonchalant, but it wasn't working very well.

The biggest problem I had when going for aloof?

I never knew what to do with my hands. On the hips? Clasped behind my back? Resting casually at my side?

Inwardly groaning at how painfully awkward I was, I sagged against the wall, hoping I could blend in with the rustic wood panels.

While trying to maintain a cool demeanor, I overheard some of the conversation Colton and his girlfriend were having. I didn't mean to eavesdrop, but it was hard not to overhear because she was practically shouting.

"I can't believe he's being such a douche!"

"He's not being a douche. I told you he never wanted to go on that date," Colton said, his voice much more calm than hers. "She upchucked on his shoes, Tara."

"It didn't stop him from sleeping with her! I know she stayed over at your place last Friday night," Tara said.

Colton's voice got too low for me to hear what he said next.

Travis slept with Kendra last weekend?

I suddenly felt kind of sick to my stomach as reality came crashing down. Maybe Travis really was a player. Obviously, what he did before he met me wasn't any of my business, but it reminded me he had a life here.

One that wasn't going to include me after I left.

Glancing over at Kendra, I studied her. Honestly, she was everything I wasn't. Dark hair, brown eyes, and she was at least five inches taller than me. Her bright purple top was tight over her breasts, which were probably a cup size bigger than mine. Or maybe she just had a really good bra.

Her short black skirt showed off her long, lean legs. With her strappy high heels, she almost matched Travis's height.

Travis looked good tonight and he did it so effortlessly. He wasn't wearing his hat, and his hair looked like he'd just run his hand through it a bunch of times. The perfect combination of messy and sexy. It was so unfair how guys could pull that off.

His plain sage-green T-shirt hugged his arms and chest, showing off the definition underneath, and his worn jeans fit his narrow hips just right, accentuating his backside. I never knew I could be so attracted to a guy's butt.

Grudgingly, I had to admit Kendra and Travis would've made a good-looking couple, and that churning feeling in my stomach returned at the thought.

This was either the bitter taste of envy, or the nachos were bad. I was going to go with the former.

I'd really hate to be the second girl to throw up on Travis within a week.

I was snapped out of my small pity party when Tara stormed off to the bathroom and Colton went up to the bar for another drink.

Just as I slipped back into the booth, I saw Kendra head to the bathrooms after Tara. Travis went up to Colton at the bar and they exchanged a few words before he came to sit down next to me.

"Sorry about that," he said with an apologetic look on his face. "I went out on a date with Kendra last weekend and I think she got the wrong idea about us. There isn't going to be a second date."

Well, she probably would get the wrong idea if you slept with her.

I was insanely proud of myself for keeping that thought to myself. It wasn't my business what he did last weekend. Or *who* he did.

I tried to smile, but it probably came out more like a grimace. "You know, I'm actually feeling kind of tired," I lied. "So I'd be ready to go any time you are."

I looked down at the table and picked at a napkin.

What made me the worst liar ever? Yet again, I didn't know what to do with my freaking hands. I picked at the napkin some more, tearing it up into little pieces.

When he didn't say anything, I glanced up to find Travis studying my face. He stared at me for a beat, his dark green eyes burning into me, then nodded his head. "Yeah, okay," he said, his tone a bit defeated. "I'll just use the restroom real quick, then we can go."

I gave him a tight smile. "Thanks."

A minute later, a different waitress than the one we had before stopped by the table and set a pink-tinted drink in front of me. A cherry floated among the ice and it had a little yellow striped umbrella coming out of the top.

"Someone bought this for you," she told me with a smile.

"What is it?"

"A kiddie cocktail," she answered, then walked away.

I glanced over at the bar to see who might have sent the drink, and I didn't have to look too hard. I made brief eye contact with Kendra and Tara before they turned away, busting up with laughter.

My eyes narrowed at them. It was an obvious dig at how young I was.

The part that pissed me off the most is the fact that I *loved* kiddie cocktails. It's basically a cherry flavored 7-up. With a cherry on top.

Seriously, what's not to love?

I kind of wanted to drink it. Wanted to slurp it down while staring at Kendra, showing her I was enjoying every last drop.

But I wasn't stupid enough to do that. There was a real possibility she put something in it. Like a laxative. Or cyanide.

"What's that?" I glanced up, and Travis was pointing at the offensive beverage.

"Nothing," I said, climbing out of the booth. "You ready to go?"

CHAPTER 17

Travis

I was seeing another side to Angel. She answered me when I asked questions, but her responses were short. This Angel was quiet. Closed off.

I didn't like it.

Clearly, what went down with Kendra bothered her. Even though she tried to act like everything was fine, I knew she was lying. Angel had the worst poker face I'd ever seen.

The whole ride back to my place was silent. She chewed her bottom lip—the same bottom lip I'd had between my teeth just hours ago—while looking intently out the window. There was nothing to see out there. It was pitch black outside and all we passed were fields and a few farmhouses.

For once I'd just wanted a date to go well, but bad luck and my own stupidity had interfered again.

Hoping to finally end my streak of disaster dates, I'd wanted tonight to be perfect. Wanted to start things off right with Angel. And everything had been going great until Kendra showed up.

Sighing, I glanced over at the girl on the other side of the bench seat, wishing I could know what she was thinking.

Fortunately, I didn't have to wait long to find out. We'd just pulled up to my apartment when she spoke.

"Travis," she let out a breath and speared me with her

crystal eyes. "I didn't come here to interfere with your life."

"You're not—" She cut me off by holding up her hand.

"I don't know what this is—" she stopped and waved her hand back and forth between us. "—what this *was* with you and me… But maybe it's better if we take a step back from it."

Her use of the past tense in reference to us left me with an unfamiliar ache in my chest. We'd barely gotten started. I didn't want it to end before it could even begin.

"I don't want to take a step back from it," I told her, my voice gruff.

When she looked at me again her eyes held so many emotions. Confusion. Hurt. Lust.

"It's not any of my business who you slept with, I know that. It's just—"

"Whoa, hold up." Now I cut her off. "Who did I sleep with?"

"Kendra?" She probably meant it to sound like a statement, but her voice got higher at the end like it was a question.

I couldn't help it—I laughed. "Who said I slept with Kendra?"

Looking down, she toyed with the hem of her dress. "I overheard Colton and his girlfriend arguing. She said you and Kendra had sex last weekend after your date."

My eyebrows went up. "She said that?" I asked, wondering if Kendra lied about what went down after our date. "What were her exact words?"

Angel's face scrunched up in thought, causing an adorable wrinkle to appear on the bridge of her nose. "She said that you slept with Kendra. That she spent the night here with you." She thought for another second. "Oh, she also called you a douche. Her words, not mine," she said quickly and held up her hands. "And Colton said she up-chucked on your shoes."

"Kendra did spend the night here after our date," I

confirmed, and Angel's face fell. "But I didn't have sex with her. She didn't want to go home because she was wasted and she didn't want her parents to see her like that. I let her crash on my bed. I slept on the couch."

"Oh." Angel looked relieved, but also a bit embarrassed over the whole conversation. "Well, that makes me feel a little better about it then. I'm sorry I jumped to conclusions. And like I said, it's none of my business who you've slept with."

"Yes, it is your business," I said, and she looked surprised. "You like me. And I like you. There's something here between us and I want to figure out what it is."

Her mouth opened like she wanted to say something, but no words came out. She looked speechless, so I decided to get everything out in the open while I had the chance.

"Angel, I've never slept with anyone. I'm a virgin."

"What?" She jerked back, disbelief written all over her face. From her reaction, you'd think I told her I had bodies buried in my backyard.

Being a virgin isn't *that* weird, right?

"I've never had sex before," I repeated.

"Are you fucking with me right now?" she asked, and I almost jerked back from her use of the F-word. It seemed dirtier coming from her pretty little mouth.

Part of me wanted to tell her she shouldn't say that word. The other part of me wanted to ask her to say it again.

"I'm dead serious. You can ask Colton if you don't believe me."

"But… but…" she sputtered. "You're so… I mean, you know you're really good-looking, right? How is that even possible?"

I just shrugged. I could tell her my entire dating history, but I didn't want to talk about other girls right now. "It just never worked out. And now I'm at the point where I want it to be with someone I really care about."

Angel nodded like she understood. A brief silence fell over us as she processed my confession. "Did Kendra really throw up on your shoes?"

I grinned. Not because it was a good memory—it was actually pretty fucking gross. I just found it highly amusing how Angel wanted to confirm that random detail of the story.

"She did." I grimaced. "It took me an hour to get them clean the next day."

Angel snickered at the unfortunate incident before covering her mouth. She struggled to wipe the humor from her face, but failed. "Sorry. Totally *not* funny."

I reached over to unbuckle her seat belt and motioned her over. After scooting across the bench seat, she snuggled into my side as I put my arm around her.

"I still can't believe you're a virgin," she said, shaking her head. "But since you were so forthcoming about your history… I guess I should let you know I'm a virgin, too."

I hadn't even thought to ask. It didn't really matter to me if she was or not. But now that I knew she'd never been with anyone that way… something akin to relief flowed through me. The thought of anyone else touching her was unpleasant.

Since meeting Angel, I felt like I was learning new things about myself. I'd never been the jealous type before. There was just something about her that made me feel possessive. Protective. It was both exciting and disconcerting.

I hugged her to my side and kissed the top of her head. "I'm sorry our date sucked."

She laughed lightly and squeezed her arm around my middle. "It wasn't all that bad. Actually, I was having a really nice time until Kendra showed up." She glanced up at me and her face suddenly held a hint of outrage. "Did you know that wench sent over a kiddie cocktail?"

My laughter bellowed inside the truck. "Did you just say 'wench'?"

"Yes. Wench. It was mean." She pouted.

"Aw, baby…" I cooed teasingly.

I was mildly surprised by how easily the term of endearment slipped out. I'd meant it to be playful, but as soon as I said it, the word felt more intimate. When she didn't object to it, I was glad. Knowing Angel, if she didn't like it she would tell me. Her straightforwardness was becoming one of my favorite things about her.

Her lips were still slightly pouting when I brought my mouth down to hers. Slowly, I kissed her top lip, nipped at her bottom lip, then finished the kiss with one more soft peck on her full mouth.

As much as I wanted to go further, I knew we needed to ease into whatever this was. The last thing I wanted to do was ruin it by rushing into the physical stuff. We were both in uncharted territory.

Cupping her face with one hand, I ran the tip of my nose down the length of hers. I'd done that on the couch earlier today. I had no idea what made me do it then, and I didn't know why I did it now. I'd never done that to anyone before.

It just felt right with Angel. Natural. Like it was an act of affection meant just for her.

Holding her tighter to my body, I placed another kiss on top of her head. She melted further into me as her fingers drew lazy circles over my ribs. We sat like that for a few minutes in comfortable silence, the only light coming from the glow of the clock on the dash. The darkness outside made me feel like we were in our own world inside the cab of my truck.

Although it wasn't really that late, I couldn't help the yawn that escaped. Since yawning always seems to be contagious, Angel followed right after me and I chuckled.

"I don't know about you, but I'm beat," I said.

She simply nodded, her eyes looking heavy.

Once we got inside my apartment, Angel excused herself to the bathroom to change into her pajamas. I went to my bedroom and started to build a pillow wall in the middle of the bed that could rival any impenetrable wall ever built.

Sleeping in a bed next to Angel was going to be hard for me.

I already knew what it was like to sleep next to her, to wake up with her body pressed against me. We had an excuse for the night before. Falling asleep next to each other had been an accident, and waking up without an inch of space between us couldn't have been helped due to the size of the sleeper bed mattress.

But now... now I knew what her lips tasted like and how the soft flesh of her hips felt underneath my fingers.

However, it wasn't what I knew about her that made sleeping next to her so difficult. The hardest part was the unknown.

There was so much more I wanted to find out.

Like what it would feel like to run my thumbs over her stiff nipples. Or how her ass would feel underneath my palms as I squeezed.

An obnoxious scoffing sound behind me made me turn around. Looking amused, Angel was standing there shaking her head at my construction efforts.

I groaned out loud because I could see her nipples through the white fitted T-shirt she was wearing. But my groan quickly turned to laughter when I got a look at her tiny shorts. I would've thought they were sexy if it hadn't been for the design printed on them.

The light purple fabric was decorated with rainbows, clouds, and unicorns.

Fucking unicorns. Seriously, what were the odds?

Angels hands went to her hips as she glared at me. "Are you making fun of my PJs? These happen to be my favorite," she said, self-consciously tugging at the bottom of her shorts.

"No." I chuckled. "It's just… unicorns and I have a sketchy past."

While we got into bed, I quickly told her the story I'd named "the great unicorn massacre of 2010" and by the end, she was laughing, too.

"I can't believe you just left!" she exclaimed. "That's terrible."

We were lying on our sides, facing each other with a pillow wall in between, and the mounds were so tall we almost couldn't see each other over the top.

"I know. Think I should send them an apology card?" I asked as I turned out the lamp. "I've seriously considered it."

"I think it might be too late. An apology won't bring the unicorns back," she replied with mock seriousness.

Angel's hand was resting on top of a pillow in front of me and I couldn't resist touching her. I slid my hand over hers and lightly ran my thumb across her knuckles. Her hand turned so she could link her fingers with mine and she let out a contented sigh.

"So… what are we going to do about this?" she whispered into the darkness. She didn't have to clarify what she meant. I knew she was talking about what was happening between us.

"I don't know, but I like it. I like you," I said. "And we have three weeks to figure it out."

CHAPTER 18

Angel

For the second morning in a row, I woke up surrounded by Travis.

Although he agreed to share the bed with me, he insisted on building that ridiculous pillow wall I'd suggested.

A lot of good that did.

I was curled up on my right side and Travis was behind me with his arm slung over my middle. His face was buried in my hair and I could feel each exhale against the skin on my neck.

My body was flush up against his and I felt a rigid bulge behind me. I'd always wondered if morning wood was a myth. Now I knew it was *very* real.

The day before, I'd felt his hardness when I was straddling him on the couch, but that was just for a second. Now I could feel the entire length of him along the small of my back.

And I do mean *length*.

The pillows that had been separating us were haphazardly strewn around the room, as if sometime during the night one or both of us decided to blow the barrier to smithereens.

Even during sleep we were drawn to each other like magnets.

I was glad Travis wasn't awake yet because it gave me some time to think about how much my life had changed in the last week.

Although I'd temporarily found a place to stay, I still felt lost. I had no idea how I would ever be able to pay Travis back. I didn't enjoy feeling like a mooch. Plus, what was I supposed to do on days when Travis worked at the shop? I couldn't just sit around his apartment all day.

Well, I could, but that would be really boring. I wondered if there was a business in town looking for temporary help. Although I didn't have a lot of skills, I was a hard worker.

I was drawn from my thoughts when Travis's arm tightened around me and his hips thrust forward. He stiffened as though he just realized what he did. Slowly, his hand traveled down the bare skin of my thigh, then back up to my stomach where one of his fingers grazed the underside of my breast over my shirt. My nipples tightened, and I involuntarily arched back into him.

"Baby… you're killing me," he croaked into my neck, and the heat from his breath sent shivers down my spine.

I felt a swooping sensation in my stomach and throbbing heat in my center that made me press my thighs together and squirm against him.

"Angel," he warned.

I laughed and wiggled again because he was kind of sexy when he got all growly.

Suddenly, I was on my back and Travis was over me. My legs parted of their own accord, making room for him between my thighs. I could feel his erection right where I needed it and my breathing picked up.

"What happened to the pillow wall?" he grumped, and it made me smile.

"It's over there." I pointed across the room. "And over there." I pointed to the other side of the room. "And over—" I gasped loudly when he rocked forward once.

He was in *just* the right spot.

"Do it again," I pleaded, my voice no louder than a whisper.

The expression on his face was pained, but he obliged when he rocked once. Twice. Three times.

My mouth fell open and my eyes closed at the sensations from his hardness rubbing against my clit.

Last night, Travis had changed into a pair of gym shorts and the material was thin and slinky, making it easier for me to feel him. He let out a tortured moan and rested his forehead on mine.

"Angel," he rasped. "I want this. God, I want this, but…"

"It's too soon," I finished for him and he nodded.

My stomach chose that moment to growl, asserting its need for breakfast and giving him an easy out.

"Come on." Travis smiled before planting a quick kiss on the tip of my nose. "We'll need to go shopping if you want to eat."

∾

It's amazing how much you can learn about a person by going grocery shopping with them. At the store, Travis insisted I pick out whatever I want and I told him I would make my famous sloppy joes for lunch.

Well, they weren't actually famous, but they should be. They were that good.

We walked through the aisles picking out our favorite foods, and I raised my eyebrows at Travis when he loaded the cart with five frozen pizzas.

He shrugged. "Colt and I like pizza."

In the cereal aisle, I learned his favorite was Fruity Pebbles and told him about my love for waffles with Nutella. Or just waffles in general.

When he dropped a carton of coffee ice cream into the cart, I couldn't stop smiling because he'd remembered it was my favorite.

At check out, I cringed when the cashier announced the total and Travis got out his wallet to pay.

It reminded me that I needed to find a way to make money somehow. The dog-walking and pet-sitting I'd done in Maine had been a great way to make extra cash.

"You're being quiet," Travis pointed out as we drove back to his apartment.

"I was just brainstorming. Do you know anyone who wants their house cleaned? Or I could be a dog-walker. I want to be able to pay for stuff while I'm here. I already owe you for the past few days."

"Don't think of it like that." He shook his head. "You don't owe me anything."

"Yes, I do." I gave him my best 'I mean business' look. "I was serious about paying you back. Plus, it would be nice to have something to do. To feel useful."

"Okay. I can understand that. I tell you what—ask my mom tonight. She has a lot of friends at church who might be looking for some help."

The sloppy joes were a hit. Colton staggered out of his room sometime before noon, grumbling about being hungover. His grumbling turned to words of praise as he devoured at least four sloppy joe sandwiches.

"These are amazing," he said around a big bite. I snickered because his face was a mess and a big glob of sloppy joe meat was smeared down the front of his shirt. "I think I might need you to marry me."

"Hey," Travis said sharply. "You've got your own girl."

Colton just grunted in response. After the argument I'd witnessed last night, I wasn't sure how stable things were with Tara, and I didn't want to ask in case it was a sore subject.

I went over to the counter to get two paper towels for the guys because gooey hamburger meat was spattered all over their faces. Travis tore his paper towel in half and crooked his finger at me.

"What?" I asked, walking over to him.

"You've got a little something right here," he smirked as he wiped at a spot near my mouth.

Dang. I thought I got it all.

I shrugged, trying to play off my embarrassment. "They're called sloppy joes for a reason."

"Crack-joes. They should be called crack-joes." Colton laughed at his own joke before leaning back and patting his stomach.

"They're really easy to make. I can write down the recipe for you, so when I'm gone you can make them whenever you want," I said, and the room got quiet.

I'd meant the suggestion to be helpful, but all I'd managed to do was remind everyone, including myself, that my time here was temporary.

CHAPTER 19

Travis

"**S**o Tara and Kendra showing up last night…" Colton began. "That was a crapshoot, huh?"

Beads of sweat dripped from my forehead as I finished my last set at the bench press.

Every Saturday, Colton and I went to the gym if our schedules allowed. We'd asked Angel if she wanted to come with us but she said she had laundry to do and felt like staying in for the afternoon, which was cool with me.

I kind of liked the idea of her being at my place even when I wasn't.

"Yeah," I said as I racked the weights and sat upright. "Not gonna lie, that sucked pretty bad. How much trouble are you in with Tara?"

Colton grunted and shrugged. "She gave me a ride home last night, so I guess things are alright. Speaking of which, can you drop me by my car? Left it at Brick House last night."

I laughed. "I guess if I had to hang around those two, I would've drunk myself into oblivion, too. I thought Kendra was supposed to work at Buck's last night."

"She was," he said. "She called in sick."

"Seriously?" I asked, a little shocked that she would risk her job like that. If word got back to Buck, she could get fired.

He nodded. "I'm really sorry, man. I never should've had

you go out with her. I knew that shit was a bad idea from the start." He made a sound of frustration. "I thought setting up that date would finally get Tara off my back, but it just made things worse."

"You *should* be sorry," I said as we made our way to the pull-up bar. I couldn't help giving him a hard time about it. He seriously owed me big time.

"How much trouble did that cause with Angel?" he asked, concerned. "You guys left pretty early last night."

"We talked things out. It's cool," I told him, and we finished the rest of our workout in silence.

After leaving the gym, I spilled my feelings about Angel. "I've dated before but it's never been this intense. Is it too soon for me to be feeling like this? Am I crazy?" I asked, gripping the steering wheel a little too tight. Waking up with Angel this morning still had me all wound up. "I've never met anyone like her. I didn't even know it was possible to feel this way."

"Is it fast? Yeah," he confirmed. "But I've never felt the way you're feeling. Hell, I've been with Tara almost a year…" He trailed off because he didn't need to finish the sentence. It wasn't a secret that their relationship wasn't great. "You and Angel have known each other less than three days and you have a connection I've never experienced. Fact is, I like Angel and I think she's good for you. She's genuine. And she makes kickass sloppy joes." He grinned.

"Damn right, she does," I agreed.

"You said things aren't so good with her mom?" Colton asked. I just nodded because I didn't want to give away too many details without Angel's permission. We never told Hank or Colton that her mom was in jail. "Well, maybe you could convince her to stay here." He voiced the best-case scenario I was too afraid to hope for.

The thought had crossed my mind, but it was way too

soon to bring it up to Angel, so I decided to switch to a different topic.

"I think we're having trouble controlling ourselves… physically," I admitted, and I grimaced because it made me feel like a total pussy. "We're both not very experienced, you know…" I shook my head, feeling frustrated. "I just don't want to rush it."

Colton guffawed and clapped me on the back. "Welcome to being in lust, my friend."

CHAPTER 20

Angel

Instead of driving to Travis's mom's house, we walked. Everything in Tolson was within walking distance, so when the weather allowed that was the preferred method of transportation.

It was a beautiful evening as we walked up the driveway to a cute one-story home with light yellow siding and white shutters. A small garage sat behind the house and a white fence lined the backyard. Colton came along, too, because apparently he would never miss lasagna night.

Travis said I should dress casual when he saw me debating between the dress from last night and a T-shirt with jeans, so I went with the latter. I was wearing my white off the shoulder tee and Travis couldn't seem to stop touching the exposed skin.

I wasn't complaining.

He had his arm around me and every time his thumb brushed my shoulder, I felt a swooping sensation in my stomach.

"You were wearing this the first time I saw you," he whispered into my ear.

Before I could respond, Colton waltzed in the front door of the house and shouted "Yo, Karen! Travis has someone he wants you to meet!"

I rolled my eyes. *Subtle.*

Travis shrugged and smiled, giving me the dimples.

I hesitated at the threshold and he noticed. "Don't worry, she's going to love you," he promised as he linked our hands together.

Ready or not, he tugged me inside. The front door led right into a small living room with walls painted a pale yellow. A floral couch and loveseat took up most of the space, but instead of looking crowded it was cozy. The coffee table and TV stand were made from some kind of weathered wood, giving it a rustic, shabby chic style. It was nice. Homey.

The smell of lasagna and garlic bread filled the air and my mouth watered. A petite woman wearing a pink and white chevron print apron over yoga pants and an oversized T-shirt came out of the kitchen.

She was pretty—beautiful, even—and didn't look older than early-forties. Her light brown hair was pulled into a low ponytail. Though she was much smaller than Travis, the resemblance was definitely there.

Something about her immediately put me at ease. Maybe it was the casual clothes.

Or the fact that she was so dang happy to see me.

After noticing I was holding Travis's hand, she smiled brightly, showing a very familiar set of dimples. And it was no ordinary smile—her face lit up like the Fourth of July. The woman was ecstatic.

"Mom, this is Angel," Travis introduced me.

Thinking we would shake hands, I started to extend my arm her way. I realized a simple handshake wasn't going to happen when I was engulfed in her arms. My hand got caught awkwardly between us against my stomach, and my breath left my body with a whoosh with how hard she squeezed.

Travis obviously came from a family of huggers.

"I'm Karen," she said, still squeezing. She abruptly pulled back, putting me at arms-length. With her hands on my shoulders, she looked me up and down. "She's gorgeous, Travis. How did you two meet?" she asked, finally leaving my personal space.

"We met while I was on the road," he said vaguely. "Angel needed a place to crash for a few weeks before she goes to California to find her mom."

Karen quickly hugged Travis, then Colton, before turning back to me.

"Well, you boys go watch some TV. Isn't there a baseball game on or something? Angel and I are going to have some girl time." She made a shooing motion at them before looping an arm around my shoulders and ushering me to the kitchen.

I sent Travis a pleading look, but he just smiled and gave me a thumbs-up sign.

Traitor.

The kitchen held the same rustic theme as the living room. The cabinets were painted white and the counter was made from wood butcher block. Fancy floral tea cups decorated the shelves above the kitchen sink. There was a nook on the far end of the room that held the dining area with a round wooden pedestal table and five chairs.

"I'm gonna need details," Karen sang.

"Details?"

"Of course. We're women. It's what we do," she explained as she slipped her hands into oven mitts. After taking the lasagna and garlic bread out of the oven, Karen faced me. "So, you're trying to find your mom?" she fished.

I nodded and took a deep breath. I didn't want to be dishonest to Travis's mother, so I went for the truth. "I won't have to look very hard. I know where she is." I paused, and she waited patiently for me to continue. "She's in prison."

Karen didn't miss a beat. "And you and Travis met on the road…?"

"In Ohio," I finished for her. "I was hitchhiking. He took pity on me and picked me up."

"Well," she breathed out as she sagged back against the counter, oven mitts still on her hands. I braced myself for the disapproval that was sure to come. Would she give me a lecture? Tell me to stay away from her son? "That's one hell of a love story, if I've ever heard one."

Two things happened—my jaw dropped open because that was the last thing I expected her to say. And I also turned ten shades of red because she implied her son and I were in love.

"Oh… Uhh…" I stammered and let out a nervous laugh. "We've only known each other for, like, three days…"

She made a dismissive sound and started to take the aluminum foil off the lasagna.

"Here, you can slice the garlic bread." She patted the space on the counter next to her and handed me a bread knife.

As I started cutting the loaf into thick slices, I glanced at Karen out of the corner of my eye. I'd forgotten what it felt like to make dinner with a mother-type figure. It was nice. Claire wasn't much of a cook. She said slaving away in the kitchen stifled her creative mind—whatever that means.

Working side by side with Karen felt more comfortable than it should, considering I'd just met the woman.

"So you don't think my situation is weird?" I asked, hesitantly.

She paused. "How much did Travis tell you about me?"

"Some." I glanced at her. I wasn't sure if I should tell her I knew about her drinking problems. "He said you're a great mom and he's proud of you."

"He's a good boy," she said warmly. "I'll be the last one

108 | JAMIE SCHLOSSER

to throw stones. If you think I'm gonna judge you because of where you came from, you're wrong. I'm an alcoholic. Been sober for seven months and sixteen days."

"That's really great. The sober part, I mean," I added, and she laughed.

"I'll bet Travis didn't tell you you're the first girl he's ever brought home," she said while she heaped lasagna onto four plates.

I added a few pieces of garlic bread to each plate as I tried to hide my surprise. "No, he didn't tell me that."

"I've been waiting for this day," she beamed at me then turned to yell into the living room. "Dinner's up, boys!"

CHAPTER 21

Travis

Dinner at my mom's house went just as well as I knew it would. Angel fit right in. Colton and I discussed some business at the shop and the Mount Vernon delivery he had to haul in the morning, until Mom told us to stop talking about work at the dinner table.

Before our plates were even clean, Mom had out the photo albums.

"And this one is Travis in the baby tub. He had the cutest little tushy…" she pointed out, and Angel laughed so hard her eyes watered.

Seriously, naked baby pictures?

Kill me now.

I sent a scowl in Angel's direction, but she just smiled and gave me a thumbs-up. The corners of my lips twitched. I guess I deserved that.

As we were getting ready to leave, I turned to my mom. "Angel wants to find some temporary work while she's here. You got any ideas?"

"Well, we don't need any help at the post office. That's where I work," she informed Angel. "It would be difficult to find a job for such a short amount of time."

"I was thinking more along the lines of house-cleaning, babysitting, or dog-walking," Angel told her. "I've done some pet-sitting before."

"You know, Beverly Johnson is looking for someone to do some yard work. She's almost eighty and she's having trouble getting around these days. Have you ever mowed a lawn before?" my mom asked.

"No, but I could do it," she replied with confidence.

"I'll see Beverly at church tomorrow morning. I'll tell her you'll stop by. Is Monday around noon okay?"

"That would be perfect." Angel smiled brightly.

After my mom wrote down Beverly's address and landline phone number—because she didn't have a cell phone—we said our goodbyes.

Before we could get out the door, my mom loaded us down with leftovers, hugged Angel again, and told her to come visit any time.

As we got ready for bed, I didn't even bother with the pillow wall. We both knew it wouldn't keep us apart.

Angel changed into gray leggings, which made her ass look phenomenal, and a plain black tank top.

Hoping the extra layers would help me keep my hands to myself, I put on a T-shirt and baggy sweatpants. I seriously doubted it would do any good, though.

Without thinking, I always gave Angel the side of the bed that butted up against the wall and I took the side closest to the door. I don't know why I did it. For some reason, I felt the need to protect her even when there wasn't any danger.

Leaving a couple feet of space between us, I slid under the covers after I turned out the lamp.

"Your mom is pretty great. She's awesome, actually," Angel said quietly.

The moonlight came through the window, and a silvery glow radiated off her light hair.

"She loved you. I knew she would," I told her.

"Has she ever dated? You know, since your dad?" She turned onto her side to face me.

"No. Colt and I tried to set her up with Hank once. We thought it would be the coolest thing ever to be stepbrothers." I laughed at the memory.

"I take it the date didn't go so well?" she concluded. Even in the shadows, I could see her smile.

"Well, it might've helped if we told them we were setting them up," I said. "We were twelve at the time and I guess we didn't understand what a blind date was. I invited Hank over for dinner one night but I didn't tell Mom about it. We thought we were being so sly." I laughed. "They caught on pretty quick."

"What happened?" she urged.

"We'd all had dinner together before, so that wasn't new. With Colt and me being such good friends and we were neighbors… But this time we lit candles and shit." I cringed. "And we may have put on some Marvin Gaye…"

Angel burst out laughing. "Oh my God! Way to be subtle about it." She poked me in the ribs. I wanted to keep touching her so I grabbed her hand and held it between us.

"I think Hank always had a little crush on her. They had a lot in common—single parents, both widowed."

"What happened to Colton's mom?" she asked.

"Breast cancer. She was only thirty. I never met her because Colt and Hank moved here after she passed away. They wanted a new start," I explained. "Anyway, the blind date… Mom ended up having one too many drinks and she fell asleep on the couch. Hank understood she wasn't ready. He took me aside and told me he didn't have to be with my mom to stay in my life. Told me he loved me like a son."

Angel sighed wistfully. "You're so lucky. You have so much here."

"You're here now," I stated, wanting her to know she had a place in my life, too.

"Yeah. I'm here now," she quietly agreed.

～

Sunday morning started exactly how I thought it would. Lying on my back, Angel's leg was hooked over my hip and her head rested on my chest. This was the first time I'd woken up before her, and it gave me some time to study her without her knowing it. She looked even more innocent when she slept.

I felt something tickling my cheek and realized it was a strand of her hair.

Actually, her hair was everywhere. Last night it had been sleek and straight but now it was a wild, chaotic mess, spanning out in all directions. It tumbled over the pillow we were sharing and covered half her face.

She was beautiful.

Outside I heard the rumbling of thunder, and raindrops pelted the window pane.

Damn. That ruined my plans for today.

I thought about getting out of bed but I didn't want to wake Angel. Her deep, even breathing and the rhythmic pattering of the rain lulled me back to sleep. I drifted in and out for a while, feeling peaceful with her in my arms.

One crash of thunder was particularly loud and it woke Angel, making her jump.

"Shhh. It's just a thunderstorm," I murmured and kissed the top of her head.

She relaxed back into me.

After a minute, she groaned. "I don't want to get out of bed. Rainy days always make me feel lazy."

"We could just stay here all day." I wiggled my eyebrows.

She laughed and playfully smacked my chest. Then her face turned mischievous.

"And what would you do if I wanted to stay right here…" She sat up and swung her leg over me so she was straddling my hips. "All day?" She batted her eyelashes innocently at me.

Fuuuuuck.

Days ago, she'd been shy. Hesitant.

She was getting bolder with me and I liked it. I liked it a little too much. I went from slight morning wood to raging hard-on in an instant.

Without a doubt, we were going to have sex at some point. There was no way I could last three weeks with Angel in my bed, and I could tell she was having trouble controlling herself, too.

I didn't stand a chance. But it wasn't going to happen today.

It was killing me to put the brakes on like this, but I already knew I wanted something real with her. If she was going to be living two-thousand miles away, our relationship would need a solid foundation to stand on. I was determined to make that happen. Unfortunately, we needed time but that wasn't something we had a lot of.

I decided to diffuse the sexual tension with humor.

"I'm a little scared," I told her.

Her face immediately changed to concerned. "Of what?"

"I'm like ninety percent sure your hair has a life force of its own and I might be attacked," I teased, cracking a smile.

She gasped. "I can't believe you!"

Angel picked up a pillow and hit me with it. Scrambling, she tried to make it off the bed, but I grabbed her around the waist and held her to me, pulling her back against my chest.

"Kidding! I'm just kidding." I laughed as she put up a half-hearted struggle to get away. "Baby…" I whispered.

As soon as I said that, she melted. Obviously, she liked being called *baby*. Noted.

Although I gave her a hard time about her hair, Angel was still the most gorgeous girl I'd ever seen, bedhead and all.

"I had big plans for us today, but the rain kind of ruined it," I grumped.

"Oh yeah? What plans?" She looked back at me over her shoulder.

"I wanted to make up for our bad date. I was going to take you fishing."

"I love fishing!" She squirmed until she turned around to face me. "I won a fishing derby when I was eight. I caught the biggest fish," she said proudly.

"We'll have to do that another time, then. I want to see these mad fishing skills." I placed my hand on her side and rubbed my thumb back and forth over her hipbone.

"What do you normally do on Sundays?" she asked, raising her hand up to lightly rub her fingers over the stubble on my jaw.

I shrugged. "Laundry. Sometimes I get some cleaning done."

"I can help with all that."

"I'm not making you do my laundry, Angel."

"You're not *making* me. I want to. It's the least I could do. Please?" she pleaded.

When she looked at me like that with those big eyes, how could I say no?

CHAPTER 22

Angel

Since Colton was gone on a delivery, it was just Travis and me in the apartment. We worked well together as a team. I did the laundry and wiped down the counter tops while he washed the dishes and took out the garbage.

I'm one of those weird people who actually likes doing laundry. There was just something satisfying about taking the warm bundles out of the dryer and folding everything into neat piles.

As I sniffed the clean clothes, I realized the fresh smell reminded me of Travis. The scent of the laundry detergent wafted from the fabric, but so did something else. Something that was distinctly him.

Could I be any creepier?

I'd been reduced to sniffing the guy's clothes.

After all the cleaning was done, Travis suggested we watch a movie since the rain hadn't stopped.

He was sifting through his DVDs when I saw my favorite movie was on TV.

"*Fried Green Tomatoes* is on!" I said happily.

"Tomatoes, what?" He made a face.

"*Fried Green Tomatoes*. It's the best movie of all time," I said, but he looked skeptical.

"It's a chick movie, isn't it?" he accused.

"Technically, yes."

He dropped all the DVDs and came to sit next to me on the couch. "All right. I'll give it a chance. For you." He bopped me on the nose with his index finger then put his arm around me.

Somehow we ended up cuddled in the spooning position, my back to his front, and I was having trouble concentrating because sometimes his hand would brush over my lower stomach, which sent a jolt of lust straight to my core. Travis seemed completely oblivious to the effect he was having on me.

Or maybe he was torturing me on purpose. Was sexual frustration considered a legit form of torture? It definitely should be.

It didn't take Travis long to be totally into the movie, and towards the end he started getting impatient for answers.

"Who killed Frank Bennett?" he pestered me. "It was Idgie, wasn't it?"

"I'm not spoiling it for you. You'll have to watch and see."

"Are you ticklish?" He propped himself up to look down at me and snaked his hand over my ribs. "I bet I could tickle it out of you."

"You wouldn't dare," I challenged.

"Oh, I would," he said as his fingers started to dance along the sides of my stomach.

I laughed and squirmed uncontrollably while yelling incoherent words of protest. At one point I threatened to pee my pants, and he just laughed.

The playful moment suddenly turned serious as our eyes locked and we both noticed the position we'd ended up in. Travis had moved on top of me and our faces were so close our breath mingled. The laughter faded, and we just stared at each other.

His brown hair was messy and the strands fell over his forehead, almost falling into his eyes. I reached up to run my fingers through it, brushing it to the side, but it just flopped back into the same place.

A few seconds went by before he closed the gap between us. Soft, firm lips met mine.

I hadn't kissed a lot of guys, but my lack of vast experience didn't stop me from realizing Travis was a *really* good kisser.

As he nipped at my lips, I opened my mouth to invite him in. His tongue slowly brushed mine and he repeated the action over and over again. This wasn't frenzied like before.

It was painfully, wonderfully slow. We delved deeply into each other, enjoying every sensation, every taste.

Every now and then he would pull back to suck my bottom lip, then I would do the same to him. My hands curled into his shirt and I pulled at him, wanting him closer.

Wetness pooled between my thighs and I started to shift uncomfortably beneath him, trying to get the friction I needed. I was so turned on it was almost painful.

The room was dark except for the light flickering from the TV. I wasn't sure how much time had passed, but the movie was long over and forgotten.

Travis broke our connection as he lifted his head and put enough space between us to look at me. Breathing hard, I begged him with my eyes not to stop.

I'd noticed he had been pulling back every time things started to get too heated, making sure we didn't go too far. I wasn't sure if it was his virtue or mine he was trying to protect, but it was becoming very frustrating.

Just as I thought he was going to say we should stop, he flipped us so he was lying on his back and I was straddling him. I moaned when his rigid length pressed against my throbbing center.

Travis seemed to know what I needed as he put his hands on my hips and pulled me forward slightly, dragging my core over his hardness. My mouth fell open and I gasped.

"Move," he whispered, nodding his head encouragingly.

I started rocking back and forth over him, reveling in the perfect pressure it put on my clit.

"Come here," Travis said as he pulled my face down to his.

I continued to move my hips over him as our lips and tongues moved together. He seemed to be enjoying it just as much as I was, and he started to thrust forward to match my movements.

His hands came up to cup my breasts over my shirt and he lightly ran his thumbs back and forth over my painfully hard nipples.

I moaned and rocked faster, being driven by need, and the rhythm of our kissing faltered.

My body had taken over and I could feel a familiar tightening in my belly and tension building between my thighs.

I'd had an orgasm before. By myself, of course.

Never like this. It never occurred to me this could be done with all our clothes on.

Burying my face in Travis's shoulder, I cried out as I came harder than I ever had before. I actually think I might have blacked out for a second.

Travis's hips jerked forward one last time and he groaned. We stayed that way for several minutes, panting and holding onto each other.

Well, he held onto me, and I just lay on top of him in a boneless heap.

CHAPTER 23

Travis

Holyfuckingshit.

I came in my pants.

Like a fucking teenager.

I didn't expect that to happen. I'd wanted to let Angel use my body for her own gratification, but my good intentions went to shit when she started grinding herself on my dick.

And when she started making all those sexy sounds, it took everything I had not to explode right then and there. I wasn't even sure if she was aware of the whimpers and moans coming out of her mouth, but it drove me crazy. Then I felt her stiff nipples through her shirt and realized she wasn't wearing a bra.

When she came apart on top of me, I just lost it.

I couldn't even feel embarrassed about it because it'd been the best orgasm of my life. It made me wonder if it was this good over our clothes, what would it be like to experience the real thing?

We cuddled on the couch for a while as I stroked her hair. Neither of us said anything, but it didn't feel awkward. Just peaceful.

I heard the key turn in the door before Angel did. I was really glad Colton hadn't come home ten minutes earlier because that would have been one hell of an interruption.

Quickly, I pulled the blanket off the back of the couch to cover us before he walked in. Even though we were fully clothed, I still felt the need to shield Angel because of the intimacy of the moment.

Surprised by the front door swinging open, Angel squeaked and slid behind me on the couch. I put my arm around her so she could rest her head on my chest.

"Hey," Colton said casually as he went by to the kitchen. To him, it probably just looked like we were lying down watching a movie.

Angel looked at me with wide eyes and we both had to fight off the goofy grins on our faces when he came back into the room, chugging a bottle of water. He flopped down into the chair by the couch.

"So, what did you guys do today?" he asked.

"Just hung around here. Did some cleaning," I told him, and I was proud of myself for being able to keep a straight face. "And we watched a kickass movie about an old lady who liked to tell stories about people getting killed and shit."

Angel elbowed me in the stomach and snickered at my summary of her favorite movie.

"Sounds awesome," Colton said, and he filled us in on the details of the Mount Vernon pick up—which was pretty uneventful—then, finally, said he was headed to bed.

Shooting the shit with Colton while I had sticky jizz inside my boxers wasn't something I ever cared to do again. To say it was awkward was an understatement.

As we got into bed that night, Angel and I didn't bother putting space between us as we fell asleep. Meeting in the middle of the bed, Angel curled up next to me as I put my arms around her.

CHAPTER 24

Angel

I knocked on the old screen door a second time as I stood on Beverly Johnson's porch. Maybe she didn't hear it. Old people had trouble hearing sometimes, right?

I unfolded the piece of paper Karen gave me to make sure I had the right address.

204 Walnut Street

I looked up at the house number, then the street sign on the corner. I was definitely at the right place.

The house was tiny, with a white painted brick exterior. Dark green trim lined the windows, reminding me of the color of Travis's eyes. I rolled my eyes at myself because my infatuation with him was reaching new levels.

I was about to knock a third time when the inside door swung open.

"Can I help you?" the old woman said through the screen.

She was very small—probably two inches shorter than me. She had thick rimmed glasses and her short, curly hair was a dyed a shade of black that almost looked blue.

Even though it was almost ninety degrees outside, she wore a fuzzy pink housecoat that looked really warm. I would've been burning up in that thing. I had on shorts and a tank top, but I was still sweating bullets.

"Hi, I'm Angel," I introduced myself. "Karen Hawkins

sent me over to mow your lawn?"

"Oh, yes." She smiled and came out to join me on the porch. "You can just call me Beverly. Calling me 'ma'am' makes me feel too fucking old," she said sweetly, and I did a double-take.

Did she just say what I think she said?

Beverly started down the steps and I followed her around the house to the backyard while she continued to talk. "The mower's in the shed. The little boy from down the street usually cuts my grass, but he's away at summer camp. My fucking yard looks like shit."

I pressed my lips together to keep from laughing, but inside I was *dying*.

Beverly had a potty-mouth. I was under the impression little old ladies didn't cuss. Obviously, I was wrong.

Despite my efforts to keep the laughter in, a giggle escape anyway and I tried to cover it with a cough.

"Yeah, it does look like it needs some work," I agreed. Not only was the grass overgrown, but dandelions and weeds were scattered everywhere.

She guided me to a shed, which looked like it might not hold up for much longer. White paint peeled off the rotted wooden siding, and the hinges screeched as the door opened. Inside was an ancient-looking push mower.

"You know how to work this thing?" Beverly asked as she gave it a light kick with the toe of her pink house slippers.

I shrugged. "I can figure it out."

∽

I couldn't figure it out.

There had been instructions on the mower at one time, but it was too faded and scratched up to make out the words.

Not helpful.

I pulled at the cord for what had to be the twentieth time, putting all my strength into it. This time it actually started to sputter to life and I let out a triumphant shout.

Unfortunately, it didn't last more than a couple seconds before it died. I let out a frustrated groan and wiped the sweat from my forehead. The long, green blades tickled the back of my thighs when I sat down in the grass, and I wondered what I should do next.

Maybe I should wave the white flag and admit defeat.

I picked an overgrown dandelion from amongst the weeds. Spinning it between my fingers, I blew the fuzz into the breeze and made a wish.

It was a simple wish. Home and happiness. The two things I wanted most.

"Looks like you might need some help," a gravelly voice said behind me.

I turned to see an old man—probably in his eighties—standing on a concrete patio in the backyard next door. He was wearing khaki pants that were being held up by suspenders over a white button-up shirt. On top of his head was a weathered-looking hat that said 'Army'.

"Yeah. This thing is trying to kill me," I sighed dramatically as I pointed to the uncooperative piece of machinery.

He barked out a laugh. "It can be tricky. First thing you gotta do is check to make sure it's got gas in it."

Oh.

"Well, that would make sense," I said, feeling a bit dense for not thinking of something so obvious.

The man got down to his knees to unscrew the gas cap and he peered inside. "Yep. Got gas," he confirmed and put the cap back on. "Next, you gotta push this button here three times. It pumps the gas into the lines so it can start."

He pointed to the button and I did what he said.

"Now," he said as he stood up, "gotta hold onto this lever, unless you want the engine to stop. Then you pull the cord. And you gotta pull it fast." He whipped his arm back, mimicking the motion.

I grabbed the lever and brought it down to the handle with one hand, while I reached for the cord with the other. Pulling as hard as I could, I yanked on the cord and the mower roared to life.

I squealed as it lurched forward and I had no choice but to hang on and walk along with it. The man was laughing so loud I could hear it over the noise of the mower.

"Thank you!" I yelled back at him as I continued to stumble forward.

Once I got going, it really wasn't that hard. The worst part was the heat. Earlier, I had put my hair up in a messy bun and I was glad to have it off my neck and shoulders, which were dripping with sweat.

Beverly's yard wasn't huge, so my job was done in about twenty minutes. After I was finished, I was putting the mower back in the shed when the man from next door came back over.

"Not bad, little lady, not bad," he said as he stuck out his hand. "Name's Ernie."

I wiped my hand on my shorts before returning the handshake. "Angel."

"Any chance you're looking for more yards to mow?" he asked.

"Yeah, definitely," I said, excited at the possibility of getting more work. More work meant more money.

"My yard's bigger, but I've got a riding mower," he boasted, hitching his thumbs under his suspenders. "When are you free?"

"Um, right now?"

"You're hired!" he exclaimed, and his smile was contagious.

"I'll just go let Beverly know I'm done and then I'll be right over," I told him.

"I won't expect you for at least half an hour." He started back towards his house. "Beverly loves company. She's probably got lemonade and cookies set out already."

Funny thing was, Ernie was right. Well, he was right about the lemonade. Not so much the cookies, but he was close. Sitting on a fancy plate in the middle of Beverly's kitchen table were a bunch of unwrapped Twinkies.

The inside of her house smelled like an interesting combination of Bengay and cupcakes, and all the rooms looked like they hadn't been redecorated since the '70s. She showed me to the bathroom so I could wash my hands and I was amused by the fact that everything was pink—the walls, sink, toilet, and carpet.

In the kitchen, her appliances were an avocado green and the walls were plastered with wallpaper full of bright orange flowers.

"So, how did you end up in Tolson?" Beverly asked as we sat down at the table for our snack.

"I'm just sort of passing through. I'm going to California to see my mom," I explained. "Travis, Karen's son, is letting me stay with him for a few weeks."

"Ah, yes," she hummed. "That boy is one fine piece of ass."

Shocked by her brash statement, I inhaled some of the lemonade I was drinking and started coughing violently.

She continued speaking, completely ignoring my inability to breathe properly. "Now, don't get your panties in a twist. I'm not gonna try to take your man. He's too young for me anyhow."

I switched between coughing and laughing while I tried to clear my airway.

After getting myself under control, Beverly and I chatted for a while. She told me she'd been a widow for fifteen years and she had three sons, all who lived in different parts of the country. She also had five adult grandchildren.

"They keep telling me I need to get a cell phone so I can FaceTime. I don't even know what that is. Some days, I can't even figure out how the hell to work my own damn television!" She laughed, shaking her head. "As long as they call me once a week and come home every Christmas, I'm happy."

She paid me thirty dollars—which was more than I thought I'd get—and I told her I'd mow for her next Monday as well.

"Thank you for the lemonade and Twinkies," I said, slipping the money into my back pocket.

"Any time. And I mean that. I don't get many visitors," she told me as we stood on her front porch. "I'd love it if you came by more. I'm always here."

Although she smiled, I could see something behind her eyes—not quite sadness, but something else. I understood that look because I had it, too. It was loneliness.

"I'd love to come back," I said, and her face brightened. "Most of my days are free. Travis works at the shop during the week, and I don't have many friends in town." I shrugged.

"Well, you have at least one now," she beamed.

∽

After mowing Ernie's yard, I could fully appreciate the luxury of a riding mower. Not only was it much easier to start, but the grass was cut in no time. With the breeze, I didn't even break a sweat.

Ernie was waiting for me on the back patio with a bottle of water when I finished. A large oak tree shaded the area, and

I was grateful to be out of the hot sun.

I greedily gulped at the cold water until it was almost gone.

"Thank you for the water," I said, remembering my manners. "And thanks for taking a chance on someone who's obviously a hazard around heavy machinery."

He laughed. "Ah, you did just fine. I'm just glad you didn't mow over my marigolds."

As we sat we made light conversation about the weather, and he mentioned how well the fields were doing this summer—not something I knew a lot about, but apparently that was great for the local farmers.

He didn't ask me what my story was, and I had to admit it was refreshing. He didn't care about where I came from or how I got here. He just seemed grateful for the company.

But that didn't mean I wasn't a bit curious about him. I couldn't stop myself from asking a few questions about his life, even though I knew I was being nosy.

"So do you have any kids?" I asked.

"Nope, no kids. Never married either," he stated.

"Why not?" I blurted out before I could stop myself.

Way to pry into the man's business, Angel.

"I had a high school sweetheart once. She was the prettiest thing this town ever saw," he said with a distant look on his face. "But I messed it up."

Now I was completely enthralled with his history. My butt scooted to the edge of the plastic lawn chair. "What happened?"

"I was a year ahead of her in school. After graduation, I joined the military. I knew I would be away for a while... I was in love with her, but I was scared. Young and stupid. Broke things off and told her not to wait for me." He sighed. "By the time I realized I'd made a mistake, she'd moved on—just like I told her to."

"That's so sad." I frowned.

He barked out a humorless laugh. "You're telling me. She still lives in town," he added.

"Really?" I asked, shocked. "Where?"

"Right next door," he tilted his head toward Beverly's house.

"What?!" I gasped. "No way!"

"Yes way," he nodded, regret painting his face.

"You know she's totally single, right?" I asked, pointing at the house next door. "You should do something about that."

"Bah," he made a dismissive sound and waved his hand as if chasing the notion away. "Say, do you like balloon animals?"

It took me a second to catch up with the abrupt change of subject.

So random.

"Sure." I shrugged. "Who doesn't?"

He went inside his house and came back out with a pink balloon. After blowing it up, he started twisting and turning it until it resembled a poodle, and handed it to me.

"That's so cool," I said, turning it this way and that, trying to figure out how he did it.

"As much as I'd like to pay you with balloons, I believe I owe you some money." He pulled out his wallet. "What did Beverly pay you?"

"Thirty."

"Here's thirty-five." He handed me the cash. "I gotta one-up her. That'll really get her goat." He grinned.

As I walked down Main Street, I smiled. I'd gained sixty-five dollars, a pink poodle, and two new friends.

CHAPTER 25

Travis

"Hey," I heard Angel say behind me while I was under the hood of an old Buick.

Just the sound of her voice caused my pulse to skyrocket. I turned to face her as I wiped my hands on my coveralls. "Hey, you. How did the mowing go?"

"It was a rough start, but Beverly's neighbor helped me figure it out. Aaaand he had me mow his lawn, too, so I made extra." She beamed as she rocked on her heels.

I went to kiss her, but she held up her hand and took a step back.

"I stink really bad right now," she stated.

She did smell, but I didn't think it was bad. She smelled like sunlight, summer air, and fresh-cut grass. Her hair was a mess piled on top of her head and pink tinted her face and shoulders from being in the sun.

Like always, I thought she looked gorgeous.

"I stink, too. We can stink together." I grinned as I picked her up by the waist. My hands were coated with dark grease and I liked the idea of leaving my handprints on her.

Her legs automatically made their way around me and linked behind my back as I brought my lips to hers. She immediately sighed and opened her mouth to let me slip my tongue past her lips.

Unfortunately, the kiss didn't last long because we heard someone loudly clear their throat.

"None of that in here," Hank said with a hint of amusement as he walked past us to his office. "Don't want to attract the wrong kind of business."

When I put Angel down I noticed she was holding something in her hand.

"Is that a balloon animal?" I pointed at the pink object.

She looked at it like she'd forgotten she had it. "Yeah. Ernie, Beverly's neighbor, made it for me. Neat, huh?" she asked, holding it up for me to see. Then she reached into her back pocket and handed me something. "Here. This is for you."

I looked down and counted sixty-five dollars.

"No way." I tried to hand it back but she wouldn't take it. "I'm not taking your money, Angel."

"You've already spent that much on food for me. You have to. I won't take it back," she said stubbornly. "Please?" she begged as she gazed up at me.

Shit.

Why did I have such a hard time saying no to her?

I sighed and ran a hand through my hair. I could tell this was going to be an issue. There was no way in hell I would take her money when she needed it so badly.

I decided to placate her—for now—and she let out a sigh of relief when I put the cash in my wallet.

∾

That night when we got into bed Angel told me Beverly swore like a sailor, and I laughed when she told me about their first encounter. Dropping the F-bomb when you first met someone was a bold move. I guess when you're that old, you just don't give a fuck.

Nighttime was becoming my favorite time of the day. Sure, I liked lying next to Angel, liked touching her, but it wasn't about physical contact.

After the lights went out, we talked. We got to know each other. I learned random details about her. Like the fact that her favorite number was eleven, but she had an irrational fear of the number twenty-three. And how she hated the color orange because it made her look 'washed out'.

It didn't matter how insignificant the detail was—if it was about her, I wanted to know.

We were lying in bed, facing each other as I traced her face with my finger. I slid the tip of my finger over her brows, down her cheek, and across her lips.

When I remembered this weekend's plans, I thought I should let her know what was going on.

"So this weekend is the annual Tolson Summer Fest," I said, running my finger down the length of her nose. "There's a parade on Saturday and I'm supposed to drive the semi. You want to ride shotgun?"

"You want me to be in a parade? Am I just supposed to wave to everyone?" She did an exaggerated beauty queen wave.

"You get to be the candy-thrower," I told her, amused. "That's a very important job. Kids are going to love you. And it would be a big help to Hank," I added, knowing it was going to persuade her. "Even though the shop is closed for business, the garage doors will be open. Hank and Colton usually give out discount coupons and free keychains. It's really good for promoting the business."

Truth was, although we did need a candy-thrower, I really just wanted people to see Angel riding with me. I wanted everyone to know she was mine, even if she didn't know it yet.

"And I'll even let you honk my horn." I smirked and waggled my eyebrows.

"Oh, I'll honk your horn so hard," she said, her tone completely serious.

I grunted, trying not to laugh. "Baby, I love it when you talk trucker to me."

∽

Over the next few days, Angel and I developed a comfortable routine. I would leave for the shop in the morning, and she made daily visits to Beverly's. Sometimes she would come back with a new balloon animal, so I knew she saw Ernie, too.

In the evening, she would cook dinner for Colt and me—it was either that, or frozen pizzas—and at night we would lie down in bed together with zero space between us as we talked.

She told me about how Ernie and Beverly were high school sweethearts and how she thought they should get married.

Angel was really cute when she gossiped. Her eyes got really big and her voice would get hushed as though she was in danger of being overheard.

Besides some hot make-out sessions and a little over-the-clothes touching, nothing more physical happened.

I was both relieved and frustrated by that.

Relieved because I didn't want to jump into anything we might not be ready for.

And frustrated because I was sporting the worst case of blue balls ever.

Thursday afternoon, I got done at the garage early and came home to an empty apartment. Angel had been losing track of time while she was at Beverly's lately and it was only two o'clock, so I figured I'd find her there.

As I walked toward the little white house, I smiled because I could hear their laughter from a block away.

I found Angel and Beverly sitting on the porch, drinking lemonade from oversized mason jars. The rusty metal overhang kept them shaded from the sun, but it was still hot as hell outside.

Whether it was from the heat or laughing so hard, Angel's cheeks were flushed. The sight of her took my breath away. She looked so happy. She'd made quite the transformation from the lost girl I'd picked up off the side of the road just seven days ago. I liked to think I had something to do with that.

"Did you spike the lemonade again, Beverly?" I teased.

"Well, it is thirsty Thursday," she deadpanned.

Angel smirked. "Don't go giving her ideas, Travis."

I stepped up onto the porch and plucked a Swiss Roll off the plate between them.

"I came to get you because my mom wants to take you shopping for a new dress for Saturday," I told Angel around a big bite.

"She wants to take me shopping?" she asked, taken aback.

"Her idea, not mine. I think you always look great." I flashed her the dimples and she blushed. "You'll be in the parade this weekend," I reminded her. "It's kind of a big deal around here."

She turned to Beverly. "Are you coming to the summer festival?"

"I suppose I have to. They block off all of Main Street. People come from all over, and for some reason, you can get into town but it's almost impossible to get out," she chuckled.

Angel stood and thanked Beverly for hanging out before turning to me. Her hair was in that sexy side-braid again and I tucked some loose strands behind her ear.

"Hi," I said.

"Hi," she said back as a small smile played on her lips.

I brought my thumb up to the corner of her mouth. "You have a little chocolate right here."

"Oh." She blushed and tried to rub the spot, but I'd already wiped it off.

The air crackled with sexual tension, like it always seemed to when we were around each other.

Beverly made her way back into the house, muttering something about young love and what sounded like 'a fine piece of ass'.

I had no idea what that was about but Angel snickered, so it must've been some kind of inside joke.

As we walked down the sidewalk, I grabbed her hand and laced our fingers.

"I'd love to go with your mom, but I don't have a lot of money for new clothes," she said, our hands swinging between us.

"Don't be surprised if my mom insists on buying. But don't worry. Mom never pays full price for anything. I think she plans to go to the thrift store over in Daywood. They're having an eighty-eight cent sale."

"Eighty-eight cents?! Like, for a dress?" She stopped on the sidewalk, gaping.

Had she never been to a thrift store before?

"For anything. Everything in the whole store," I informed her.

Angel squealed, then started doing that hopping thing she did whenever she got really excited, which made her tits bounce up and down.

I felt my cock start to thicken and I groaned under my breath.

Fuck.

I was wound up so tight from holding myself back with

her all week. Sleeping next to her. Kissing her. Touching her. But never going any further. It was the best kind of agony I'd ever experienced.

However, rocking a boner while walking down Main Street wasn't on my to-do list today.

"Here." I turned and offered her my back. "Hop on."

Maybe if I couldn't see her, my suffering would be over. A piggy-back ride was the only thing I could think of at the time, and I quickly realized my mistake when her legs wrapped around me and I could feel her breasts pressed against my back.

Motherfuckingshit.

I looked to the sky in frustration, then tried to make it back to my apartment before anyone saw the bulge straining in my pants.

CHAPTER 26

Angel

I slipped on the black bomber jacket I'd found, and I was thrilled when it fit me perfectly. As I ran my hands over the smooth exterior, I realized it was *real* leather. I almost didn't want to take it off, scared that someone else would try to snatch it from me.

Seriously, who would give this away?

"It's crazy what people throw away, isn't it? One man's trash is another man's treasure," Karen said, reading my thoughts as we shopped.

I nodded enthusiastically. "This would cost hundreds of dollars new," I whispered at her as I kept a tight grip on the jacket.

As I continued my search for the perfect dress, I sorted through the endless racks of clothes. Racks and racks of clothes everywhere. The small thrift store was bustling with activity—probably because of the sale—and everyone seemed to be talking about the upcoming festival.

Beverly wasn't exaggerating when she said it was a big deal. We were in a town ten miles away and people were still talking about the tiny town of Tolson as though it was hosting the event of the year.

A woman close to Karen's age approached us. "Karen, it's so good to see you," she said. The woman attempted to give

Karen a hug but it didn't work very well because her arms were so full of clothes.

"You, too, Rita." Karen smiled and motioned towards me. "This is Angel, Travis's girlfriend."

My eyes went wide at the title she gave me, and the woman gasped. "I didn't realize he was dating anyone."

Karen nodded and put her arm around me. "He brought her over for lasagna night."

"It's nice to meet you," I said weakly.

"I think I just heard hearts breaking all over town." The woman giggled, Karen laughed, and I stood there mutely, like a deer in the headlights.

A few more people came up to us to chat and exchange pleasantries. And every single time, Karen introduced me as *Travis's girlfriend*.

And she sounded so *proud*.

I didn't correct her, and I had to admit it made a warm feeling spread through my chest every time she said it. But after the third time, I started to feel a little awkward about it because I wasn't sure how Travis would feel about our new assumed relationship status.

Karen found a coral short sleeve, knee-length wrap dress, and went to the changing room to try it on along with a pair of wedge sandals.

Much like her son, she was able to pull off the simple look so well. Today she was wearing a plain gray T-shirt and jeans. Her hair was down and she didn't have much makeup on. Everything about her was understated, yet beautiful at the same time.

When she stepped out of the dressing room to show me her new outfit, my jaw fell open.

"That looks great. You have to get that dress," I gushed.

"You think?" she asked, twirling in front of the mirror.

"Definitely." I nodded.

Honestly, she was a knock-out. It was baffling that she hadn't dated in so long, and I wondered how many hearts she'd unintentionally broken over the years. It's not like it was too late for her. People dated in their forties all the time.

I ended up finding the perfect off-the-shoulder sundress. It was white with a cinched waist, flowy skirt ending at mid-thigh, and it had lace detail around the shoulders and bottom hemline.

"Oh, you definitely have to get that," Karen said when she saw me holding the dress up to my body. "And the jacket, too. Do you want to go check out the shoes?"

I shook my head. "These are good enough."

"I'm buying," she insisted as we walked over to the counter to pay. "And don't even think about feeling bad. Travis said you might give me a hard time about it but, I'll tell you right now, I'm just as stubborn as my son." She grinned.

"Okay, okay," I surrendered with a laugh.

Actually, I didn't feel that bad about the clothes because the cost was less than two dollars and it seemed to make Karen really happy.

"Do you know how long it's been since I had a girls' shopping day?" she asked as we walked back out to her car.

"It's been forever for me, too. This was really fun," I said sincerely.

On the short ride back to Tolson, she told me some fun stories from Travis's childhood.

"He had so much energy. Some days I swore he was trying to drive me crazy," she said fondly. "Oh, guess what he wanted to be when he grew up!" She reached over and tapped my knee excitedly.

"Um, something to do with trucks?" I guessed, amused.

"Close! Real close. He wanted to be a garbage truck. Not

a person who drove it, but the *actual truck*." Her laughter was contagious. It was like she'd been dying to tell this story, and I felt special because she wanted to share it with me.

"And have you heard him singing in the shower yet?" she asked.

"Oh, it's the *worst*! The first time I heard it, I actually thought someone was being attacked," I admitted, laughing so hard my stomach muscles ached. "It happens all the time, so I'm pretty much used to it now."

"He's done that since he was a little thing. I always knew when it was shower time."

The horrendous shower singing had continued to happen every day. And every time, he came out of the bathroom wearing nothing but a towel. He didn't even bother to dry himself off all the way, and seeing his toned upper body slick and wet left me tongue-tied.

When Travis sang, it sounded like a pack of dying coyotes, but I couldn't make fun of him. Not when he looked like *that*.

I suspected he was doing it on purpose. It's not like he couldn't bring clothes into the bathroom with him. If he was trying to distract me, it was a very effective tactic.

All too quickly, the ride ended and we were pulling up in front of Travis's apartment. I was a little sad our time to hang out was over.

"Thank you for the clothes. And I had a really good time," I said, not making a move to get out of the car yet. I wanted her to know how much I appreciated spending time with her. "Travis is so lucky to have you as a mom."

The look she gave me was sympathetic, and I wondered if she could tell how much I missed having my own mother in my life.

"I'd love to get together any time." She reached over the

middle console to give me a hug and I returned it.

Tolson was doing funny things to me. It seemed I was getting used to this hugging thing.

CHAPTER 27

Travis

"**S**o…" Angel began, sounding hesitant as we lay facing each other in my bed. The pause was so long, I wondered if she was actually going to continue talking. "Your mom kept telling everyone I was your girlfriend today."

"Oh yeah?" I asked, keeping my face impassive. "And what did you tell her when she said that?"

She looked at me for a beat, trying to gauge my reaction, and brief frustration flitted over her face when she couldn't get a good read on me.

"Nothing." She shrugged and looked down at her hands as she picked at imaginary lint on the blanket. "I didn't want to contradict her in front of her friends. And she sounded so happy about it, I didn't have the heart to tell her it wasn't true."

"Good," I grunted, and her eyes flew up to mine. "Because it is true."

I'd been wanting to broach the subject all week, so it was kind of perfect that she was bringing it up. I'd have to thank my mom later.

"It is?" Her eyebrows went up.

I nodded as I moved my body over hers, and her knees automatically fell open to make room for me.

"Do you want that?" I asked, and I could hear a hint of vulnerability in my voice.

"Yes." She started to smile, but in the next second her face fell. "But is that what you want? Because I'm still leaving in a couple weeks…"

"There's nothing I want more," I stated. "Even if you're far away, at least I'll still know you're mine."

Yeah, I knew she was leaving. But wherever she was, I wanted her to belong to me.

Her face softened, the worry disappearing. And the way she looked at me… No one had ever looked at me like that.

Innocence. Desire. Trust.

I framed her face with my hands then I kissed her. I loved the way her mouth welcomed me. My tongue ran along the seam of her lips and delved inside where her soft tongue tangled with mine. I sucked on her plump bottom lip—one of my favorite things to do—and her hands slid under my shirt. Her nails dragged down the skin of my lower back, and goosebumps spread over my entire body.

I moaned as I slanted my mouth over hers again and again and again.

Breaking the connection, Angel trailed soft kisses along my jaw. Her teeth scraped over the skin on my neck, causing a shudder to ripple through my body. At the same time, she wrapped her legs around my waist, linking her ankles behind my back.

"Baby…" I rasped, reluctantly moving back a little. It was too easy to lose control with her.

"I know, I know. Too soon and all that jazz." She sighed. I recognized her frustration because it mirrored my own. "Who would have thought *you* would be the one putting on the brakes when it comes to this stuff? I thought that was my job," she teased as she poked me in the ribs.

"And it's my job to protect you," I said, my tone serious.

"What are you protecting me from? Is it because I'm

younger than you?" she asked, her insecurity bleeding through. "Because it's not my fault I was born three years after you. And my birthday is literally in, like, six days."

"No," I told her honestly. "It's because I want to do this right. I've never felt this way about anyone before."

"Neither have I," she whispered, and I moved to lie down beside her, placing one more kiss at her temple.

What I didn't tell her is that I was trying to protect myself, too. It was weird to refer to myself as innocent—because I was a twenty-one-year-old dude—but that's what I was.

Maybe not completely innocent, but definitely inexperienced.

Not just my body, but my heart, too.

I'd never been in love before. My heart was in one piece because it'd never been broken. I had a feeling Angel had the power to wreck me, which was kind of terrifying considering the short time we'd known each other.

From the beginning, all I'd wanted to do was help her. Keep her safe.

But now I felt like I was the one in danger.

CHAPTER 28

Angel

"Is it always like this?" I wondered out loud as I stood in front of Hank's shop, looking up and down Main Street. I couldn't believe the crowds that gathered in the front yards and along the sidewalks of this tiny town.

Tolson only had a few hundred residents, but the summer festival drew *thousands*.

"Yep. Every year," Colton replied behind me. "Just wait 'til the parade starts."

"It's crazy," I said, amazed.

An ice cream truck was parked in front of the empty building next door, and the mass of people waiting in line went halfway down the block.

Orange construction cones lined the sides of the entire length of Main Street, blocking it off for the parade.

"Angel, I better show you this map. I already told Travis but he's liable to get lost." Hank winked at me.

I knew he wasn't serious, but it felt nice to be included.

Hank held out a piece of paper that had the parade route outlined. "Now, this is us—right behind the Herman's tractor and in front of the Wilson's golf cart." He moved his finger to the starting point. "You'll get in line here on Oak Street and take a left onto Main. Just follow the line until you get to Elm, then you'll loop around to the back of the shop."

"I think we can handle that. What's up with all the golf carts?" I pointed to all the small yellow icons on the map.

Hank chuckled. "Don't let anyone catch you questioning their cart. It's serious business around here."

I smiled, and gave him a questioning look because he couldn't possibly be serious.

"He's not joking," Travis piped up from the other side of the garage. "Remember that show 'Pimp My Ride'? Well, it's like that. But with golf carts."

Call my curiosity piqued. I wanted to see these pimp carts.

Colton came over to hand me a basket full of candy—mostly bubble gum and taffy—then ruffled my hair. I shot him a half-hearted glare and he just laughed.

I felt the heat of a familiar body come up behind me and callused fingertips grazed over my exposed shoulders.

"Have I told you how much I love this dress?" Travis whispered by my ear, causing butterflies in my stomach.

"Maybe you can show me later," I suggested quietly so no one else could hear me.

I wanted him to stop holding back with me, to stop handling me as though I was innocent—even though I was. I wanted to throw all caution to the wind and just *get it on* already. I just wanted *him*.

"Anything for you." He kissed the tip of my nose.

I sighed, feeling all swoony. Every time he did that it felt like my insides melted into a pile of mush.

Across the street, the taverns were giving out free ice water. Long white tables littered with disposable cups lined the sidewalk in front of the buildings. It was a great idea, considering the heat. People flocked to the tables, picking up the cups with grateful words I couldn't hear.

It had to be close to ninety degrees outside. With the cloudless sky and stagnant breeze, the air felt a little suffocating. I went to stand by an oscillating fan Hank had put by the open garage door, hoping it would give me some relief.

An unsettling feeling came over me when I got a weird, hair-raising feeling of being watched. I glanced around before I caught the sight of a slightly familiar face. Kendra was one of the people behind one of the water tables in front of Buck's.

And she was staring right at me. Not just staring. Glaring was more like it. Aside from the fact that she obviously had feelings for Travis, she didn't have any reason to hate me, but there she was, glowering at me.

If looks could kill...

I almost laughed when I wondered if she was going to give me another kiddie cocktail. Maybe I should've been creeped out by the seething looks she was sending my way, but it was just so ridiculous. She and Travis had one date, and he told me they never even kissed. She had no reason to believe she had any sort of claim on him.

"You ready for this?" Travis interrupted the stare-down I'd been having with Kendra. "We've got about thirty minutes until start time, so we need to get in line."

"I'm totally ready," I said, holding up the candy basket.

In no time, we were driving down Main Street and kids squealed with delight as we drove by.

"Me! Me! Over here!" they shouted with outstretched hands, and I obliged by throwing handfuls of candy their way.

About halfway through the parade, Travis asked me if I wanted to sit on his lap and steer.

"I don't know how to drive this thing!" I yelled over the loud cheering coming from both sides of the street.

Travis laughed. "We're going like five miles per hour. You'll do fine."

He pulled me onto his lap and put his hands over mine on the wheel. He took off his hat and plopped it onto my head backwards. "Every trucker's gotta have a hat." He winked.

It was a good thing Travis was helping me steer because I honestly wasn't sure I'd be able to do it on my own. Everything felt so big—the wheel, the windshield, and the pedals (which I definitely couldn't reach with my feet).

The only vehicle I'd ever driven was the Driver's Ed. car, which was a small sedan, and Claire's Prius.

"There's Hank." Travis pointed out as we slowly passed by the auto shop.

Leaning out the window, I waved my hand wildly. "Hey, Hank!"

Travis hooked his arm around my waist and planted me back into his lap. "Gotta keep both hands on the wheel, baby." He chuckled against the back of my neck before taking over with the steering and pointing up at the ceiling. "Here, pull that."

Wrapping my hand around the rope, I pulled down and the horn blasted. Unrestrained laughter burst from me as I bounced on Travis's lap, causing him to groan.

"Sorry!" I said over my shoulder. "Did I hurt you?"

"No, baby." He kissed the side of my neck and smiled against my skin. "But Hank expects that basket to be empty when we get back. I'll steer, you throw candy."

Remaining in Travis's lap, I resumed my assignment and allowed him to take over the task of driving.

I honked the horn again when I saw Ernie making balloon animals for some kids.

"Hi, Ernie!" I shouted, then tossed the last of the candy out the window.

Our part in the parade only lasted about fifteen minutes. Once we got back to the shop, Travis parked the semi and we went into the garage to help hand out coupons and key chains.

The pimp carts, as I'd so eloquently named them, were

impressively decorated. Each one seemed to have a theme. The patriotic cart had dozens of mini American flags sticking out, waving in the wind, and all four family members wore red, white, and blue. A very loud cart had bells, whistles, and bicycle horns attached. People cheered as it made all kinds of obnoxious noises. My favorite was the musical cart that had a father and son dueling banjos in the backseat while an amused-looking woman drove.

Halfway through the afternoon, we ran out of the goodies and the crowds in the streets started to clear.

At some point, Ernie stopped by and handed me a yellow giraffe. "It's my last one. Ran out sooner than I thought I would."

It wasn't a big deal—just a silly balloon animal. A kid's toy. But it still meant a lot to me. He'd saved the last one for me.

"Thank you." I hugged it to my chest.

"I'll see you Monday? My grass needs a trim," he said.

"Definitely." I nodded, and he left with a salute-like wave.

He was walking away when I caught sight of Kendra and Tara approaching the shop with a tray of ice waters.

This was the first time I was getting a good look at Tara. Last time I'd seen her it was at The Brick House, and she was too busy laughing at me behind her hands for me to see her face.

She was pretty, with a short blonde bob and brown eyes. It was hard to tell how tall she was because her heels were sky high. She and Kendra wore black polo shirts with the Buck's logo and black shorts.

Tara was a mystery to me. I never heard Colton talk about her, and she hadn't been over to the apartment at all since I'd been staying there.

"We thought maybe you guys would be thirsty over here," Tara said with a shrug. She attempted to smile, but it looked fake to me.

"No kiddie cocktail this time?" I raised an eyebrow.

"Oh, come on, that was just a joke," Tara said with a forced laugh. When she was met with stony silence she changed the subject. "Where are the guys?"

"In the office going over the plans for the next transport job," I told her, keeping our exchange short.

She set a glass down for me, then went to the office to give the rest to the guys. Unfortunately, with Tara gone, I was left alone with Kendra. Her glare was still in place and I wondered if she always looked that way.

Resting-Bitch-Face was a real thing.

"You think you're so special. Riding in the parade. Pretending you and Travis are together. Acting like you belong here," she sneered. "But everyone knows all about you."

Man, she really didn't waste any time letting me know how she really felt, which was fine. I didn't exactly have warm feelings for her either.

"What do you mean 'everyone knows all about me'?" I asked warily, putting air quotes around her words, although I wasn't sure I really wanted to know the answer.

"Rumor in town is you're a hitchhiker." Her voice dripped with malice. "And Travis just picked you up off the side of the road like some lost, helpless kitten."

My cheeks burned with embarrassment. I couldn't deny what she said, so I just stayed silent and hoped she would go away. But she just had to dig the knife in a little further.

"That can't be true, right? I mean, that would be ridiculous…" she trailed off.

She didn't really need me to confirm the story. Obviously, the hitchhiking thing was true and she knew it. I resented the lost kitten comment, though. It was another low blow about the fact that I was young.

"Anyone ever tell you that your conversational skills need a little work?" I gritted through my teeth, but she continued as if I hadn't said anything.

"What I do know for sure is you're that leaving. And when you're gone, I'll still be here."

The truth of her words stung. I didn't need a reminder that my time here was limited. Although, she was delusional with that last part. If she was implying she had a chance with Travis, she'd obviously lost her marbles.

I hadn't known him that long, but I knew he would never be with someone like her.

He was too good.

I didn't see the sense in arguing with her, though. I'd never been very good at defending myself. The best comebacks always seemed to come to me hours later. I'd probably think of the perfect witty retort when I was in the shower tonight. What I really wanted to do was slap that bitchy look right off her face.

Instead, I just stated the truth. "You puked on his shoes."

I could tell I hit a nerve with that one because Kendra's face got bright red. I'd be pretty embarrassed, too, if I threw up on a guy I liked.

The office door opened and Travis came over, looking back and forth between us.

"Hey, Kendra," he greeted her as he put his arm around me. Although his tone was casual, I could feel the tension in his muscles. "What's going on?"

"Travis! So good to see you. We thought you might be thirsty." She plastered on an obnoxious smile, and I rolled my eyes so hard I felt it through my entire body. I was sure Travis felt it, too.

"Thanks. That was nice of you," he said politely, and an awkward silence followed.

"Well," Kendra started to back away, "I should get back to Buck's. See you at the street dance later?"

"We'll be there," he told her while possessively rubbing my shoulder.

It was really hard not to feel triumphant in that moment. *Point for Angel.*

Travis just made it very clear where his interests were, and I might've even felt bad for her if she wasn't so mean.

Her words from earlier still stung, but I didn't want it to ruin my day. Luckily, Travis had the perfect distraction.

"Are you hungry? There's a barbeque going on over at the community building. Hotdogs and hamburgers," he said. "That sound good to you?"

I was already nodding before he could finish. "You had me at hotdogs."

Laughing, he looped an arm around my waist before steering me down the street and dropping a kiss to the top of my head.

CHAPTER 29

Angel

The sun was sinking below the horizon when the music started, and the intense heat of the day began to ease up. The DJ was set up in the community building parking lot and Main Street was blocked off for everyone who wanted to dance.

Groups of people stood off to the side to talk while children ran around with glow sticks and tried to catch the thousands of fireflies that lit up the surrounding fields of the town.

Travis stood behind me, with his arms wrapped around my middle as he made small talk with some of the auto shop customers. They asked about the trucking business and he told them about the upcoming trip to Colorado. *Our* trip to Colorado.

Oh yeah, and he told several people I was his girlfriend, which made me feel all warm and fuzzy inside. It almost didn't seem real.

Wanting to dance with Travis again, I planned to drag him out into the mass of moving bodies as soon as a slow song came on. It seemed as though he had the same idea because when the first chords of 'Silver Wings' played through the giant speakers, he intertwined our fingers and pulled me out into the middle of the street.

I wrapped my arms around his neck and ran my fingers

through the short hairs on the back of his head. I loved the way they prickled against my skin.

Travis put his hands on the small of my back and pressed my body against his until I couldn't get any closer. I swayed with him, resting my head on his chest where I could hear his steady heartbeat over the music.

Rising up on my tiptoes, I placed a chaste kiss on the side of his neck and his hands tightened around my waist.

Okay, so maybe the kiss wasn't that chaste. Maybe I wanted to drive him crazy. Maybe I wanted to make him to lose control.

He pulled back and rubbed his nose over mine. I loved it when he did that. It made me feel special. Cherished.

"Wanna get out of here?" he said against my lips.

I nodded eagerly. Travis grabbed my hand and hauled me away from the crowds of people. We were practically running when we came to his apartment, but we didn't go inside. Instead, he opened the passenger door to his pickup truck and planted me inside.

"Where are we going?" I asked breathlessly after he started it up.

"Country cruising." He smiled, dimples on full display.

We took a back road out of town and headed south until the lights from the festival were far off in the distance. After slowing to a stop on a deserted country road, he turned off the ignition, then reached beneath the bench seat to pull out a folded-up blanket.

"Come on," he said, hopping out of the truck.

I followed him around to the back where he lowered the tailgate and spread the fuzzy blue blanket over the bed of the truck.

After helping me up, Travis laid down and I curled into his side as he put his arm around me.

"What are we doing?" I asked through the sounds of the night, which was mostly the breeze rustling through the corn-fields and the crickets chirping.

"Star-gazing." He looked up into the sky.

Looking up in the same direction, I noticed how bright the stars seemed now that they weren't drowned out by city lights.

"That's the Big Dipper. And there's the North Star." He pointed out. "And those three in a line, that's Orion's Belt."

"You know a lot about this stuff, huh?" I looked at his face.

He gave me a sheepish smile. "Not really. That's about all I know. Hank knows a lot more about it. He knows all the constellations, and every year in August there's a few days of meteor showers. Sometimes you can see ten shooting stars in an hour…"

He was babbling, and I wondered if he was trying to distract himself from the sexual tension. I wasn't going to let him get away with it.

"Travis?"

"Yeah?"

"That's all really great, but if I'm being honest, I don't really want to talk about the stars right now."

He barked out a laugh. "Neither do I."

Rolling onto his side, he faced me and tilted my chin up with his thumb and forefinger. There was no hesitation to our kiss as my tongue eagerly met his.

He bit down on my bottom lip before trailing kisses over my cheek and down to my neck. He sucked at my pulse point and a whimper escaped from me.

Softly, he ran the tips of his fingers over my shoulder before bringing his mouth to my skin. This was another first. I'd never been kissed on the shoulder before and I had no idea it could be so erotic.

A continuous pulsing started between my thighs and I felt myself getting wet. My hand played along the bottom of his shirt, then slipped underneath to feel his abs. I traced the lines with my fingers, until I moved up high enough to graze his nipple.

Travis gasped against my neck. His breath fanned over my skin as he started to pull down on the top of my dress.

Just as I thought we were finally—*finally*—getting somewhere, I felt a sting and an itch at my temple.

"Ow," I hissed and swatted at the air.

"What's wrong?" Travis asked, concerned.

"Mosquito bit me," I said, scratching at the bump by my hairline. As the haze of lust started to clear, I realized I was itching in other spots, too. "I think I'm getting eaten up out here."

"Damn. Maybe we should get home," he suggested.

With a heavy sigh, I agreed. I should've remembered bug spray, but in the heat of the moment, I'd forgotten how much mosquitoes love me.

Travis rolled the blanket up while I got back into the truck.

On the drive back, I itched all over. I found I had bites on my arms, hands, knees, ankles and several on my toes. Mosquito bites on toes were the *worst*.

"What kind of mosquitos do you have in Tolson?" I asked, baffled by the number of bites I'd obtained in such a short amount of time.

Travis glanced over at me as I furiously scratched at my body. "Did you seriously get bit that much?"

I grunted unattractively as I found another bite on my face. "It's my blood type. O negative." Travis had a skeptical expression on his face, so I insisted. "I'm serious. That's a real thing."

When we got into the apartment, he turned the lights on

and his eyes widened when he saw all the welts on my skin.

"Holy shit," he hissed. "You weren't kidding."

I just made a pathetic whining sound while I sat down on the couch and scraped at my skin some more.

"Don't scratch so much. You're gonna make them bleed," he said, and I shot him a dirty look. "Hold on, I think we have some Calamine lotion."

Travis went into the bathroom and when he returned, he held up the pink bottle like it was some kind of trophy.

"Last year, Colton walked through some poison oak," he said, applying it to all the red bumps on my legs and arms with a cotton ball. "This stuff works wonders."

The cool cream felt good on my skin and I let out a sigh of relief as it started soothing the itch.

"I thought making out in the back of your truck under the stars was so romantic," I grumped. "This—" I gestured to all the bumps, which were now covered with big pink splotches of lotion. "—is so not what I was hoping for."

"Lift up your dress." Travis's voice came out huskily.

"I think it's a little too late to bring the mood back," I quipped, arching an eyebrow.

"I bet you have bites under here." Flicking at the hem of my dress, he smirked. "I'm just trying to be thorough."

Standing up to give him better access, I watched him as he kneeled in front of me. My breath caught in my throat as he searched my skin. His fingertips grazed the edge of my white cotton panties, lifting them in certain places, but not removing them from my body.

He was right. I had two bites on my inner thigh, one on my butt, and one on my hip. He seemed to take extra care with those, going as far as applying the lotion twice.

I wasn't sure which was worse—the itchy welts on my skin or the sexual frustration I was feeling.

Just as Travis was finishing up with the last untreated bumps on my face, Colton walked through the door.

"What the hell happened to you?" he asked, looking me up and down.

"Country cruising happened," I said, and Colton guffawed obnoxiously. "You guys have some seriously aggressive mosquitos in this town," I informed him as I resisted the urge to claw at my skin.

CHAPTER 30

Travis

Three really is a crowd.

Don't get me wrong. Colton was my best friend and I loved him like a brother. But the dude was a cock-block.

It was another rainy Sunday, only this time, Colton hung with Angel and me at the apartment. All day.

She didn't seem to mind his company. In fact, they even spent a good hour making random comments about some ridiculous romantic comedy on TV.

The only good thing about that was having Angel next to me. Every now and then, she would absentmindedly graze her fingers over my stomach and I kept getting a whiff of the scent coming from her hair. Honey and vanilla.

At least Colton wasn't trying to sit on the couch with us.

"Gerard Butler was way better in *300*. That movie was epic," he told Angel.

"You would say that." She smirked. "Every guy thinks that movie was epic."

"The special effects alone made it awesome. Although, it didn't have Katherine Heigl in it. She's pretty hot." Colton grinned, and Angel rolled her eyes at his typical guy observation.

"What's Tara up to today?" I hinted, hoping he would leave.

"Hell if I know," he replied with a shrug.

He and Angel resumed their friendly banter while I wallowed in my grumpy mood.

Last night, I'd been ready to take things to the next level with Angel. Maybe not sex, but definitely more than what we'd been doing.

And shit, I was still ready. But it wasn't going to happen with my roommate hanging around.

Even though Angel's mosquito bites looked better this morning, I'd insisted on applying the lotion again. I told her it was because I didn't want her to be itchy, but I might've had ulterior motives.

There was something so sexy about seeing her in those little white panties. They were innocent-looking and completely unpretentious. They made me so hard it hurt.

The day passed slowly as we all pitched in cleaning around the apartment. After that was done, we watched some baseball on TV. Angel admitted she didn't know anything about sports, but she took interest in the game, asking questions about rules and certain players.

Sometime during the afternoon, I got the idea that I might take Angel for another country drive, only this time, we'd stay inside the truck. We had the perfect opportunity to leave because dinner at my mom's had gotten pushed back a day due to the festival. And since it was raining, we'd have to drive anyway.

Much to my dismay, Colt slid into the passenger side of my Chevy before we could take off and Angel scooted to the middle of the bench seat to make room for him.

On the short ride, he was completely oblivious to my seething as he rubbed his hands together and talked about how much he was looking forward to lasagna night.

Angel gave me a knowing look as she squeezed my thigh

with her hand. Just that one touch made my cock twitch.

Colton bolted from the truck as soon as we got into the driveway, finally leaving me alone with Angel.

"Give the guy a break." She rubbed her hand up and down my leg, which did nothing to help the uncontrollable need I felt. "You've been spending a lot of time with me and he probably just misses you."

I sighed, suddenly feeling bad. "Ah, you're right. I'm being a dick."

I'd never been one to think with the wrong head before, but it was definitely the one in control today. Hell, I even tried to push Colton off on Tara. That was a whole new low for me.

Angel giggled. "I never said you were a dick."

"Mmm, baby. Say dick again." I nuzzled the side of her neck.

"Dick," she whispered.

"Fuck." I laughed as I not-so-discreetly adjusted the front of my pants. "You're driving me crazy, you know that? Like, I'm losing my shit here."

The smirk on her face said she knew exactly what she was doing to me.

"You're not the only one. I've never hated mosquitoes more than I do right now." She huffed.

"Maybe I'll see if Colt wants to go to the gym with me tonight," I suggested, thinking a workout would help me blow off some steam.

"I'm sure he would like that." She placed a loud smooching kiss on my cheek and smiled. "Let's go eat before we steam up the windows."

A sense of déjà vu washed over me as I walked into my mom's house holding Angel's hand, only this time she didn't seem so skittish. In fact, she abandoned me as soon as we got inside, heading straight to the kitchen to hang out with my mom.

Colton was sitting down on the couch and I took a seat on the opposite end.

"Hey, you wanna head to the gym tonight?" I asked. I wasn't sure if he'd been aware of my shitty attitude today, but I wanted to make it up to him.

"Hell, yeah." He extended his arm out to me and we fist-bumped, then his face turned serious. "So, what was up with Kendra yesterday at the shop? She been giving Angel a hard time?" he asked, keeping his voice low.

"I don't know." I frowned at the reminder. "It didn't look like they were having a very friendly conversation."

I didn't know what transpired between them, but I didn't need to. It was obvious Kendra was trying to intimidate Angel, and that didn't sit well with me.

"Chick is bat-shit crazy, man," Colton said. "Even Tara's starting to feel weird about hanging out with her. I guess all she ever does is talk about you."

"I've sent the message loud and clear," I said, frustration evident in my tone. "I've flat-out told her I don't want to date her. I don't know what else I can do to show her I'm not interested."

"I'm sorry," he apologized. "I never should've asked you to take her out. That's on me."

I was about to tell him he was forgiven, but feminine laughter floated out into the living room followed by the dinner announcement. It made me smile and all thoughts of Kendra were forgotten.

CHAPTER 31

Angel

After Travis headed over to the shop Monday morning, I went to mow for Beverly and Ernie earlier than usual. I wanted to get done before lunch so I would have some time to hang out with them afterwards.

Mowing the second time around went much better than the first. Beverly's mower and I seemed to have come to an understanding.

Meaning, I finally understood how to start the dang thing.

Ernie's yard came next and I was done before noon. As usual, Beverly had a lemonade and a plate full of zingers waiting for me. The woman seemed to have an endless supply of snack cakes.

Ernie said he didn't have any balloon animals, but he tipped me an extra five dollars to make up for it. I had no complaints about that.

I said my goodbyes sometime after two o'clock so I could go back to the apartment and shower.

That happiness I'd wished for a week ago? I was starting to feel it. There was an extra hop in my step as I walked the streets of Tolson.

I even found myself singing in the shower. As I scrubbed my body, I belted out 'Wouldn't It Be Nice' by the Beach Boys. I wasn't going to win any awards, but if Travis could do it I could, too.

I continued to hum the happy tune as I got dressed and threw a load of laundry into the washing machine.

My hair was still wet when I heard a knock at the door.

That was odd. People never stopped by here during the day. If they wanted to talk to Travis or Colton, they just found them at the shop.

A second knock echoed through the apartment and I rubbed a towel over my hair one more time before I opened the door to a smug-faced Kendra.

"Travis and Colton aren't here," I informed her, before shutting the door in her face. Her hand slapped the surface before I could close it all the way.

"Well, that's just fine, because I came here to talk to you," she said.

"What do you want, Kendra?" I sighed tiredly. I wasn't in the mood for her antics.

She looked like she always did—impeccably put together in a green halter top paired with a short jean skirt, and her long legs were perfectly balanced on four-inch heels.

"Do you have a Facebook account?" Her random question threw me off a bit.

"Not an active one." I narrowed my eyes at her suspiciously, wondering what she was getting at. "Why? You want to be friends?"

I couldn't help the snide remark. I was pretty sure there was no chance of a friendship in our future. That ship had already sailed.

Kendra turned her phone towards me so I could see her profile. Was it petty of me for wanting to scoff at her picture? She was doing one of those ridiculous duck faces while her boobs spilled out of her shirt.

How cliché.

I was still confused as to why she was here when she turned her phone back around, pressed the touch screen a few times with her manicured fingertips, then turned it back to me.

Shock caused my stomach to drop and I felt the blood leave my face. A picture of myself was staring back at me. Not just any picture—it was a missing person poster.

My mouth was gaping as I rudely snatched the phone from her hand to get a closer look. It was my senior yearbook photo. The information stated that I was a runaway—or that I had possibly been abducted—and to contact the authorities immediately if anyone had information on my whereabouts.

"Where did you get this?" I whispered harshly as I tried to regulate my breathing. Hyperventilating would be extremely inconvenient right now.

"Looks like you've gone viral, honey," she announced in a congratulatory voice. "Saw it in my newsfeed this morning. Must be that pretty face of yours."

"You're not going to say anything, are you?" I practically begged as I clutched her phone against my chest. I hated how desperate I sounded. "Travis could get into trouble. You wouldn't want that."

It was a bluff. I wasn't sure if there would be any consequences for Travis, and I didn't like appealing to her feelings for him, but it was the only card I had to play.

"Oh, gosh." Kendra feigned concern. "You're right. He could get into big trouble. He might even lose his license. I think it's sort of illegal to pick up a hitchhiker, especially with you being a minor and all."

"And that's why you shouldn't tell anyone," I confirmed. "Besides, my birthday is the day after tomorrow. After I turn eighteen, they won't care about where I am."

I silently begged her with my eyes as she pried her phone

out of my hands. She shrugged, completely nonchalant. "Too bad I already called the cops."

"You... wh-what?" I stuttered as I tried to comprehend what she was saying. She couldn't possibly be that much of a bitch, right?

"I already told them. They're probably on their way here," she said, her face filled with triumph. "Maybe you should get going. If you hurry, they might miss you."

Kendra stood casually with her hands in her back pockets, relaxing against the door frame as though she hadn't just decimated my world.

Okay, so maybe she really was that much of a bitch. I slammed the door in her bitchy face without bothering to say one more word.

"*Shit*. Shit shit shit," I chanted as I ran around the apartment stuffing my belongings into my backpack. I didn't swear very often—at least, not out loud—but maybe Beverly's bad-language habits were rubbing off on me.

Or maybe this situation just called for a few 'shits'.

What was I going to do? Where could I go?

If I went to Travis, there was no way he would let me leave and I couldn't let him lose everything he'd worked so hard for.

Now that I thought about it, Kendra was right—he could get into big trouble for helping me.

If they found me, what would they do? Drag me back to Maine? Honestly, I didn't even care about that at this point. But I couldn't let them find me here, in Travis's apartment.

This was my mess and I wouldn't let him get dragged into it.

CHAPTER 32

Angel

"Beverly?" I frantically rapped on the door then continued knocking when she didn't answer right away. "Beverly!"

I heard shuffling of feet and a 'hold your horses!' from inside before the door swung open. The screen door creaked as Beverly opened it to peer into my face.

"What's wrong?" She looked worried as she took in my haggard appearance.

"Do you have a car?" I asked, breathless from running the whole way. "And a driver's license?" I added, wondering if people her age could still drive. I didn't have time to consider the possibility she might be offended.

"Of course I do," she said haughtily as she straightened her shoulders. "I passed the test just last year, and I won't stop driving 'til they tell me I can't anymore."

A sigh of relief left me. "Good. That's great. Could you possibly drive me to a bus station? Or a train station?"

"Are you in some kind of trouble?" Her eyes narrowed at me through her thick glasses.

I probably looked as panicked as I felt. My hair was still slightly damp and sticking to the sweat on my neck and forehead. My cheeks felt flushed and I was still breathing heavily.

"Something like that." I nodded.

She stared at me for a few seconds before seeming to come to a decision. "All right. Let me get my things together."

I followed her inside as she gathered her purse and took off her housecoat. I never knew what she wore underneath it—she always had it on. I'd just assumed she liked to be comfortable. If I was her age, I'd stay in my pajamas all day, too.

Imagine my surprise when I saw the woman was dressed to impress. She wore black slacks and a white blouse with a black floral design. It was like she was ready for action at any moment. I would've been able to appreciate the hilarity of it if the circumstances had been different.

Beverly tied a white scarf over her head and smiled, seeming oblivious to my inner torment. "I haven't had a trip into the city in ages. This is going to be so fun!"

An air freshener in the shape of a palm tree dangled from the rearview mirror, filling the car with a tropical scent as we drove out of Tolson.

Beverly squinted through her giant glasses and adjusted them on her face. Her white-knuckled hands were positioned at ten and two on the wheel, and I suddenly wondered if asking her for a ride had been a very bad idea.

Moving along at a snail's pace, some very pissed-off people passed us. Some laid on their horns, a few yelled obscenities out their windows, and we were on the receiving end of one middle finger.

I peered over at the speedometer and noticed we were barely going twenty on a road with a fifty-five-mile-per-hour speed limit.

"People are always in such a hurry these days," she muttered, shaking her head and clucking her tongue.

With the radio off the silence was unnerving, and there was nothing to distract me from my current situation. I thought about making conversation with Beverly, but I didn't want to distract her from driving. Obviously, she was concentrating very hard on not running us off the road.

My hands twisted in my lap and I pressed my lips together to keep from urging her to go faster. Anxiously, I looked into the rearview mirror several times, expecting to see red and blue flashing lights behind us, but, thankfully, that never happened.

A trip that should've taken twenty-five minutes took closer to an hour, and I finally let out the breath I'd been holding when we pulled into the train station's parking lot. Beverly shut off the car and started to get out.

"Oh, you don't have to come in with me," I said, feeling like I'd already inconvenienced her enough. "I'm really grateful for the ride."

"Of course I'm coming in with you," she insisted. "What kind of friend would I be if I didn't make sure you got your ticket?"

Once we were inside, I looked at the large clock over the ticket counter. It was 3:50pm and the next train to St. Louis didn't leave until 5:15. Travis would already know I was gone by then. In fact, he would probably find out within the next fifteen minutes because he was supposed to get done at the shop at four.

My heart squeezed painfully when I thought about him coming home to find me gone. I'd been in such a hurry that I didn't even leave a note.

Would he hate me for this? It was a possibility.

But he'd hate me more if my careless decisions got him arrested or made him lose his job.

I scanned the train station, wondering if anyone would

recognize me. Every time someone looked up from their phone, I was afraid they would point at me and say I was that missing girl they saw on the internet, but no one even gave me a second glance.

I wasn't even sure what my plan was, but I'd have time to think about it on the train.

Once I purchased my ticket, Beverly handed me a piece of paper with her phone number written on it. "Don't be a stranger. Call me soon, ya hear?"

"I will," I promised, trying to keep the tears at bay. Blinking rapidly, I watched her walk out the sliding doors. In such a short time, she had become my best friend.

I'd known my time in Tolson was limited, but I hadn't expected it to end this soon. Not like this.

Feeling defeated, I trudged over to a bench, away from most of the people so I could be alone. As I sat down, I let the first tear fall.

CHAPTER 33

Travis

Coming home to an empty apartment wasn't unusual, so when Angel wasn't there, I didn't think anything of it. I figured she'd lost track of time over at Beverly's, so I decided to walk the few blocks to her house. She'd been spending a lot of time over there during the day and it made me smile when I thought about how well she fit in here.

Sixty-year age difference aside, those two were thick as thieves.

As I approached the little white house, my heart raced at the thought of seeing Angel. It was always this way.

I missed her all day while I was at the shop, and the anticipation of being with her, touching her, talking to her—it made my whole body feel energized, like I'd just downed a whole pot of coffee.

The strangest part was that once I was with her, she had the opposite effect—I felt calm. Peaceful. My body seemed to be addicted to the whiplash she unknowingly gave me.

I was knocking on the screen door when I heard tires squealing. Looking over my shoulder, I was shocked to see Beverly's ancient Cadillac careening around the corner. The old car bounced and groaned as she came to a screeching halt in her driveway.

She flew out of the driver's seat and moved way faster

than any person her age should.

"You better go get your girl. I had to drive like a bat outta hell to get back in time to tell you," she practically shouted at me.

"Tell me what?" I asked as an unpleasant feeling came over me.

"She's at the train station. Poor thing was terrified. Something scared her real bad and she's leaving." Beverly's chest heaved with exertion.

"Shit," I swore as I started running down the porch steps.

"Her train leaves at 5:15. You better hurry!" she called after me, but I was already halfway down the block.

I shoved my keys into the ignition of my Chevy and it rumbled to life. Gravel went flying as I tore out of the parking lot.

When I got out onto the open road, I pushed the pedal down to the floor. I'd be breaking a lot of speed limits if I wanted to make it to the train station on time.

Hopefully I didn't get pulled over. I didn't even care about a speeding ticket, but I didn't have the time to stop. The clock on the dash told me it was almost 4:25.

What could have made Angel run like this? Beverly said she'd been scared. Terrified.

My phone started vibrating in my pocket and I took it out to see who it was. Even though Angel didn't have a phone, I got my hopes up that it might be her.

Colton.

Ignoring the call, I set my phone down in the cup holder. I'd just have to call him back later. When it lit up again with his name flashing across the screen, I decided to answer. I put it on speaker and set it back down.

"I can't talk right now," I told him quickly. "Angel took off, and I have to go find her."

"I know. Fuck."

"What do you mean you know?" I asked, confused.

"That's what I'm calling to tell you. This is Kendra's hand-iwork. Tara just told me what happened," he sighed and con-tinued. "Apparently, Kendra saw some missing person's report for Angel on the internet or something. She went to your apartment and told Angel she called the cops and that they were coming after her. And you. The both of you."

"Did she seriously call the fucking cops?" I asked, unable to contain the rage in my voice.

"No, that's the thing. She didn't really call them. She just wanted to spook Angel enough to get her to leave town."

"Well, it worked. Why the fuck would she do this?" I an-grily slammed my hand down on the steering wheel.

"I don't know. Bitches be crazy, man."

"If you see Kendra, you tell her she'd better hope Angel makes it back safely," I warned. "Did Tara have anything to do with this?"

"She says she didn't." I could hear a hint of doubt in his voice. "Says she called me as soon as she found out what Kendra did."

"I gotta go," I told him, reeling from the information he'd given me.

"Okay. Let me know as soon as you find her. And Travis? You will find her."

Walking through the doors of the train station, not knowing if I would find Angel or not, was one of the scariest moments of my life. Because, if she wasn't here, I had no idea where else to look.

The inside was fancy with marble flooring and decorative

pillars throughout the large lobby. Bright sunlight came through pristine floor-to-ceiling windows lining the front of the building.

I couldn't have looked more out of place, standing there in my auto shop coveralls, covered in grease and motor oil up to my elbows.

My head whipped back and forth as I sorted through all the people milling about.

Men in business suits impatiently checked their watches while towing their luggage behind them. Frazzled parents attempted to entertain their young kids with iPads and crossword puzzles. A small group of people around my age talked excitedly, probably going over plans for a fun trip.

I spun in a circle, my eyes desperately seeking the one person I wanted to find.

Time seemed to stop as I spotted wild blonde hair. It was the back of her head, but I'd recognize it anywhere. It looked exactly the same as it did the day I first saw her walking along the side of the road.

Angel was sitting alone on a bench that was far away from the main waiting area. Her head was tilted down and her shoulders were hunched.

The call for St. Louis boarding sounded over the speaker system. She slowly lifted her backpack from the bench beside her and slung it over her shoulder. When she turned around, her eyes went straight to me—eyes that were red-rimmed and puffy from crying.

Her mouth fell open in surprise as she realized I was thirty feet in front of her, and we stared at each other for a good ten seconds.

With steady strides, I closed the space between us because she seemed to be glued in place.

I felt an array of emotions. Relief, anger, hurt. Relief

because I found Angel before she left, anger at Kendra's deception, and hurt because my girlfriend was going to leave without even saying goodbye.

"Travis," she breathed out, nervously glancing around. "I have to go. It's a long story—"

"We're going home. Now," I stated, and Angel flinched at my tone. I didn't mean to sound so harsh, but damn it, she wasn't getting on that train.

She shook her head and her voice lowered to a whisper. "You don't understand. The police are looking for me."

"No, they're not. Kendra lied. She never called them."

"She… lied?" she asked in disbelief, and I recalled our very first conversation—the one where she told me she was a bad judge of character. She definitely wasn't kidding about that.

"Come on." I grabbed her hand and started walking towards the exit. "We can talk about this later, but you're safe," I assured her. "No one is coming after you."

I felt resistance as she planted her feet on the floor, and I was forced to stop. "What if someone reports me? That could still happen," she said, her eyes darting around the train station.

"Just lay low tomorrow. Then on Wednesday, call your case worker and let them know you're safe. They won't be able to make you do anything at that point."

"I don't even care about me. I just don't want to get you in trouble," she said vehemently.

"Baby," I whispered as my grease-stained hands came up to cradle her face and she leaned into my touch. I loved that she never cared about how dirty I was when I got done with work. "Nothing will happen to me. The only thing I want is to have you back at my place. Safe. We'll sort this out, okay? Together."

Angel chewed on her lip as she thought it over, and relief

hit me when I could see her come to the decision I was hoping for—her face gave away everything. Her features relaxed and her eyes filled with hope. She finally nodded, and I gave her a swift kiss on the forehead.

The ride home was silent. Angel spent most of the time anxiously twisting her hands together in her lap while looking out the window. I felt her eyes on me several times, but she never said anything.

I gripped the wheel and clenched my jaw every time I thought about what Kendra did. Now that I knew Angel was safe, the anger I was feeling had my full attention.

When we pulled into the parking lot by my apartment, Angel glanced around with a paranoid expression on her face. I wasn't sure what she was looking for, but she let out a relieved sigh and unclasped her seatbelt when she realized there was no one else in sight.

We exited the car and made our way back into the apartment. Angel's backpack hit the floor with a thud while I shot Colton a text.

Me: Found her. Back home now.
Colton: Thank fuck. I'm staying at Tara's tonight. I'll try to find out more details.
Me: Thanks.

I was glad we had the apartment to ourselves. Angel and I still needed to talk, and I'd rather do it without an audience.

After sliding my phone back into my pocket, I looked up to find Angel staring at me, and my cock responded to the look on her face. Her eyes flared with heat as they roamed over my body, then up to my face. Pink tinged her cheeks as her lips parted and her breathing picked up.

For a short time, we'd both thought we might never see

each other again. And now we were back at my apartment. Safe. Together. Alone.

The charged emotions of the day—fear, anger, confusion—turned into white-hot lust.

She licked her lips and my body suddenly felt electrified, like a soda can after it got shaken up, ready to combust.

I moved toward her as she launched herself at me. Angel's jean-clad legs wrapped around my waist while my hands when down to her ass.

Our teeth clashed as our mouths moved together at a feverish pace. I moved to the closest available surface, which happened to be the kitchen counter, and set her down.

Angel's hand tugged at the zipper of my coveralls and I let her pull it down. Her hands slipped under my T-shirt. Smooth fingertips grazed over my chest and stomach as her mouth sucked at my neck.

My hands went into her hair and I pulled her head back so I could take her mouth with mine.

We were seconds away from losing control.

This had been on my mind since the day I met her. It was what I wanted, eventually.

But not now. Not when I was still upset about everything that happened.

Forcing myself to let go of the grip I had on her hair, I stepped back and the lustful expression on Angel's face cleared a little. "What's wrong?" she asked.

"We can't do this right now."

"Why not?" She sounded disappointed. Frustrated. I could definitely relate to those feelings.

"Damn it, Angel." I ran a hand through my hair. "Because I'm still pissed at you." While my words were harsh, my tone was soft.

I still couldn't believe she'd left the way she did.

"I'm sorry," she squeaked and looked down.

Oh, fuck.

I knew that squeak.

"Baby, no. Please don't cry." I stepped close to her and lifted her chin to make her look at me. Fat tears spilled from her eyes and trailed down her cheeks. I gently wiped them away with my thumbs. "I'm sorry, okay? Do you have any idea how scared I was? Scared I'd never see you again? What would've happened if I'd been too late?"

"I was going to call you… As soon as I figured things out, I was going to call Hank's shop to let you know I was okay," she said softly as she reached up to run her fingers through my hair.

Overwhelmed with emotion, I closed my eyes and dropped my forehead down to hers.

"Please don't do that to me again," I pleaded in a whisper.

"I won't," she promised. "I just panicked. I'm sorry."

I gave her a kiss before lifting her down from the kitchen counter. "Let's watch some movies or something. Might be a good distraction," I suggested.

I tossed a bag of popcorn into the microwave before heading off to take a quick shower while Angel sorted through the DVDs.

Once we were sitting on the couch, Angel faced me, draping her legs over my lap. "How did you find me so fast?"

"Beverly. That woman drives like a NASCAR racer."

"What?" She huffed out a laugh. "No she doesn't. It took us almost an hour to get to the train station…" she trailed off and realization dawned on her face. "Oh my God. She totally played me. I'm like the most gullible person ever," she complained as her hands went up cover her face, muffling her words.

"You're trusting." I tried to phrase it differently to make

her feel better.

I pulled her hands away from her face and laced our fingers.

"I'm just way in over my head with this whole thing. I should've known better. I never could get away with anything. While all the other kids were skipping class and sneaking out..." She huffed. "I always followed the rules because I knew I'd get caught. Like it was the universe's way of keeping me in line. Foster kids run away all the time, especially so close to aging out. I just assumed no one would care..."

"You haven't been caught," I reminded her. "We can just hang around here tomorrow. I only have to go into the shop for a couple hours in the afternoon."

"Hiding away with you does sound nice," she admitted with a shrug.

"Then let's start right now."

Pulling her close to me, I pressed her back to my front. She relaxed into me with a sigh as I ran my thumb back and forth over the smooth skin on the inside of her wrist.

We spent the rest of the evening making light conversation and flirting with each other, avoiding any talk of train stations or missing persons reports.

After we got into bed, I held Angel against my chest a little tighter than usual, thankful that she was still here.

CHAPTER 34

Travis

Early morning light filtered through the window blinds, casting a pinkish glow over the room. Angel's deep, even breathing was soothing as I held my arm around her. I was lying on my back and her head rested in the place where my shoulder met my chest—my favorite way to wake up.

A content sigh left me as I peered down at her face.

The hurt and anger from the day before had melted away, and it was replaced with something else—something I'd never felt before.

My heart swelled in my chest when I realized what it was. *Love.*

I was in love with her. The realization nearly took my breath away.

My arms held her tighter and I placed a kiss on the top of her head, making her sigh in her sleep.

I wanted to tell her, but it was way too soon to be making that kind of declaration. The last thing I wanted to do was scare her away. Obviously, she was a flight risk. I decided it was best to keep my feelings to myself for now.

Angel started waking up and I decided that even though I wasn't going to tell her, maybe I could show her how I felt.

When she stretched, I moved over her and started playfully nipping at her neck. She squealed and giggled until I moved my mouth up to her face, gently brushing my lips over hers.

Kissing her was always great—it was something we'd done a lot of, but I knew we both wanted more.

Tentatively, my hand slipped underneath her shirt and I brushed my fingers over the soft skin of her stomach. I moved my mouth to the place on her neck that I knew drove her crazy as my hand went a little higher. The tip of my middle finger brushed the underside of her breast and she gasped.

"Is this okay?" I looked up into her heavy-lidded eyes.

She nodded rapidly and bit her lower lip. I slowly slid her shirt up until I could see her pink nipple peeking out. I circled my thumb over the hard pebble and she moaned.

I was about to ask her to take the shirt off, but she beat me to it. After she pulled it over her head, she leaned back to look at me but I was too busy staring at her bare skin.

Angel's tits were amazing. Not more than a handful, but round and firm. Perky.

With both of them exposed, I had full access to do what I wanted. I sucked one peak into my mouth while gently pinching the other with my thumb and forefinger. Angel's fingers tangled in my hair as she held me to her.

My cock throbbed painfully in my gym shorts but I ignored it. This was about her.

Her hips started shifting underneath me and I knew what she needed. My hands went to the waistband of her sleep shorts and I looked up at her in question.

She nodded her permission and I slipped them down her smooth legs. Apparently Angel hadn't been wearing panties, because she was completely bare to me now.

Angel in my bed. Naked.

I slowly slid my fingers up to the trimmed blond hair at the apex of her thighs.

"We're not having sex," I blurted out. I felt the need to let her know I didn't plan on doing that yet. "We don't have to do anything you don't want to do."

"Travis, I might die if you don't touch me right now," she said dramatically as she fisted the sheets in her hands.

I chuckled but my amusement didn't last long. I think my brain short-circuited when I ran a finger through her slit and felt her wetness. She was soaked.

She tensed as I rubbed my finger over her entrance, but I didn't push inside. I collected some of the slickness there and moved up through her folds to her clit where I started drawing tight circles.

Angel whimpered and spread her legs wider, baring every part of her to me. Her perfect pink folds glistened with wetness, and I licked my lips when I thought about what it would be like to taste her there. While continuing the movements with my fingers, I kissed the inside of her thigh, so close to the place I really wanted to be.

I moved my fingers back down to her wet opening and played there, stroking and circling while I brought my mouth to her clit and licked.

She arched off the bed, writhing and panting.

Her scent and sweet taste hit me like a ton of bricks. I could feel pre-cum leaking from the tip of my cock and I hoped I didn't come in my pants again. Once was embarrassing enough.

"Oh… Oh my God…" she moaned.

I pushed one finger inside of her while latching onto her clit, sucking it into my mouth while flicking my tongue back and forth. Back and forth. Back and forth.

Her legs started to shake and the sound of her whimpers filled the room.

I continued the constant rhythm and a minute later, I felt her silky walls start to spasm around my finger.

A harsh breath left her mouth as her shoulders came up off the bed before slamming back down. Her back arched off the bed and a strangled cry ripped from her throat.

Not ready to stop, I lapped at her, tasting her a few more times before she jolted from the oversensitivity.

After kissing my way up her body, I left one more lingering kiss on her mouth.

"Well, that was…" Angel seemed at a loss for words.

"Awesome? Fantastic? Life-changing?" I said cockily, causing her to playfully pinch one of my nipples through my shirt. "Ow," I complained as I rubbed at the abused flesh.

It didn't really hurt—I just wanted her sympathy. When she got a mischievous glint in her eye, I knew I was in trouble.

"Take this off," she demanded, clawing at my shirt.

After whipping it over my head, she pushed on my chest until I was lying on my back. Her hands trailed down my chest and stopped at the waistband of my shorts.

I reached out to grab her hand. "Angel, if you touch me, I'm going to explode."

"That's kind of the point," she quipped with a smirk before eagerly tugging my shorts and boxers off.

She stared at my dick with an expression of awe on her face. She was still completely naked, and seeing her hover over me caused another bead of pre-cum to gather at the tip.

Slowly reaching out, she spread the wetness around the head of my cock with her index finger. Then she leaned down to lick it once while wrapping her delicate hand around the base.

"Fuck," I rasped. Now it was my turn to fist the sheets.

Her warm, wet mouth engulfed the tip, testing and tasting. She let out a quiet moan in the back of her throat, so quiet I almost didn't hear it.

It was a sound of satisfaction. She liked the way I tasted.

That alone was enough to make me clench my jaw in effort to hold off coming all over her beautiful face.

Angel looked up at me with innocent eyes.

"Tell me what you like," she whispered.

The heat of her breath licked over my sensitive skin and my dick twitched in her hand.

The realization hit me that she'd probably never done this before.

"Wrap your hand around it. Yeah, just like that," I encouraged. "Suck it into your mouth as far as you can and use your hand, too. Shit, that's good."

Her golden waves fell around her face like a curtain and I lifted some of it out of out of the way so I could watch my cock disappear into her mouth.

She did everything I said perfectly.

Too perfectly.

Angel bobbed up and down a few times when I felt my balls draw up tight to my body.

I wasn't kidding when I told her I was close.

"Fuck, baby... I'm gonna come," I grunted, and tapped her shoulder in warning so she could take me out of her mouth.

But she didn't. If anything, she sucked me harder, took me in deeper.

My entire body tensed up as the orgasm slammed through me. Letting out a hoarse shout, I emptied into the back of her throat as she swallowed every drop.

Angel sat back on her heels, shyly wiping at her grinning mouth, then crawled up my body so I could wrap my arms around her.

"Well, I hope you're proud of yourself," I said, still breathing hard. "That was... perfect."

I loved the feel of her naked body against mine. Skin on

skin. I brought my lips to hers for a kiss, then affectionately brushed my nose over hers.

Angel smirked and threw my words back at me. "Life-changing?"

"Definitely," I told her without a doubt.

I wasn't sure if she had any idea how true those words were. Because that's what she was for me.

Life-changing.

∽

After breakfast, we watched some morning talk shows before I decided to take a shower, and Angel went into the bedroom to read a book she'd borrowed from Beverly last week.

Being with Angel was easy like that. Comfortable.

We'd quickly developed a relationship where being around each other didn't mean constant conversation, and we didn't feel the need to spend every second together. My mom always told me the best relationships included companionable silences. I never knew what she meant until now.

I guess that's what happened when you basically moved in with someone right off the bat.

Was it normal? No. But that didn't make it any less awesome.

I was walking through the living room, running a towel over my wet hair, when my phone started ringing on the coffee table. Seeing it was Colton, I picked up right away.

"What's up, man?"

As he quickly explained what he learned from Tara the night before, my hand gripped the phone tightly. Every word he said caused the anger to build and I had to restrain myself from saying something shitty to him. None of this was his fault—he was just the messenger.

When we ended the call, my hands shook from the rage I was feeling.

I set the phone back down to keep myself from hurling it into the wall. I was a pretty laid-back guy and it took a lot to make me angry. Kendra had officially crossed the line.

After taking a deep breath, I went to the bedroom to find Angel. She was lying on the bed on her stomach, propping the book up in front of her so I could clearly see the cover. It was one of those smut books with an oiled-up man torso on the front.

I'd been so pissed off a second ago, but I couldn't help smiling as I watched her. Her eyebrows were drawn together and she was biting her nails—something she never did. The story must've been at one of the really good parts.

I almost didn't want to interrupt her. Didn't want to ruin the peace she might finally be feeling. But she had a right to know and maybe it would make her feel better to find out the truth.

I cleared my throat to get her attention and she looked up at me.

"Hey," I said.

"Hi." She dog-eared the page she was on. "What's wrong?"

I went to sit on the bed with her, resting my back against the headboard, and she sat up next to me.

"I just got off the phone with Colton. He found out some stuff from Tara about what went down yesterday," I said, and she waited for me to continue with an impatient expression on her face. "Kendra lied about everything. All of it. There was no missing person's report. She made that poster herself."

"She made the whole thing up?" Angel wanted confirmation, and I nodded my head. "But it had my senior picture… And it sounded so real."

"I know. Apparently, Kendra's a lot smarter than I thought.

She must've done some serious Googling on you. That poster she made—it was never even on Facebook. It never went viral. You didn't actually see it on her profile page, did you?"

Angel shook her head. "She just pulled up a picture of it on her phone."

"I'm really fucking pissed at her for this. That's some devious shit right there. But I'm also a little relieved now that I think about it. That means you can relax. There's no missing person's poster out there."

"I'm *so stupid*." She started thumping herself on the forehead with the book. "I can't believe I believed her!"

"Hey, you're not stupid." I took the book away from her and set it on the nightstand. "This is all on Kendra. I never would've expected her to do something like this either."

"Well." Angel sighed. "I'll still call my case worker, just in case anyone really is looking for me. But I guess I feel better now knowing the poster was fake."

"I'm so sorry this happened, baby." I picked up her hand and absentmindedly fiddled with her fingers.

Her face screwed up. "It's not your fault Kendra's a psycho."

"No." I shook my head. "But I feel like I should've seen this coming. I knew she was giving you a hard time and I should've done something about it sooner."

Angel moved onto my lap, sitting sideways, and looped her arms around my neck. "Let's just both agree to stop blaming ourselves. Okay?"

"Okay." I smiled. Like there was any chance I could say no to her.

～

After suiting up in my coveralls, I told Angel I was heading into the shop for a couple hours and that I'd be back around three. Before I left, she kissed me, looked me in the eye, and told me she would be here.

It was like she could read my mind. Maybe she could tell I felt reluctant to leave her, afraid that when I came home she'd be gone.

I walked quickly down the block, eager to get my work done at the shop, but as soon as I got there Hank sent me home. He'd heard about what happened yesterday from Colton.

"You go be with your girl. Sounds like she needs you right now," he said as he affectionately squeezed my shoulder.

I did leave the shop, but I didn't go straight home. There was something I had to take care of first.

I saw Kendra's car parked behind Buck's so I knew she was there.

I'd known Kendra wasn't the nicest person, but I didn't think she was cruel. One thing was for sure—I'd underestimated her intelligence and overestimated her decency as a person.

Some people made the mistake of thinking that just because I was a nice guy, I was a pushover. They mistook kindness for weakness. I wasn't a fucking pushover and Kendra was about to find that out right now.

Buck's was the same as always. Long bar off to the right and some tables to the left. The place was pretty empty—just one older man sitting at the bar and a young couple at a table by the front window—and I was glad. I didn't want a lot of people hearing what I was about to say.

Kendra was wiping down a table in the back and she looked surprised when I approached her. Surprise gave way to a satisfaction. She obviously didn't know my purpose for coming here. She thought she'd won.

Her smile faded as I got closer, and she saw the cold look

in my eyes.

"Are you proud of yourself?" I asked, shoving my hands into my pockets. I would never physically harm a woman, but that didn't mean I didn't have the urge to throttle her.

I held eye contact with her, my hard stare unwavering. She nervously glanced away before deciding to play clueless. "What are you talking about?"

"Are you proud of yourself," I repeated, annunciating the words. "You took a girl who didn't have anything, didn't have *anyone*—" I slashed my hand through the air, then pointed it at her. "—and you ran her out of town."

Her mouth opened and closed but no words came out. I didn't need her to talk. There wasn't anything I wanted to hear her say.

"You need to listen to me." I leaned forward and flattened my hand on the table between us. "There will never be anything with you and me. Even if I'd never met Angel, that wouldn't change."

"She's leaving." She glared at me. "But I'll still be here, Travis."

"I love her." The confession left my mouth without warning and warmth spread through my chest. It was bittersweet because, although it felt good to say the words, the wrong person got to hear it.

"That's ridiculous," she scoffed and laughed humorlessly. "You've known her for, like, two weeks."

"And what does that tell you, Kendra? I've known you for how many years? Yet, I feel nothing for you. I've been with Angel for two weeks and I'm in love with her. *I love her,*" I said vehemently before continuing. "And how much does it suck that you're the first person to know? The first time I've ever been in love and you're the first person I tell... It. Fucking. Sucks."

Kendra's face was stricken and tears glistened in her eyes. I couldn't even feel bad about it. Not after what she did to Angel.

"Are you going to ruin this for her, too?" I demanded. "Are you going to run and tell her?"

"No," she whispered, her voice wobbly.

"Good. Stay the fuck away."

She called after me as I was leaving. "I'll be waiting for you after she breaks your heart."

I thought about letting her have the last word—it was the only thing she would ever get from me.

But fuck that.

I turned on my heel and went back over to where she was standing until our faces were inches apart. "No. Not now. Not ever. Not under any circumstances. This is a small town, Kendra. Psycho doesn't look very good on you. Got it?"

I didn't wait for her to respond before walking away. Short and sweet. Well, not really sweet, but clear as day.

After leaving Buck's I made a quick trip to the next town over. I had to get Angel's birthday present and I had the perfect gift in mind.

CHAPTER 35

Angel

I wasn't used to waking up alone anymore, so I was briefly disappointed when I felt the cold, empty sheets next to me.

Burying my face in Travis's T-shirt, I breathed in his scent. I'd started wearing his clothes at night. My particular favorite was an old high school baseball tee. The light blue fabric was worn and super soft from years of use.

Without bothering to put on pants—because the shirt was basically a nightgown—I sleepily puttered out to the kitchen, following the smell of bacon and a hint of cinnamon.

Mmm bacon.

Travis was standing at the stove, wielding a spatula in one hand and a fork in the other. He was shirtless and his track pants rode dangerously low on his hips, showing off the low back dimples I liked so much. My mouth watered, and I wasn't sure if it was from the smell of breakfast or the view.

"What's going on?" I asked as I rubbed my eyes and attempted to smooth out my bedhead.

He turned around and shot me a grin, complete with the other set of dimples I couldn't get enough of.

"Happy birthday, baby." He came over to place a kiss on my lips. "I was planning to bring you breakfast in bed."

"This works just fine." I smiled as I plucked a perfectly cooked piece of bacon off the plate on the counter. "Mmm.

You made it extra crispy, too."

"Just how you like it. The waffles are almost done."

I sat at the table while Travis served up the best waffles I'd ever had. While it was clearly a waffle, it tasted like a cinnamon roll. Instead of syrup, icing was drizzled on top, collecting in the square pattern made by the waffle iron.

"How did you do this? This is amazing," I mumbled around a huge bite.

"It's actually really easy. It's premade cinnamon rolls that come in a can. I just flatten them out and put them in the waffle iron."

"Where did you learn that?" I shoveled another fork-full into my mouth. Unbelievable. Travis had successfully made a hybrid of my two favorite breakfast foods.

"Pinterest."

A surprised laugh burst from my mouth, along with several particles of food. I grimaced and felt my face heat from embarrassment as I covered my mouth with a hand.

Travis just laughed and handed me a napkin.

"Well, you nailed it," I said after making sure I didn't have any food in my mouth. "It's just... The sexy trucker browsing Pinterest is kind of hilarious to me."

"Sexy truckers like Pinterest, too. But don't tell anyone. It's kind of a secret," he teased.

I just made an incoherent sound of agreement and kept eating. After I finished every bite, I had to resist the urge to lick the plate.

Just as I took my dishes over to the sink, Travis walked by. "You'd better go get ready," he said by my ear before lightly swatting my butt. "Got big plans today."

"What big plans?"

"Well, first we have to drop the trailer off in Bloomington for the Colorado trip. Then I thought we could go to the zoo, since we'll already be close to there."

"I love the zoo." My heart melted a little.

"I know." He grinned. "So, do you want your present now or later?"

"There's more? Um, now of course." I gave him my best 'you should know the answer to that' tone.

Travis grabbed a small gray plastic bag off the counter and handed it to me. I reached inside and picked up a sleek black cell phone. Complete with a touch screen, it was fancy. Probably not top of the line, but way better than the one I used to have.

"You got me a phone?" I asked with disbelief. It was an expensive gift. Honestly, I expected a keychain or something.

I swiped my finger across the screen to unlock it and burst into a fit of laughter. The background picture was of Travis, cocky grin and dimples in place while he gave a 'thumbs-up' sign.

He shrugged. "Figured you'd need it. Plus, I like the idea of being able to get ahold of you. You know, for when you're running off to train stations and stuff," he joked.

I raised an eyebrow and gave him a pointed look.

"Too soon?" he asked cheekily.

I poked his chest playfully before rising up to give him a kiss. "Thank you for the gift. Really, it's way more than you should have spent."

"It's practical. I'm a practical guy." He smiled then his face got serious and his hand came up to toy with a wild strand of my hair. "But mostly, I want to be able to talk to you when you're in California, so it would mean a lot to me if you keep it."

We rarely mentioned my upcoming departure. It was as if we'd come to some unspoken agreement not to talk about it.

Glancing up to his face, I held his stare for a few

seconds—not because I needed to think it over—but because I wanted to soak up the way he looked right now. Every now and then, I saw a side to Travis that he tried to hide. It wasn't insecurity—he was one of the most self-assured people I'd ever met.

It was vulnerability. And every time I got a glimpse of it, I felt like I was seeing into his heart, into the deepest part of him.

"I'll keep it," I promised.

CHAPTER 36

Travis

I hadn't been to this zoo—or any zoo, for that matter—in over ten years. When I'd come here as a kid it seemed so big. Huge. Epic.

But now that I was seeing it from adult eyes, it seemed so small and I suddenly felt silly for bringing Angel here. That is, until I saw her face.

Her face held an expression of awe as she walked towards the wallaby exhibit. My eyes followed the innocent, yet seductive sway of her hips as her dress swished around her thighs.

"Look!" She pointed to the gate. "It says we can go inside."

I swung our laced hands between us as we walked, and Angel chattered on about how cute the wallabies were—most of which were hiding behind the logs and bushes.

She got out her phone to snap some pictures and after she was done, I took it from her hands to turn it around on us. I wanted a selfie with my girl.

When we came to the otters, Angel did some sort of spastic happy dance, which was really fucking cute, then practically fell over the wall of the habitat trying to get a closer look.

Because her dress—the white dress that drove me crazy—was already short, it rode up way too high for my liking while we were in public. I came up behind her to make sure no one got a peek at what was mine.

Unfortunately, it meant she was bent over in front of me and I felt my cock stiffen immediately. By now, I should've been used to getting hard at awkward times. Being around her did that to me.

But no amount of being used to it was going to change the fact that public boners were awkward, not to mention inappropriate.

When she finally stood up, I encased her body with my arms and linked my hands around her stomach. We stood that way for several minutes, Angel watching the otters, and me holding her while I rested my chin on top of her head.

"Aren't they just the cutest?" she gushed.

"They are pretty cute." I had to agree. "Kinda smelly, though."

She laughed at my honest observation and leaned her head to one side to look at me. "You're kinda smelly, too, sometimes, but I still like you."

Grinning, I started tickling her sides. She squealed and spun away from me toward the petting zoo. When I caught up to her, I gave her a long kiss that was borderline indecent for a public place.

The goats were definitely my favorite. There was a food dispenser where you could get a handful of pellets for twenty-five cents.

"How genius is this?" I asked Angel as I inserted a quarter into the machine. "We pay the zoo to feed their animals."

"It's a win-win for everyone. Looks like they're not hurting for a meal." She hitched a thumb over her shoulder at the groups of people crowding the area waiting for their turn.

The goats eagerly stuck their heads through the wide slats of the fence, necks stretched out to reach the closest hand.

"It feels so weird." Angel snickered as the soft muzzle nibbled at her palm. "Now, now. You have to share with the others," she softly scolded the greediest one and offered the rest of the food to a smaller goat.

After our hands were empty, we attempted to pet their heads, scratching them behind the ears. But once they realized their snack was gone, they moved on to other people who were willing to give them what they really wanted.

It only took us about forty-five minutes to get through the entire zoo. Before we left, Angel excused herself to the restroom and I sat down on a bench to wait for her. Since I had the bench to myself, I was able to man-spread as I relaxed into the seat.

Don't judge. Man-spreading was comfortable.

A squawking sound came from somewhere close behind me and I turned around to find my face mere inches away from a goose standing on the other side of a chain link fence.

Laughing, I looked my new companion in the beady eye he had cocked in my direction.

"Well, hi," I said, and he honked in response. "Sorry, I don't have any food for you." I held up my empty hands so he could see I was telling the truth.

He flapped his brown and white wings, wiggled his tail feathers, and let out a shrill squawk. I wasn't sure what he wanted from me.

Thinking maybe he wanted me to pet him, I started to stick my fingers through the hole in the fence.

"I wouldn't do that if I were you," Angel warned as she stepped up beside me, a smirk on her face.

"I think he likes me." I went back to poking my finger through the chain link fence.

"I think he wants to bite your finger off," she retorted.

As if to prove she was right, the goose stuck his beak through the hole and snapped at the tip of my finger.

"Ow." I pulled my hand back and glared at him. "I thought

we were friends. Not cool, dude."

Angel laughed, then kissed the end of my smarting finger. *All better*.

After we left the zoo, I drove to a small town called Elmer, which was about twenty minutes away from Tolson. My plans for the day weren't finished yet but I refused to tell Angel what we were doing, no matter how much she pestered me.

I'd just parked the semi when Hank called.

"What's up?" I answered.

"Travis, what's your twenty?" he asked professionally, making me chuckle.

Angel started bouncing in her seat and motioning for me to give her the phone. Smiling, I handed it over. I'd taught her some trucker lingo on the way to the drop-off this morning and it seemed she wanted to put it to good use.

"Hi, Hank?" she said after putting the phone up to her ear. "What's our twenty?" With raised eyebrows, Angel sent me a look that said 'I've totally got this'. The sun glinted off the sequins on her flip-flops as she propped her feet up on the dash, then proceeded to babble random trucker talk. "We're double nickels in the hammer lane and a dragon wagon."

I had to stifle a laugh with my hand, playing it off like I had an itch because I didn't want her to know I was laughing at her.

She had it completely wrong. More or less, she'd just told Hank we were going fifty-five-miles-per-hour in the fast lane of the highway with a tow truck.

So, not even close since we were parked in front of the grocery store in Elmer.

Even though the phone wasn't on speaker, I could hear Hank laughing on the other end. Angel laughed along with him before turning to me.

"He said I did good!" she whisper-yelled at me with a

proud expression on her face.

That time I did laugh out loud. She spouted off a few more nonsensical phrases then said "Ten-four" and hung up. At least she got that last one right.

I gazed over at her, entirely amused and caught up in how gorgeous she was. I must have been staring too long because she started to look uncomfortable.

"What?" she asked, self-consciously pawing at her face and hair.

"You're beautiful," I told her with tenderness in my voice.

"Thank you." Her lips tipped up and her cheeks pinked.

Fuck, yeah. I loved that I could still make her blush like that.

"You ready for this?" I asked, getting out of the semi.

She made a face at me. "Well, I could answer that question if you told me what we're doing."

"Not a chance," I replied before kissing the scowl off her face.

I made my way through the store to the deli section and picked up a package of bologna.

Angel raised her eyebrows. "Are we making sandwiches?"

"No." I chuckled.

"Are you going to tell me what we're doing?"

"No."

"Just a hint?" she begged.

"Nope." I laughed and she huffed.

～

The gentle sway of the paddle boat was calming as Angel and I drifted on the water of Elmer Lake. I was sitting patiently with my line in the water, waiting to get a nibble.

Something tugged on the hook, causing the bobber to

briefly dip into the water. After reeling in my fishing line, I was annoyed when I saw my bait was gone, yet I had no fish.

"Maybe you're not doing it right," Angel suggested with a teasing smile as I loaded the hook with another strip of bologna.

I shot her a look. Before I could respond, Angel's bobber got tugged under the water as she caught another fish. She squealed with happiness as she lifted the good-sized catfish out of the water.

"I can't believe how good the fishing is here!" she exclaimed, handing me her catch, which was still on the hook.

Shaking my head in amusement, I carefully removed the hook from its mouth because Angel couldn't do it. Said she couldn't stand the thought of hurting them. My girl was a sweetheart.

As I placed the new addition into the five-gallon bucket, I counted the six fish we'd caught. Well, Angel caught most of them. The smallest bluegill flapping around in the shallow water was my only accomplishment.

I frowned. "If this were a contest, you'd totally kick my ass."

"What can I say?" She shrugged. "Fish love me. Probably because I won't eat them."

"You won't eat fish? Even if it's cooked?" I asked, remembering her adorable rant about sushi on the first day we met.

"Don't look at me like that. Not everyone likes fish. Try hating seafood while living in Maine. I was basically a social pariah," she joked.

"This isn't seafood." I pointed out at the water. "That's a *lake*."

"It's still fish." She wrinkled her nose.

"So you're saying we have to throw them back?"

"Of course." She looked shocked that I would even

suggest otherwise.

"Colton will be disappointed. He loves a good fish fry."

She waved her hand dismissively. "I'll just make him sloppy joes and he'll be happy again."

"Okay. But not tonight. You're not cooking on your birthday."

∽

We finished off the day with dinner from Pizza Palace.

"It smells so good," Angel said, holding the large pepperoni pizza on her lap as we drove back to my apartment.

"Best pizza you'll ever have," I told her. "Let's just hope Colton isn't home. He'll eat half of it himself."

Trying to look as inconspicuous as possible, she slowly lifted the lid on the cardboard box, snuck her hand in to pull out a corner piece and started nibbling on it. I wasn't sure why she was trying to be sneaky about it, but it made me smile.

"If you're hungry, you don't have to wait for me," I encouraged.

She smiled gratefully before flinging the lid off and digging in. After she devoured at least a quarter of the pizza, she held a small square piece out to me.

"Do you want some?" she offered, but since her mouth was full, it came out more like 'ju ju wum shum'.

I laughed. "I'll wait, thanks. It's kinda hard to eat and drive."

"I could feed it to you." She extended her arm toward me again.

Now there was an idea. As innocent as her suggestion was, it conjured up all kinds of images in my mind.

"As much as I would love to get kinky with you, now's not the best time." I smirked, hoping to make her blush again.

"It's a pizza, not a dildo."

Her crude statement took me by surprise and I barked out a laugh.

"Okay, one piece." I tilted my head in her direction and she unceremoniously shoved it into my mouth.

CHAPTER 37

Angel

I laughed as Travis chewed happily on his pizza while he drove. One piece turned into several and I was having way too much fun feeding him.

"So, tell me something about Claire or your dad," he requested between bites. "Or is it too hard to talk about it?" he asked cautiously.

"My dad and I weren't really close," I replied. "He worked a lot. Cops have weird hours sometimes and he usually worked at night. I spent a lot of nights at Claire's. She was already pretty involved in my life before he died, and that's probably why the transition was so easy for me when I moved in with her." As I talked, I was pleasantly surprised to notice it didn't hurt to talk about my crazy aunt. "She was wacky. Kind of a hippie-type. Spontaneous. Fun."

I searched my mind for a favorite memory. It was hard to narrow it down to just one.

"When I was fourteen, we dyed our hair together—red." I laughed and ran my hands through my hair as I recalled our love for *Anne of Green Gables*. "It was one of those cheap box dyes you can buy at the pharmacy. It was supposed to be temporary—the kind that washed out after six weeks. Only, it didn't. Claire and I had to wait almost two years for our hair to grow out back to our natural color. For a while, the top half of my hair was blonde and the bottom had red tips. It almost looked like I did it on purpose."

Now that I'd started to talk about her, I felt like I couldn't stop. It felt good to be able to share stories about her with someone else.

"She wasn't squeamish about sex talks. At all." I shuddered when I thought about the time she demonstrated how to put a condom on, using a banana. "And she had the worst luck on dates, so you would have been able to swap stories with her. A few years ago, she went on a date with a man she met at the grocery store. They bonded over the avocado sale." I waved my hand at the unnecessary detail. "Anyway, he invited his mother along on their date to the pumpkin patch. I mean, it was sweet that he wanted to include his mom and all, but he was *forty*. And it was a *first date*. He even made Claire sit in the backseat of his car so his mom could ride shotgun. She totally felt like the third wheel." I laughed, remembering how pissed she was when she got home from the date.

Travis was grinning. "She sounds awesome. You must miss her a lot."

"I think I'll always miss her. She was my best friend."

"You've made quite a few new friends," he pointed out. "That Beverly's a handful."

"That's an understatement," I agreed with a smile.

Tolson came into view as we drove down Main Street and Travis pulled the semi up to the designated spot beside the shop. Before we could get out, I stopped him by reaching over and grabbing his hand.

"Travis?"

"Yeah?"

"Thanks for today. It was the best day ever."

After unbuckling my seatbelt, he tugged me over until I was sitting on his lap. He didn't have to tug very hard. I'd always go to him willingly.

Framing my face with his hands, he kissed me long and deep until I felt breathless.

"It was the best day for me, too," he whispered before rubbing his nose over mine. "Happy birthday, baby."

$\sim$

The next morning, I couldn't put off reality any longer and I finally called my case worker. And I was really glad I did. The weight of my guilty conscience lifted when I apologized profusely for leaving the way I did. I informed her that I was staying with a friend and when I told her about my plan to find my mom, she was extremely helpful about the process.

Apparently, there were forms I needed to fill out in order to be added to my mom's approved visitors list. She sent the paperwork to my email, along with the correctional facility website, which had a list of rules including visiting hours and a dress code for guests.

I had no idea visiting an inmate could be so complicated. It would've been a horrible disappointment to get there and be turned away.

Now, I found myself back on Beverly's porch.

"Why, Angel," she exclaimed, pretending to be shocked as I stepped inside. "What a pleasant surprise. Back so soon?"

"You must think you're pretty sneaky, huh?" I scolded with my hands on my hips, but my tone was a mixture of amused and impressed.

"Whatever do you mean?" Her eyes danced with mirth.

She might be able to fool other people with the sweet old lady act. In fact, she was quite good at it. But I knew better.

"You know what I mean. I spent the whole ride to the train station wondering how you possibly passed a driver's test! I seriously feared for our safety, Beverly."

Beverly cackled. "Oh, please. There was no way we could've been injured going that slow. Hell, I could probably ride a bicycle faster than that," she said as I followed her to the kitchen.

"Why did you agree to take me to the train station?" I asked. "You didn't even try to talk me out of it."

"If I'd tried to change your mind, would it have worked?"

I shrugged. "Maybe not. I probably would've tried to find a different way."

"Exactly." She pointed at me.

"Well, anyway, thanks for sticking your nose where it doesn't belong," I teased.

All joking aside, I really was extremely grateful for her meddling. If she hadn't interfered, who knows where I would've been right now.

"Maybe I should be thanking you. I haven't had that much excitement in years. Would you like some Oatmeal Crème Pies? Or…" She opened the fridge and took out a round container. "How about some cake?"

She beamed as she took off the white plastic top to reveal a round, vanilla frosted cake with a big number '18' drawn in pink icing in the middle.

"You made me a birthday cake?" I asked, touched by her thoughtfulness.

"Of course I did. We're friends, aren't we?" She raised her eyebrows, giving me a look that meant she actually wanted me to answer her question.

"Yeah, of course we are. I just didn't expect anything special."

"We're led to believe that expectations are our enemy," she said as she placed the cake on the counter, then she turned to look at me. "The greatest expectations lead to the greatest disappointments, right? Well that's a bunch of bullshit. In this life, you expect nothing, you get nothing. Expect great things, Angel. Expect everything. Don't ever sell yourself short. You got me?"

I'd never heard Beverly sound so passionate about something before. And the words she was saying… I had to admit it was great advice. No one had ever said that to me before.

The problem was, disappointment was something I'd gotten used to over the years. I wasn't the kind of person people went out of their way for. I once saw someone make a Facebook post declaring they had a case of the sniffles and fifteen people commented, offering soup and home remedies.

That kind of stuff didn't happen to me. And I didn't expect it to. But I felt like I was getting some sort of priceless wisdom, so I absorbed her words and nodded my head.

"Good." She turned back to the cake. "By the way, my birthday is April twenty-fifth and I expect a card and a phone call, at the very least."

I laughed, even though I knew she was completely serious.

Then I had to swallow around the lump in my throat when I realized a card and a phone call was probably all she would get from me, since I wouldn't be here. I was going to miss her so much after I was gone.

Maybe I could teach her how to Skype.

Pushing all thoughts of leaving aside, I forced myself to live in this moment. Thinking about moving on was just too painful.

After cutting two giant pieces of cake, she handed me a plate and we went to sit on the front porch. As we were getting settled, I quickly filled her in on all-things-Kendra, and lamented about the fact that my panicked trip to the train station was all for nothing.

"Sometimes women are bitches," Beverly stated very

matter-of-factly.

I nodded in agreement. "It never even occurred to me that she was lying. I'm too gullible."

"I like you just the way you are." She waved her fork at me and her expression got soft. "Don't ever change. Especially not because of the Kendras of the world."

We sat quietly, enjoying the cake while I mulled over some of the thoughts and feelings I'd been plagued with lately, most of them revolving around Travis.

The way I felt about him… I'd never felt that way about anyone before. I thought about him constantly and I loved everything about him.

It didn't hurt that he looked really hot driving a semi. Scratch that—he looked hot all the time.

It wasn't just his looks, though. Yeah, the physical attraction was off the charts, but he was funny and protective and kind. He was fiercely loyal to the people he loved.

He was a truly good person. I might have been naïve about the world, but I knew people like Travis were rare.

And it wasn't all about the way *I* felt about *him*, but the way he made me feel about myself. When I was with him, I felt special.

Important.

Loved.

Even though he hadn't told me he loved me, there were times when I felt it. It came through in the way he looked at me, when he touched me.

I didn't plan on telling him, though. Just the thought of it made me uncomfortable. *Love* was one thing my filter insisted on keeping inside.

I knew it was a modern world, and women could be the first to declare their feelings in a relationship. But much like physical affection, *I love you* wasn't something we did in my family. I couldn't remember the last time I'd uttered those words—or the last time they were said to me.

My insides felt all twisted up and I needed someone to confide in. Since Beverly insisted on hanging out with me, she was pretty much volunteering. 'Confidante' fell under the job description of friends, right?

"I think I'm in love with Travis." The words ran together as they rushed from my mouth.

Beverly guffawed. "Well, of course you are. Like I said—fine piece of ass."

"Beverly!" I scolded while laughing. "I'm serious."

"Well, what's the problem? You sound like you're complaining."

"I don't know." I wrung my hands together while I tried to think of a way to explain how I was feeling. "I'm leaving in a week. I didn't expect this and it just happened really fast."

"Despite what you might believe, love doesn't adhere to a schedule," she said wisely. "And sometimes it pops up when you least expect it."

I nodded, but I didn't really get it. I had zero experience with this type of love. "I guess I always thought when I fell in love it would be a slow, gradual process. One that made sense and had some sort of timeline. I thought the term 'whirlwind romance' only happened in movies or books."

Beverly sat back in her chair and folded her weathered hands in her lap. She was silent for a minute as she gazed out into the distance, unfocused, as though she was lost in thought.

"I knew my William for two weeks before he asked my father for my hand in marriage. I was seventeen and he was twenty-three. My daddy didn't like that." She chuckled. "Said I was too young to know what love was. He made a rule that we could send letters back and forth, but we weren't allowed to see each other until I turned eighteen, which was three months away. Seemed like a lifetime to me back then." She smiled and shook her head. "I think my daddy thought he was being sly. Thought one or both of us would lose interest. But guess who showed up on my doorstep with a ring on my birthday?"

"William," I sighed, because it was so romantic.

"You bet your ass," Beverly confirmed. "I may have been young, but I wasn't inexperienced. Before I met William, I'd already been in love once. Already had my heart broken."

"Ernie," I said knowingly as I glanced at the house next door.

"He told you about that, did he?" She chuckled.

"He still has a thing for you." I swung my eyes back to her.

"Oh *pssh*. It's been over sixty years."

"Weren't you the one who just told me love doesn't adhere to a schedule?" I asked, putting obnoxious air quotes around her words of wisdom.

"Touché, my dear, touché."

CHAPTER 38

Angel

"**A**re you sure you don't want to try out the showers?" Travis teased as he tugged on the ends of my hair.

"I had one this morning, thank you very much," I replied with an exaggerated pout and he made it better with a kiss. "Maybe on the way back, though."

In all honesty, I really was curious about these truck stop showers. Apparently, they were super nice.

It was Friday afternoon and we were at a truck stop somewhere in Kansas. We still had a couple more hours of driving before we stopped for the night, then we would arrive in Denver late tomorrow morning.

After we picked out some snacks, Travis said he was going to pay then use the restroom, so I could just go wait for him in the truck. I was walking around the back of the building through the parking lot when I noticed my shoelace was untied.

I'd just finished tying it when a shadow fell over me. Thinking it was Travis, I stood up to face him.

It wasn't Travis.

The man standing before me was the epitome of trucker stereotypes.

He was probably twice my age, with a scraggly beard and a dark mullet streaked with gray. The red plaid shirt he was wearing had the sleeves torn off and his arms were covered in faded tattoos. His big stomach hung over the belt of his beat-up jeans and dark sunglasses concealed his eyes.

"Well, hi there, sweet cheeks. I suppose it's my lucky day." He grinned, revealing brown-stained teeth.

"What?" I whipped my head around to make sure he wasn't talking to someone else. We were the only people in this part of the parking lot and a feeling of unease came over me.

"You come on back to my rig. I promise I'll make it worth your while."

I started to back away because—creepy—but he wrapped his large hand around my forearm and started pulling me along with him.

"Hey! What are you doing?" I protested. "Wait." I tried to pull my arm free from his grasp but he just held on tighter, completely ignoring me.

We were probably about forty feet away from the blue eighteen-wheeler he was dragging me toward, too far for me to make out the company name on the side of the driver's door.

I dug my heels into the ground but my shoes skidded on the asphalt, causing me to stumble.

Thirty feet away.

My heart started to pound, my body kicking into fight or flight mode. I kept trying to yank my arm from his grasp, but he wouldn't let go.

Twenty feet.

I remembered something Claire told me. She said if I was ever attacked, to scream as long and loud as I could. *Be loud*, she'd said. *The louder the better. Most attackers won't want the attention drawn to them and they'll run away.*

"Stop!" I yelled in the most commanding tone I could muster.

The man's footsteps faltered, but he didn't loosen his grip. He started to turn around to face me but before he could, he was tackled to the ground.

I saw a blur of bodies colliding and it took me a second to realize Travis was on top of the man, raining blows to his face. My hands flew up to my mouth as I gasped in shock.

Travis got three or four solid punches in before he pushed off him and stood up. The fight—if you could even call it that—was over before I could make sense of what was happening.

"Don't touch my girlfriend, you sick fuck," Travis said in a voice I'd never heard him use before. The muscles in his arms and back bulged and strained against his white shirt.

"Fuckin' shit," the guy moaned and grumbled before rolling over and spitting blood on the ground. "What the fuck."

He managed to sit up on his knees and he swayed a bit while trying to regain his balance.

My heart was still pounding, and I felt like I couldn't catch my breath as the man pulled a red bandana from his back pocket and held it up to his bleeding lip.

Body tense and fists clenched, Travis was still braced for a fight as the man wobbled to his feet.

"I didn't mean no harm," the man said as he backed away in defeat and spit more blood off to the side.

His sunglasses had been knocked off in the scuffle and I could tell his left eye was already swelling shut. He tried to glance my way, but Travis stepped in front of me.

"Don't even fucking look at her," he growled.

"I thought she was a lot lizard," the man explained, as if that should be enough to clarify why he was dragging me off to his truck caveman-style.

"You thought wrong." There was a finality to Travis's

tone and if this guy knew what was good for him, he would walk away.

The man made the right choice. He bent over to pick up the broken pieces of his sunglasses off the ground and staggered towards his semi, seeming dazed.

I'd never seen Travis violent before, but it was obvious he knew how to throw a punch. I'd also never seen him so angry. So threatening.

The aggression seemed to leave him immediately as he turned to me and hugged my body to his. After picking up the bag of our snacks, he quickly steered me toward his semi at the other end of the lot.

When he stopped with me by the passenger side, a mix of emotions painted his face—fear, anger, guilt.

He ran his hands over me as if assessing me for injuries. "Are you okay?" he asked, sounding distressed. "I leave you alone for two minutes… Fuck! I'm so sorry, Angel. I should've been there…"

"I'm okay." I finally found my voice. "I'm just really confused. What happened back there?" I motioned with my thumb toward the empty parking lot.

Instead of answering my question, he continued to search my body with his hands. "Did he hurt you?"

"Not really. I mean, he grabbed me…" I rubbed at the place where he'd had his meaty fingers wrapped around my arm. It didn't look like there would be any bruising, but there was a red streak on my skin, probably caused by the friction when I tried to pull away from him.

Travis's face turned murderous when he saw the mark on my skin. "*Motherfucker*. I should've hit that sick bastard a few more times," he growled.

When he started to look around like he was trying to find the guy again, I brought my hand up to his face to make him look at me.

"It's okay. I'm okay. Let's just get out of here?" I pleaded.

He nodded and briefly touched his forehead to mine before opening the passenger door and helping me up into the seat.

CHAPTER 39

Travis

That sack of shit touched Angel. When I saw him manhandling her, saw her struggling against him, my vision went *red*.

My hands were still shaking from the adrenaline and rage as I started the engine.

I didn't think she would run into any trouble here. The big-name truck stops got a lot of traffic and usually had parking lot surveillance, which discouraged the customers from certain behaviors.

I knew what he planned to do with her. It didn't take a genius to figure it out.

"Hey, you're bleeding." Angel pointed at my bloody knuckles with a trembling finger.

I flexed my hand, noting that it would be sore, but my skin wasn't broken.

"It's not my blood," I said, looking over at her and noticing she looked a little pale. "Are you sure you're okay?"

She nodded. "We should clean it. Do you have a first aid kit?"

"Glove compartment."

She found the small square case then tore open a few alcohol wipes before passing them to me.

"What's a lot lizard?" Angel's curious voice piped up

beside me as I thoroughly disinfected the back of my hand.

I hated that she had to see this side of the business, but there was no way to sugarcoat it. "A hooker who hangs out at truck stops."

"He thought I was a prostitute?" she gasped. Sounding insulted, she sat back in her seat and looked down at her clothes.

She was wearing skinny jeans, and her Beach Boys shirt. Nothing about her outfit suggested she was for sale.

"He made an assumption based on what *he* wanted. You didn't do anything wrong, okay?" I made eye contact with her, wanting to make sure she heard me loud and clear.

"I told him to stop." She paused, then shivered as she quietly asked the sickening question I'd been wondering myself. "Do you think he would have taken no for an answer?"

"I don't know," I said, wanting to be honest with her. "I'm not sure if he was concerned about how willing you were."

We didn't talk much after that. Angel fiddled with the radio stations while I tried to concentrate on the road. Usually, driving was calming for me. But after what happened—or almost happened—calm was the last thing I felt.

I drove for another two hours before deciding on a rest stop.

"Are you sure you don't want to get a motel room?" I asked her after shutting off the semi. "After what happened back there… Maybe it's a better option."

"No," she said stubbornly. "This is where we spent our first night together. I want to do it again."

Well, okay then. I couldn't argue with that.

The truth was, I couldn't wait to sleep with her on the tiny sleeper bed again. I'd been looking forward to it all week and I didn't want to let some asshole to ruin our trip.

After we got changed and ready for bed, I snuggled in close to her on the narrow mattress.

Angel didn't waste any time, hungrily consuming my lips with hers. Usually, I was the one to initiate the physical stuff, so I loved it when she made the first move.

Unfortunately, I was distracted and she could tell. I was still pretty shaken up by what happened back at the truck stop. My head spun with the 'what ifs', replaying all the different ways it could have gone.

Her kissing slowed, and she pulled back to look me in the eye.

"What's wrong?"

"I just can't get it out of my head—what could've happened to you back there if I'd been one minute later. Just one minute." I shook my head. "It's on replay in my mind and I can't get it to stop."

"So let's replace it with something else," she suggested quietly as she ran her fingers through my hair.

"Like what?" I closed my eyes at the soothing gesture, the feeling of calm seeping into me with every gentle sweep of her hand.

"Let's make tonight a good memory." Her hand trailed down my chest and her fingers lingered suggestively at the waist of my pants. "Travis, how long do I have to wait?"

I knew what she wanted from me. And I wanted to give it to her.

I wanted Angel to be my first and I wanted to be hers. Although, somewhere deep down, I knew it wasn't going to be enough. Truth was, I didn't just want one part of her—I wanted it all.

I wanted her to be my first, my forever, and everything in between.

And even though I knew she didn't plan on staying, I was willing to take whatever she was willing to give, consequences be damned.

"I don't want to wait anymore either," I proclaimed.

A relieved breath whooshed from her and a huge grin spread over her face. "Good. Now take this off." She tugged at my shirt and it made me chuckle.

"Someone's impatient," I teased as I slipped my shirt over my head. "And bossy."

She ran her hands over my skin while licking her lips, and my dick instantly hardened.

Fuck. This is really happening.

After removing her shirt and bra, I came over her, loving the way her bare skin felt against mine. She eagerly clawed at my pants, pushing them down over my hips, and my erection bobbed impatiently between us.

A chuckle left me when she started using her toes to pull my pants all the way down to my feet. It was like she couldn't get me naked fast enough.

The feeling was mutual.

Next, I peeled her jeans off, revealing smooth, creamy skin. We'd been naked together before, but this time it was different.

Tonight, we would claim each other in a way no one else ever would again.

I melded my mouth with hers and a quiver ran through my body as the underside of my cock brushed against the short hairs over her center. I could feel the heat and wetness between her folds.

Running my fingers through her slit, I confirmed what I already knew. "Baby, you're soaked."

"I want you," she said breathlessly.

I thought about what it would feel like plunging into her heat, and I hoped I could last longer than a few minutes. If I'd known we were going to have sex, I would've prepared myself for it by rubbing one out before we left this morning.

Speaking of being prepared, a sudden realization came over me—I didn't have any condoms.

"I'm such an idiot," I groaned.

"What? Why?" she asked, confused.

"I don't have any condoms. I'm an idiot," I repeated.

"I'm on birth control," she said. "I have that implant thingy in my arm. Claire was pretty adamant about me getting on something even though I wasn't sexually active," she explained. "I'm covered for another year. And we've never been with anyone else so…"

"Are you sure?" I really hoped she was sure. Because I really liked the thought of being with her bare.

She nodded. "I want to feel you, Travis. I want to feel everything."

"Okay." I gave her a quick kiss, then reached into the front of the truck to grab my phone out of the cup holder.

"What are you doing?" Sitting up on her elbows, she gave me a good view of her breasts.

"Just trying to make everything perfect for you," I told her as I set it to the romantic songs station on my mobile radio app.

Angel smiled when 'From the Ground Up' by Dan + Shay came on, and I knew there couldn't have been a more perfect song for this moment.

After arranging the curtain to make sure no one could see anything behind it, I settled back over her.

Since I knew it was a real possibility I wasn't going to last very long, I decided to take care of Angel first.

I lowered myself until my face hovered right above her pussy. I nuzzled my nose over her mound while my hands came up to lightly pinch her hard nipples. Her sweet taste hit my tongue as I licked over her clit in circles.

"God, Travis," she panted. "How do you do this to me

every single time?"

It was a rhetorical question and I answered it by sucking her clit into my mouth. She whimpered, and her hands went up to grip the pillow underneath her head. My hand trailed down her stomach to the warm, wet place between her thighs. I pushed two fingers inside of her, curling them upwards, massaging her silky inner walls.

I hoped it would stretch her out a little, make it easier for her to take me in. I'd measured my dick before—every guy does it—and I knew I was well above average in size. I hated knowing it was going to cause her pain this first time.

That thought almost had me asking her again if she was really sure she wanted to do this.

But my tongue was occupied.

Her clit was still in my mouth and my fingers were still inside her when her inner muscles started to spasm and clench. Her legs shook as she arched her back and let out a long, drawn-out moan.

I slipped my fingers out of her and made my way back up her body to kiss her. The song on the radio switched over to Zac Brown Band's 'Got Whatever It Is'.

Angel licked her way into my mouth, tasting herself on me, and my cock throbbed painfully against her lower stomach between us. She spread her thighs and impatiently lifted her hips until my head was perfectly lined up at her entrance.

She was so wet that the tip slipped in a little, probably just an inch or so. My mouth fell open but no sound came out. I wasn't even close to being all the way inside her and it already felt so good. So warm. Wet. Tight.

So fucking good.

"It's not fair," I groaned into her neck.

"What's not fair?" she asked, breathlessly, and I drew back to look into her eyes.

"It already feels so good for me. And it's going to hurt you," I said, my voice filled with regret.

She placed her hand on the side of my face. "Probably just for a second. I want this so bad."

"I'll go slow, okay?"

She nodded, and I gently kissed her lips. Trembling with the effort it took to keep myself from thrusting all the way home, I slowly worked myself into her tightness, retreating then pushing back in a little further each time. Our lips were still touching, but we weren't kissing anymore—just panting into each other's mouths.

A whimper escaped Angel's mouth once I was finally seated deep inside her. I was as far as I could go, our hip bones pressing together.

Holy fuck.

I'd imagined what sex would feel like thousands of times. No fantasy or wet dream ever lived up to this. Any brief concerns I may have had about not being able to get my cock inside her vanished.

It was a perfect fit.

"Fuck," I said against her lips. "It's like you were made for me. Baby, are you okay?"

Angel nodded sharply. "Just kiss me."

She didn't need to tell me twice. I sucked her bottom lip into my mouth then stroked my tongue over hers. As though her words summoned the song, Ed Sheeran's 'Kiss Me' played through the speakers on my phone.

Snaking my hand between us, I used the pad of my thumb to massage her clit and I felt a new gush of her wetness coat my cock.

Using the tempo of the song, I started pumping myself into her in long, slow strokes. Every time I went deep, Angel gasped into my mouth. Her hands were still gripping the pillow underneath her head, so I brought my hands up to hers to link our fingers.

Being connected with Angel in this way was overwhelming—not just physically, but emotionally. We were as close as two people could get.

The love I felt for her was so overpowering. In this moment, nothing else outside of my truck existed. No time limits, no goodbyes. Everything came down to this fragile girl pinned beneath me.

She was everything.

Fingers laced, eyes locked, I rocked into her over and over again.

"You feel so fucking good," I whispered, my voice shaking.

She started to move her hips in time with mine and every time I pulled back, her walls clamped around me. It was like her pussy was squeezing me, trying to suck me back in.

Angel kissed down my jawline, then latched onto the side of my neck. As she sucked on my skin, tingles shot down my spine and I could tell it was going to leave a mark.

Good.

My thrusts sped up and the friction of her slick, tight walls around my cock caused the familiar feeling to build. My balls drew up tight and I knew I wasn't going to last much longer.

"Do you want me to pull out?" I grunted, trying to hold off the inevitable.

"No," she moaned. "I want to feel it."

Her words pushed me over the edge. My grip tightened on her hands as every muscle in my body tensed up. With a powerful thrust, I buried myself deep and let go. Angel whimpered, and I groaned into her mouth as my cock pulsed inside her.

It seemed to go on forever. I tried to keep my eyes open, wanting to hold eye contact, but the feeling was too much. My eyes slammed shut as the last of my cum spilled into her.

Resting my forehead against hers, we both tried to catch our breath.

I let go of her hands and cupped her face while I lazily kissed her forehead, her nose, and her cheeks.

Feeling dampness on my lips, I pulled back to look at her. Tears ran down the side of Angel's face into her hair, and I was surprised—shocked even—to notice wetness in my own eyelashes.

Did I just fucking cry the first time I had sex?

I thought about it for all of two seconds before deciding I didn't give a damn. This was the best experience of my life. It was worth a few tears.

"Baby, did I hurt you?" I wiped at her temples with my thumbs.

She shook her head and gave me a watery smile. "I'm just so happy."

It took everything I had in that moment to hold back telling her how I really felt. That I loved her. Needed her. Wanted her to stay with me forever.

"Me, too." That's what I said instead. Because I was a chicken shit.

We kissed slowly, leisurely, while I absorbed the importance of what we just did. It was perfect. *She* was perfect.

I was no longer a virgin and neither was she. From this moment forward—no matter what—we would always belong to each other in this way.

I started to pull out of her, but she stopped me by wrapping her hands around my lower back.

"Don't go yet," she begged.

That was completely fine with me. I pushed back into her before I could slip out. "Angel, I would live inside you if I could."

She laughed and it caused her muscles to flutter around

my softening dick. I went from being half-mast to rock-hard in two seconds flat. I took the opportunity to thrust into her again and it felt just as good as it did the first time.

Her eyes went wide with shock. "Are you seriously hard again?"

I smirked. "Yup."

CHAPTER 40

Angel

I couldn't believe Travis was up for round two already.

Literally *up*.

I started to rotate my hips underneath him, seeking the release I was so close to getting. I felt hot and needy. I was just on the brink of orgasm, but I didn't know how to get there.

"What do you want, baby? I'll do anything you want," he whispered by my ear, and his stubble rubbed against my cheek as he spoke.

"Just let me… I need…" I let out a grunt of frustration as I wiggled my body.

As though he could sense what I needed, he settled his weight on me, increasing the pressure where we were joined.

"Go ahead. Do what you need to do," Travis said as he rested his elbows on either side of my head, bracketing me in with his large frame.

He stayed still while I moved my hips in a circular grinding motion underneath him and my eyes rolled back from the sensations it caused. His cock kept nudging some place deep inside me while my clit ground against his pelvic bone. I hooked my ankles around the back of his legs to get better leverage.

Between my wetness and his cum, my core was extra slick, making it easy for me to feel every ridge, every slide of skin on skin, and with each movement my nipples rubbed against his chest.

"Fuck," Travis breathed out, clearly enjoying it as much as I was.

Beads of sweat broke out on my forehead and I couldn't stop my body from shaking. My hands clenched and un-clenched on his lower back as my hips bucked faster and faster.

Heat spiraled through my body. I felt a tightness in my center winding up, ready to snap.

An embarrassingly loud keening sound came from my throat as I exploded around him. I rode out the orgasm until the spasms subsided and my whimpers turned into a satisfied sigh.

My arms fell limply to the mattress as I panted against Travis's neck.

He resumed slowly thrusting into me while sweetly kiss-ing my lips.

This wasn't just *sex* or *fucking*. I'd never done either, but I knew enough to recognize the difference.

This was something so much more than that.

Between kisses, Travis whispered words of praise against my lips. "So perfect, baby." Kiss. "So beautiful." Kiss. "You're mine."

One song changed to the next, but I didn't hear the notes or the words. All five of my senses were focused on Travis—his masculine smell mingling with our sweat, his green eyes burn-ing into mine, the taste of his lips and his tongue, the sound of quiet gasps and raspy moans, the feeling of him moving over me, around me, and inside me.

I wasn't sure how long it went on like that before he found his release again.

I only knew two things for sure.

One, I was head-over-heels in love with Travis. And, two, he was right—I was completely his.

CHAPTER 41

Travis

Angel couldn't snowboard for shit. That much was clear after she fell off the lift at the top, landing in a heap of tangled limbs in the snow.

"Shit, are you okay?" I went over to help her up.

"Yes," she huffed as she rubbed her hip.

"We seriously could've done the bunny slopes," I offered, even though it was too late now.

"I didn't come all this way just to do that!" she said incredulously as she gestured toward the bottom of the mountain, where beginners—mostly kids—slid down the leveled slope at turtle-like speeds.

I understood where she was coming from. But now, we were half-way up a mountain with only one way to get down.

She looked so fucking cute all bundled up in my clothes. I'd brought extra sweat pants and hoodies because I knew it would be cold up here. And now I was thinking the extra padding was a good idea because I had a feeling she might be falling down a lot.

Since it was so late in the year, I almost thought we wouldn't be able to find a ski resort that was still open. I hadn't taken that into consideration when I'd promised Angel we could go snowboarding. But a promise was a promise.

I drove for two hours before I found this place. Luckily, we passed through a quaint mountain town during our search and some kind people were able to direct me to the slopes.

More people hopped off the lift, much more gracefully than Angel, and we had to move out of the way.

Angel slid three feet, then fell down again.

"Okay," I said, reaching down to help her back up. "I'll just have to give you a crash course, pun intended."

"Ha. Ha. Very funny." She rolled her eyes, then looked at me with determination. "Seriously, I can do this."

She awkwardly stood on the pink board I'd rented for her and adjusted her snow goggles, which looked way too big on her face.

I proceeded to give her tips on how to keep her balance. "Hold your arms out and use your core strength."

"I think I might be lacking in the core strength area," she grumped as she swayed to one side before catching herself.

I laughed. She wasn't even moving and she almost fell down.

I tried to show her how to lean into a turn and how to effectively stop, but it was a fruitless effort. Maybe I just really sucked at instructing. Or maybe snowboarding just wasn't Angel's sport.

Either way, I lost count of how many times her ass hit the snow. Fifty? Seventy-five? Some of the falls actually looked pretty bad, with her feet flying over her head, arms and legs tangling together. I was afraid she might've gotten hurt a couple times, but she just laughed and brushed herself off. I couldn't help feeling impressed when she got right back up, eager to try again.

Once we got to the bottom, she seemed relieved but happy.

"That was so much fun!" She bounced up and down.

"Are you sure you're okay? You really bit the dust there a

few times."

She probably didn't feel any pain right now because she was numb from the cold and high on adrenaline, but I had a feeling she was going to be in a world of hurt later.

"Nope, I feel great." She beamed.

Angel moaned as she sank down into the hot bath water, bubbles soaping up her bare skin. It was a bad time for me to get a hard-on.

"I've never been this sore in my whole life. I feel like I got hit by a bus. Even the muscles in my fingers hurt." She wiggled her fingers, then winced.

"Snowboarding will do that to you," I said, amused.

"I don't think you can call what I did snowboarding. I basically fell down a mountain for two hours."

"Nah, you did good for your first time."

She responded by making a grunting noise and sinking deeper into the water.

Earlier, Angel didn't even put up a fight when I mentioned getting a hotel room. All I had to do was tell her there would be a bathtub and a big, comfy bed and she was sold on the idea.

Not even one word of protest came out of her mouth when I pulled up to the fancy hotel. I chose one of the best hotels in Denver. I was afraid she might argue with me on how expensive it was, but she just limped beside me as we walked into the ornate lobby.

After I paid and got our room keys, I scooped her up into my arms and carried her to our room. She'd laughed and told me I was just being dramatic, but she looped her arms around my neck and relaxed into me anyway.

Now she was naked, and I debated whether or not I should join her in the oversized tub. I knew she was probably in too much pain for sex—I didn't even care about that. I just wanted to feel her against me.

"Are you getting in or are you just going to stand there and watch?" she teased, peeking at me with one eye.

I answered her by whipping my shirt over my head and unsnapping the button on my jeans. Her eyes flared with heat as they roamed over my body.

"Don't even think about it, baby." I stripped the rest of my clothes off. "You think your body hurts now? Tomorrow will be worse. You need to relax."

Sliding in behind her, I let Angel settle back against me as I massaged her aching muscles.

"Oh my God," she moaned, which made my dick twitch against her back. "You're like, the best. I mean, seriously the best boyfriend ever."

"Only for you. I feel like I've waited for you forever," I admitted, continuing to rub her shoulders.

The confession made me feel a little too exposed, which was funny, considering I was completely naked. But words like that made it feel like I was showing her my heart, which was scary as fuck.

"Me too." She sighed tiredly as she rubbed her hand up and down my thigh muscles.

I grunted in satisfaction because I was sore, too. Angel wasn't the only one who took a beating today. My snowboarding skills were pretty rusty, and I'd had a couple rough wipeouts myself.

Angel ended up dozing off in the tub. I woke her to get out, but I could tell she was exhausted.

It felt good to get to see another new side to her. Worn-out Angel was extremely agreeable. She let me dry her off, dress her, and she even let me brush out her hair.

After slipping my favorite T-shirt over her head, I sat her down on the edge of the bed. Her body swayed while I ran the comb through her long golden strands. With uncoordinated fingers, she braided her still-wet hair and collapsed onto the middle of the mattress.

Chuckling, I slipped on some gym shorts before climbing in next to her. As I gathered her close, I realized she was already asleep.

"Angel?" I said quietly, and when there was no response, I felt safe to say what I really wanted to say. I knew she wouldn't hear me. I just wanted to say the words out loud. Emotion clogged my throat as they came out in a whisper. "I love you."

CHAPTER 42

Angel

Travis was so right about my body feeling worse the next day. My muscles and joints felt stiff and achy. Any movement at all caused pain to travel through every part of my body. I was feeling muscles I didn't even know I had.

I couldn't say I regretted it, though. I wasn't sure I would be snowboarding again any time soon, but the experience was worth it. Just another amazing memory I had with Travis.

We decided to drive straight through on the ride back to Tolson. Usually, Travis liked to break up the driving time on the road, but we were both ready to be back home.

Home.

It didn't even feel weird to think of Travis's place as *home*.

Isn't it funny how that could happen in such a short amount of time?

But my time was running out. In just four short days, we would be leaving for the Sacramento delivery and when Travis returned, it would be without me.

It was late when we finally fell into his big bed. We were both so exhausted that we barely muttered "goodnight" before sleep took over.

The next morning, I woke up to the feeling of soft kisses on the back of my neck.

The Colorado trip was fun, but nothing compared to waking up in Travis's warm bed.

Spooning me from behind, Travis slid the strap of my tank top down to move his lips across my shoulder. I could feel his erection against my lower back, and my core pulsed with the need to feel him inside of me again.

I pushed my shorts off and reached behind me to wrap my hand around his hard length.

"Please," I whispered, tilting my head back to look at him.

Without moving from our position, Travis kicked his boxer briefs off then slowly slid into me from behind.

Oh.

This was new. Different than before, but just as good.

Travis groaned as he grasped my hips and pushed himself into me over and over again. His hand slid down to my center and he circled his fingers over my sensitive bud.

I tried to keep my moans quiet because I didn't know if we were alone in the apartment. Travis lifted my leg and hooked it over his, spreading me wider and giving him better access to my clit.

"That feels so good," I breathed out.

As my body started to tingle and shake, I reached my hand behind my head to grip the back of Travis's neck, needing something to hold on to.

When my climax hit, I muffled my sounds into the pillow.

In one swift movement, Travis rolled me onto my stomach and started pumping into me. I gasped because he was going so deep. He brought his hands up to clasp mine by the headboard.

"Fuck, baby. So fucking tight," he whispered by my ear before lightly sinking his teeth into the side of my neck, and I couldn't stop a loud whimper from coming out.

His thrusting sped up until he buried himself so deep it took my breath away. He moaned and panted against my shoulder as I milked him dry.

When he slipped out, I made a sound of protest at the loss. He rolled me over and hovered above me, smiling wide. The expression on his face was pure happiness, and I had a good view of his dimples. I poked each one with my finger.

"Best. Morning. Ever." He punctuated each word with a kiss.

$\sim$

Over the next couple of days, Travis and I couldn't keep our hands off each other. He didn't have to work at the shop since he had two long hauls back to back, so it gave us a lot of alone time at the apartment.

We had sex in every position and every location possible. In his bed. Against the wall in the shower. Bent over the kitchen counter. On the couch. Him on top. Me on top.

One of my favorite times was on the bench seat of his pickup truck. We'd gone out for pizza, but ended up pulled over on the side of a country road on the way back. We kept the windows rolled up to make sure no mosquitoes could ruin the moment, which resulted in some very steamed-up glass.

Sometimes it was frantic and desperate, and other times it was slow and sweet.

The only place off limits was Colton's room, for obvious reasons.

In between wearing ourselves out, we talked, watched movies, and even played some board games. I kicked his butt at Monopoly—because I was ruthless—but, to his credit, he always won at Scrabble.

"You know I don't have the money to pay rent on North Carolina Avenue," he sighed, shuffling through the multi-colored bills.

"You can always admit defeat. Again." I smiled. "Or, you can let me have Park Place." Holding out my hand, I did a 'give me' gesture.

"Ruthless." He shook his head, then placed the property in my palm.

Two more turns and the game was over. We may or may not have ended up having sex on the coffee table after I won.

`

CHAPTER 43

Travis

Wednesday morning, Angel and I woke up naked together. We didn't see the point in wearing clothes to bed anymore. Pressing my lips to her neck, I followed our normal routine where I kissed her body until she was fully awake.

Kissing down the valley between her breasts, I trailed my lips down to her belly button and she giggled.

That's when the realization hit me—this was one of the last mornings we would wake up together this way. Angel wasn't even gone yet and I already missed her. By this time next week, I'd be back in my bed. Alone.

"Stay," I said against the smooth skin above her hipbone, my mouth pausing its descent.

"What?"

She probably couldn't understand me because the word had been muffled against her stomach.

Lifting my head, I looked up at her.

"Stay," I begged. "Stay with me." I could clearly hear the desperation in my voice, but I didn't care.

Her face looked conflicted and her eyes held so much pain. Immediately, I regretted asking. I hadn't planned on begging her to stay. The plea just bubbled up and burst out.

"I want to," she responded quietly. "I really do, but I can't.

I have to try things with my mom. If I don't try, I'll never know if we could've had a relationship. I can't go my whole life wondering…"

"I know," I told her.

Because I did know. I knew from the beginning she would be leaving, but that didn't make it any easier. All along, this had been the plan. Nothing had changed.

Except *everything* changed.

I fell in love with her.

"This was always the plan." She shook her head in frustration.

"I know," I repeated. "I just wish we had more time."

Angel swallowed hard. "I'll try to come back to visit. I promise."

Our conversation was interrupted by a door slamming in the hallway, followed by Tara's voice. "What the hell is wrong with you? You don't think I'm pretty?"

"Shh, Tara. Keep it down. I don't want to wake everyone up," Colton replied much more quietly.

"Oh, right," she scoffed. "Wouldn't want everyone to find out, would we?"

Heavy footsteps stomped by my bedroom door and their voices got quieter as they walked further away. I couldn't hear what else was said, but that was probably a good thing. I had no desire to overhear their private business.

"What was that about?" Angel asked, concerned.

I shrugged. "I don't know."

"Why does he stay with her? He deserves better." A scowl marred her beautiful face, making her look like an angry kitten. Her protectiveness of my best friend was endearing, and I knew I wouldn't be the only one missing her after she was gone.

"He's a big boy. He can take care of himself," I reassured her.

I looked at the clock on my dresser and noticed we'd slept in too late. I gave Angel a quick kiss before reluctantly leaving her naked body.

CHAPTER 44

Angel

I wasn't in the best mood as I took a shower and got dressed. Sadness weighed down on me when I thought about the unexpected conversation Travis and I had earlier.

The frustration I felt wasn't because he asked me to stay— it had more to do with the fact that I really wanted it. There was a big part of me that wanted to throw all my plans away and just say *YES*.

But I had other obligations. Things I'd been looking forward to for years.

The possibilities flashed through my mind—what it would be like to rebuild a relationship with my mom. Movie nights. Shopping days. Mother-daughter manicures. The simple things so many people took for granted.

Travis came up behind me while I waited for the toaster to be done with my waffles.

"I'm sorry." His breath tickled my ear. "I shouldn't have even asked. I know how important this is to you."

I knew I'd been moping all morning, but I just couldn't help it. I turned in his arms and put my hand up to his cheek, scratching my fingers over his two-day stubble.

"I'm not mad." I shook my head and tried to give him a smile. "I wish we had more time, too."

Travis gave my lips a gentle kiss. "I have to run down to

the shop for a bit to go over some details for the Sacramento job," he said as he tucked some of my hair behind my ear. "You have lunch at Beverly's, right?"

"Yep," I replied, fighting a heavy feeling in my chest.

I couldn't believe it was the last time I would see her—at least, for a while. I had no idea when I'd be able to come back.

Before I had time to feel too sad about it, Travis stripped me down and spread me out on the rickety kitchen table. It was so small my head hung off the end, and I was afraid it might not be able to hold my weight.

But all worry flew out the window when he buried his face between my thighs until I screamed.

Afterwards, I made him promise me he would never get rid of that table.

$$\backsim$$

The walk to Beverly's was bittersweet. I remembered the first time I walked these few blocks, not realizing I was going to find such a good, foul-mouthed friend.

In the grass along the sidewalk, I spotted a fuzzy dandelion. Thinking it would be perfect for a wish, I plucked it up. Except, this time I couldn't decide what I wanted. While I was excited to see my mom, I dreaded leaving. In just three weeks, this place and these people had wormed their way into my heart.

I twirled the dandelion in my fingers.

Still unable to decide what to wish for, I blew on it anyway. The breeze caused some of the fuzz to blow back into my face and it tickled my nose. I sneezed, then I laughed.

That's what I get for wasting a wish.

As I climbed the steps to Beverly's porch, I saw a small yellow piece of paper taped to the screen door. It flapped in the breeze as I read what it said.

Come on in.

The hinges creaked as I pulled the door open and stepped into the living room. The familiar smell of Bengay and cupcakes filled my nose.

"Surprise!" a bunch of voices said in unison, and I jumped.

My mouth hung open as I took in the faces smiling at me. Beverly, Ernie, and Karen were standing by the dining room doorway, while Hank, Colton, and Travis stood in front of the couch.

A variety of balloon animals had been placed around the room, and multi-colored streamers hung from the ceiling fan.

"What's going on?" I asked pointlessly. Obviously, they were throwing me a party. But why?

"We thought we'd give you a proper send-off." Beverly beamed.

"A going-away party?" My voice cracked on the last word. This was the last thing I'd expected. I was completely blindsided. I guess that's why they called it a *surprise party*.

After a round of hugs from everyone, I excused myself to the bathroom.

I shut myself inside and turned to grasp the edge of the pink sink while I tried to get my emotions in check. Unwelcome tears filled my eyes.

A grand gesture like this should've made me happy. And it did, but it also made the thought of leaving that much harder.

The funny thing was, it had always been a secret dream of mine to have someone throw me a surprise party. Every year when my birthday came around, I'd hoped for it. And now, here I was, getting exactly what I'd always wanted.

Everyone just wanted to show me how much they cared, but it was too much for me to handle.

After grabbing some toilet paper, I mopped at my face and

blew my nose. A quiet knock came at the door.

"I'll be out in a minute," I called while fanning myself with my hands, hoping the cool air would take away the red splotches on my face.

A second later, the door swung open and Travis stepped in, shutting it behind him.

"What are you doing?" I asked incredulously. "I could've been pooping!"

"You're not pooping." He chuckled.

"But I could've been."

His expression softened. "What's wrong? You hate surprise parties?"

"I wouldn't know." I shrugged. "No one's ever thrown one for me before. I guess it just made me a little emotional."

"Come here." Travis hugged me, and I wrapped my arms around him. I ran my hands over the hard muscles of his back and buried my nose in his chest, breathing in his comforting scent.

After a couple minutes, I felt prepared to go back out there.

"Ernie grilled hamburgers and hotdogs," Travis told me with a smile.

"Mmm, hotdogs," I said, and he laughed. If anything could get me to come out of the bathroom, it was food and he knew it.

While we ate, we all sat outside on Ernie's back patio in a circle of mismatching lawn chairs. I didn't miss the way he openly flirted with Beverly. I think she even blushed once or twice, which was too cute, because Beverly never blushed.

She made an appreciative sound as she finished her food. "Ernie, that was the best fucking burger I've ever had."

Colton choked on some of his soda, and Travis slapped him on the back until he got his coughing and wheezing under control. I laughed so hard that I ended up making a very unattractive snorting noise into my napkin. I forgot some people weren't used to hearing elderly women drop the F-word in casual conversation.

After all our plates were empty, Travis handed me a pink envelope and everyone watched while I opened it. It was a card that said 'Good luck!' on the front along with a picture of an otter that looked like it was waving.

It made me laugh, because how cute is that?

On the inside it said 'You otter know we'll be thinking of you!' and it was signed by everyone.

"Thank you," I told them while hugging the card to my chest. "You guys are awesome."

There was a collective "you're welcome" and "we'll miss you" from everyone, and they started gathering their cups and plates to take inside. Travis took mine, leaving me alone with his mom.

"We sure are gonna miss you," she said as she took the chair next to me.

"I'll miss you, too. You have no idea how much."

"I always wanted a daughter. I love having a son but I wanted a daughter, too. I wanted it all. After my husband died, I found out I was pregnant," she said and my mouth opened in shock. "I never told Travis. I've never told anyone. I miscarried early, around seven weeks. It was too early to know if it was a girl or a boy, but I always felt like I knew it was a girl."

Tears glistened in her eyes and I blinked rapidly when I felt my own eyes burning.

"I guess you're probably wondering why I'm telling you this." She smiled a little.

I couldn't speak past the tightness in my throat, so I just nodded.

"You may have noticed I'm a little desperate for Travis to

settle down, and my reasons aren't completely selfless." She laughed lightly. "It's been so great getting to know you. I've never seen Travis this happy and he has such a big heart." She paused. "I just wanted you to know that you'll always have a place here. With us."

Then she hugged me.

It was the kind of hug where you could tell the person really cares. She hugged me like she meant it.

"Thank you," I managed, my voice scratchy.

"By the way." She pulled back. "You and I are having a girls' day after the party. Are you up for some shopping at our favorite thrift store?"

I laughed. "I think you know the answer to that question."

She ran her hand over the side of my head in a motherly gesture before going back inside.

I sat back in the chair and thought about everything Karen just told me. My heart broke for her and what she'd been through. And it meant a lot that she decided to share that deep part of herself with me.

She'd turned to alcohol because she'd experienced something tragic, and it made me wonder if that's what happened to my mom. Maybe she had a good explanation for leaving the way she did.

And while Karen's story was sad, it also gave me hope. If she was able to overcome addiction, that meant my mom could, too.

CHAPTER 45

Travis

I stood in Beverly's kitchen, watching my mom and Angel from the window over the sink. From what I could tell, it looked like they were having a moment.

The sunlight reflected off of Angel's hair, emitting a glow around her head. I smiled because my first impression of her had been dead-on. Somehow, I'd known she was going to be important to me, even before I ever talked to her.

A hand landed on my shoulder. "So, your girl goes to Cali this weekend."

Glancing at Colton, I gave him a nod.

"Listen," he started. "I'm sorry if I gave you shitty advice in the beginning. I didn't really think about how hard it would be for you when she left. I'm not exactly an expert on the topic."

I smirked at him. "You might not always know what you're talking about, but you were right about one thing. She's the best thing that ever happened to me."

"You gonna do the long-distance thing?"

"There isn't any other option," I said with complete certainty. "When I think about being without her... It makes me feel like I'm drowning. I fucking need her."

Colton was silent for a few seconds as he thought about my honest words.

"I wish I could say I knew what that felt like, but I don't."
He shrugged, and I could hear the envy in his voice.

"It'll happen to you someday. Speaking of that, what the
hell are you doing with Tara anyway? I heard you guys arguing
this morning," I admitted. "I don't know what it was about,
but you deserve someone better."

Colton looked unsure. He'd always been a cocky son of a
bitch. He was one of the few people I'd ever known that could
pull off cocky, yet loveable at the same time. But I'd seen some
of that slip away in recent months. I wondered if Tara and
their toxic relationship was taking a toll on his self-esteem.

Instead of answering the question, he deflected the conversation back to me. "Do you love her?"

My gaze went back to Angel and I gave another nod.
"Yeah." Colton didn't ask for details, but that didn't stop me
from gushing about it like I was on some damn talk show. "I'm
in love with her. She just fits, you know? And it's crazy how
we met." I laughed at how absurd it was. "I picked up some
random girl off the side of the road and she turned out to be
my soulmate."

Chuckling, Colton clapped me on the back. "Well, I'm
happy for you, man."

Fate. I'd never been a big believer in it. Had never really
given it much thought.

But the chances of us meeting the way we did—what
were the odds? Every event in our lives, every decision, led us
to that road in Ohio, putting us there at exactly the right time.

I knew, without a doubt, Angel was meant for me.

CHAPTER 46

Angel

Packing up my things was surreal. And also very depressing.

It felt like a lifetime had gone by since I left Maine. I folded up the same clothes—just like I'd done weeks ago—and placed them in my backpack.

Only this time, it was so different.

The night before I left the foster home, my hands shook with excitement as I covertly packed my bag and hid it under the bed. I couldn't wait to get out of there. Couldn't wait to move on. That certainly wasn't the case now.

Another difference was the fact that my backpack was no longer big enough to hold everything I owned. As I attempted to zip it shut, I realized I'd need a second bag because of all the extra clothes I'd acquired from the thrift store.

Karen had gone a little wild with the shopping. Every time I insisted she didn't need to buy clothes for me, she somehow guilt-tripped me into picking out more. By the end of it, I'd gained an entire new wardrobe. It was like some kind of Jedi mind trick.

A soft knock came at the bedroom door and I glanced up to see Travis standing there, looking sexy as always in a white T-shirt and his gray gym shorts.

He produced a black tote bag from behind his back. "I

figured you might need this when I heard my mom was taking you to the thrift store."

Grateful, I took it from him and started filling it with all my new clothes and shoes. "I don't know how your mom convinced me to get this much stuff. I went in there telling myself I would get one thing. And this—" I laughed and held up and handful of shirts. "—is what happened."

"It's just because she's going to miss you so much. I'm not the best shopping partner," he said before helping me pile the rest of the clothes into the tote bag.

After setting my luggage off to the side, I looked up at Travis's face. I studied his features, trying to memorize every detail—his thick eyelashes, the way he looked with a five o'clock shadow, the shape of his lips.

I brought my hand up to his face and with a soft touch of my finger, I traced over the places where I knew his dimples would be if he smiled.

What would happen to us after I left? We hadn't really talked much about it and I wasn't sure what he wanted. Although I didn't have much experience at dating, I knew being apart would be hard on a new relationship.

Travis must have been able to see the distress on my face because he smoothed out the area between my eyebrows with his thumb. "What's going on in that head of yours?"

"I don't want to break up," I rushed out, and he let out a low chuckle.

"Well, that's good, because we're not breaking up," he replied confidently.

"Promise?" I knew I sounded like an insecure little girl, but I couldn't help it.

He nodded. "Promise. There's a lot of ways to keep a relationship going. We'll talk on the phone every day." His face broke out in a devilish grin. "There's always sexting."

"Mmm, I love it when you talk trucker to me." I repeated his words from the week before, unable to keep a straight face.

He walked forward, gently backing me up until my butt landed on his bed. He crawled over me and his lips gently met mine before his tongue slipped inside. I sucked in a breath when his teeth scraped over my bottom lip. When he broke the kiss, his face was serious.

"I mean it. We can make this work. The distance doesn't matter," he said, looking down at me. "I might be here, but I'll still belong to you."

Swoon.

CHAPTER 47

Travis

P anic. That's what I felt when I thought about the fact that in twenty-four hours, Angel and I would part ways.

Although we said we'd stay together, there was too much unknown.

My apartment was going to feel so empty when I got home. My whole life was going to feel her absence. Angel filled a void I never even knew was there.

It was crazy. In just over three short weeks, she'd become such a huge part of my life.

Sighing, I leaned back in the driver's seat and tried to stretch a little while staying focused on the highway. It'd been a long day of driving. We were pulling some long hours so we could get to the delivery destination by the next morning.

"So, tell me about your mom. What are your favorite memories? What do you look forward to the most?" I asked Angel while keeping my eyes on the road.

I needed to know more about the person who would be taking her away from me. Although I knew it wouldn't make me feel better, maybe it would help me understand.

And I needed to understand. Because right now, all I could do was feel overwhelming dread at the inevitable goodbye coming our way.

"She named me," she said. "I mean, yeah, all moms name

their babies, so that's not special or anything. But during the whole pregnancy, she couldn't think of a name. She said as soon as she saw me—blonde hair, blue eyes, pink chubby cheeks—she knew my name should be Angel."

"I can imagine." I smiled because I was picturing her as a baby. She definitely came by her name honestly.

"She was really good at sewing," she continued. "She could take any pattern and fabric, fire up the sewing machine, and make something out of it. Like magic. She used to make all my costumes for the school plays. I've always wanted to be able to do that. Maybe she could teach me," she said hopefully. "And she was so good at piano. There was a duet we used to play together. I had the simple part, of course. You could put any music in front of her, and she could play it." She stretched her fingers out and wiggled them like she was imagining piano keys in front of her.

I laughed because she was so damn cute.

"And every Christmas morning, we had homemade cinnamon rolls," she went on. "She'd spend hours the night before getting them ready—rolling out the dough, letting it rise. I loved waking up to the smell of them baking in the oven."

"That all sounds really great," I admitted.

"She was good at baking everything. Every year we entered the cookie contest at the county fair and every year, we placed. Sometimes we won first place. Chocolate chip cookies. It was a secret family recipe, but we made them so many times, I still remember every ingredient by heart. I'll have to make them for you sometime." She stopped abruptly and then her face fell.

Tears filled her eyes as she had the same thought I did—when would it happen?

"Hey, it's gonna be okay," I told her and grabbed her hand.

"This doesn't have to be goodbye forever. We can see each other again. Maybe if I have another delivery out this way I can visit. Or once you get settled, you could come see me…" I trailed off.

She nodded like she wanted to believe it was possible, but even the words didn't sound very comforting to my own ears. The uncertainty—not knowing when I would see her again—was the worst part.

I decided that I needed to come up with future plans before we said goodbye. We needed something to count on, something to look forward to.

People made long-distance relationships work all the time. I had to believe we could do this.

I wanted Angel to be happy. If being in California with her mom was what she wanted, then I'd support her.

∾

That night, as we settled in for bed in my small sleeper cab, I felt sick knowing it was going to be our last night together. Wanting to make it count, I kissed her deeply, slowly, taking my time with her.

After our clothes were gone, she spread her legs wide for me and I slid into her, enjoying every inch of her tight pussy. I retreated until I was almost all the way out, then I would thrust back in again.

"Always so fucking good, baby," I groaned into her neck. "Every single time."

Angel made an impatient sound as she dug her heels into my back, urging me to go faster. As much as I wanted to savor the moment, it didn't take much for me to lose control. We weren't usually rough with each other, but neither of us could contain the desperation we were feeling.

It didn't help that she kept digging her fingernails into my ass and pulling me into her roughly with her hands. I pounded into her relentlessly and her moans only encouraged me further.

This was fucking.

I kept trying to ease up, but I was having trouble holding back. The urgency of knowing it was our last night together mingled with anger. The anger wasn't directed at her, but it was anger just the same.

I resented the situation. Resented the fact that I wouldn't get to kiss her every day. I hated how desolate my life was going to be without her in it.

"Harder," she demanded. "Don't stop," she begged. "I want to feel you for days," she said.

And fuck if I didn't want that, too.

I slid an arm under her lower back, causing her hips to tilt at a different angle, and she cried out at how deep I was able to go.

Sweat slicked our bodies and the only sounds that filled the cab were whimpers, moans, harsh breathing, and the slapping of skin.

Angel bit my shoulder as she came hard, her inner muscles squeezing my dick.

I pulled out of her, flipped her over onto all fours and slid into her from behind. My fingers dug into the flesh of her ass as I spread her wider for me.

"Travis," she moaned loudly. "Oh my God…"

Her front half collapsed onto her elbows and her hands gripped the sheets. I pumped into her until I felt my balls draw up tight, but I didn't want to finish this way. I wanted to look into her eyes when I came inside her.

Gently, I rolled her onto her back and I forced myself to slow my pace as I locked eyes with her. Lifting her legs higher, my thrusts went deeper and she closed her eyes at the sensation.

"Open your eyes," I demanded. "Look at me."

She did as I said, and I kissed her one more time before I let go.

"Angel. Baby…" My voice sounded hoarse as I emptied myself into her, buried as deep as I could go.

Panting into her neck, I took a minute to recover from the mind-blowing sex we'd just had. But I went from satisfied to concerned when I saw Angel's face. Her chin wobbled and I wondered if I'd been too rough with her.

"Angel?"

"I'm sorry, Travis." She choked out a sob and tears streamed from her eyes. "I'm so sorry I can't stay."

"Please don't." My voice sounded tortured as I pressed my forehead to hers. "Don't be sorry for needing to do this. I'll wait for you, okay?"

"I'll wait for you, too," she whispered.

She curled her body into mine as we waited for sleep, but it didn't come easily for either of us.

We kept waking throughout the night, reaching for each other. At some point, Angel woke me up by sucking me into her mouth. Just like that, I was ready for round two.

It was just as wild as before. Angel rode my cock until I finished with her on top of me. She collapsed onto my chest and we both fell asleep with my dick still inside her.

By the third time it happened, we were both running out of steam. I made love to her gently as the sun came up, then we passed out to get a couple more hours of sleep.

CHAPTER 48

Travis

After the drop-off in Sacramento, we found a shitty motel for Angel to stay for a few days until she was able to work out her living situation.

I didn't like it.

The L-shaped two-story building looked haggard on the outside, with pale yellow stucco and faded maroon doors.

Security was a concern of mine. It was the kind of motel where all the doors were on the outside—not the safest option. I would've felt much better about her staying at a hotel with some kind of front desk to get past.

Of course I was worried about her safety. How could I not be? But I also knew that worrying about her all the time was something I would have to get used to. I couldn't protect her when she wasn't with me. Knowing she was going to be all alone here, vulnerable, had my gut tightening.

I kept those thoughts to myself though. Angel wasn't a child, and she wouldn't appreciate being treated like one.

I tried to convince her to stay somewhere else, but I had to admit she was right when she listed the reasons that this was the most logical place for her to stay.

Not only was it incredibly cheap, but it was also near her mom. They even offered a shuttle bus that ran directly from the motel to the prison, so she wouldn't have to pay for a cab.

And it had an even cheaper rate if she paid by the week, instead of nightly, and that would be a good option if she couldn't find an apartment right away.

It was economical. It was practical. Like I said—shitty.

Once she got the key to her room, I helped her carry her bags to room 108. It smelled musty and slightly of cigarette smoke, but Angel didn't complain. She sat down on the bed and the mattress springs creaked.

"I don't have to take off right away," I told her after looking at the time. It was only three o'clock. I could stick around for another hour.

She nodded and scooted back on the bed as I grabbed the TV remote. After tossing it to her, I settled down beside her and put my arm around her shoulders, wanting to soak up the feeling of her body next to mine.

I didn't even know what she decided to watch. The only thing I was able to pay attention to was her warmth, her softness, her smell.

When our time was up, I reluctantly left my spot beside her. Angel stood up and for the first time since the first day we met, an awkward silence hung between us.

She shuffled from one foot to the other and she seemed to be unable to decide what to do with her hands. First, she tried crossing her arms over her chest. Then, she planted her hands on her hips. Finally, she just clasped her fingers together over her stomach.

I smiled because it was cute.

Deciding to put her out of her misery, I took her hands and placed them behind my neck, hauling her body against mine.

"Hi." I gazed down at her.

"Hi." She gave me a small smile.

"I'm gonna check my schedule and see if I can come out

next month sometime. If I get a plane ticket, I can spend more time with you instead of driving. I've never flown before and it scares the shit out of me, so you should feel pretty special."

She nodded excitedly. "That would be great. A month isn't too far away."

Remembering I needed to give Angel back her phone, I pulled it from my pocket. She hadn't even realized it was missing.

"Why did you have my phone?" She swiped the screen then laughed when she saw the changes I'd made. "You changed my background pic."

She turned the phone to show me what I already knew I'd see—a picture of us on her birthday. Our heads were pressed together as we smiled into the camera, the lake where we went fishing behind us.

"I also made you a playlist," I said, a little self-conscious about the cheesy gesture. "I thought maybe you could listen to it if you miss me."

"Of course I'm going to miss you." She swallowed hard.

Ah, shit.

I was trying to make a joke. I didn't mean to make her sad.

"Hey, I know." I hugged her to me. "I'm gonna miss you, too. You have no idea."

"Yes, I do," she whispered against my chest.

"Maybe I could stay another day," I said, trying to work it out in my head. Hank needed the rig back in three days for a local delivery. If I drove straight through, I might be able to pull it off.

"No. I know what you're thinking," she accused. "It's not safe for you to drive that long without sleep. Don't even think about it."

"So, you can read my mind now?" I smirked.

She nodded. "I know you."

I touched my forehead to hers. "I know you, too."

It felt like the perfect time to say *I love you*. But I didn't.

Instead, I ran the tip of my nose down the slope of hers and stepped back.

"I'll call you tomorrow night," she said. "Let you know how things went with my mom."

"Sounds good." I placed one last lingering kiss on Angel's lips and gave her a reassuring look. "Good luck tomorrow. I'll talk to you soon."

Despite the protest going on inside my body, I opened the motel door, got into the semi, and drove away.

CHAPTER 49

Angel

He made me a playlist.

I couldn't even describe what it felt like to watch Travis walk away. I almost took out my phone to call him. To beg him to come back.

Almost.

Instead, I opened the app with the songs and pushed play. The song 'Earth Angel' filled the motel room as I sat down on the bed. It made me smile because I remembered our first date.

To pass the time, I decided to unpack some of my clothes. I set the phone down on the small nightstand so I could listen to the music while I tried to distract myself from the ache inside my chest.

As 'Must Be Doing Something Right' came on, I caught a glimpse of familiar blue fabric. I pulled my favorite T-shirt—Travis's shirt—from the bag and held it up to my nose. As I inhaled the familiar scent, something fell from inside the shirt. It was a pair of my panties and there was an envelope inside.

Of course, Travis would put something inside my panties.

Inside the envelope, I found all the money I'd made from mowing over the last few weeks. All $200 of it.

I let out a frustrated growl because I'd wanted Travis to have that money. I should've known he never intended to keep it. Stubborn ass.

'Raining On Sunday' by Keith Urban was next on the play-list, and I paused because I couldn't remember a time when I heard this song with Travis. Then I remembered our first rainy Sunday together at his apartment. I felt heat rise up in my cheeks thinking of how we lost control together on the couch.

The playlist was like a soundtrack to our relationship. Every song held a memory.

Next up was 'Silver Wings', the song we danced to at the summer festival. As I listened to the words, I realized how sad the song really was.

I paused the music to make a trip down to the vending machines by the motel office. The dry Sacramento air was a sharp contrast to the humid Illinois weather. And while it would have been a great place for a vacation, it felt wrong. It didn't feel like home.

After I made my selection of unhealthy junk food, I went back to my room. Chips didn't really qualify as dinner, but homesickness had left me without much of an appetite.

After slipping on Travis's shirt, I pushed play and lay back on the bed while I listened to the music. I hugged the pillow, wishing it was Travis.

When I heard 'From the Ground Up' and 'Kiss Me', I got really turned on because it reminded me of our first time together.

When Queen's 'Another One Bites the Dust' came on, I laughed because I knew he was making fun of my pathetic snowboarding skills.

With every song, my longing for Travis grew. It had barely been an hour since we said goodbye and I already missed him so much.

It wasn't until the end of the list that I got really emotional.

The two last songs were 'Already Home' by A Great Big

World and 'Quit Your Life' by Mxpx. Neither of the songs had been a part of any event over the last few weeks. Travis added these for a reason.

I'd never even heard the last one before. But as I listened to the lyrics, I knew this was coming straight from his heart. It perfectly described our simple life in Tolson, and I was reminded of the way he asked me to stay with him. He hadn't even tried to hide the vulnerability in his eyes.

I'd wanted to say yes.

It broke my heart to say no.

The rough, scratchy hotel sheets smelled like bleach, so I buried my nose in the shirt and took a whiff. Instant comfort.

For several minutes, I shamelessly sniffed Travis's clothes. I probably looked like a lunatic, balled up on the bed, smelling a shirt.

After the last notes rang out, I burrowed into the covers and prayed for sleep to come.

CHAPTER 50

Travis

Driving away from Angel was the hardest thing I'd ever had to do. I had to force myself not to look back at her as I was walking away, because if I did, I wouldn't have been able to leave.

Every mile marker on the highway mocked me. The further away I got, the heavier my chest felt. It felt like there was a weight sitting on me, and with every mile that stretched between us, another pound was added.

My body rebelled at the idea of leaving her behind. Everything inside of me told me to turn back.

But I just kept driving, leaving jagged pieces of my heart along the way.

CHAPTER 51

Angel

Drifting in that place between asleep and awake, I had about ten blissful seconds before I remembered where I was.

It was a happy place.

A place where Travis had his arms around me. A place that smelled like fresh cut grass and the wind rustled the cornfields. A place where I could feel dandelion fuzz tickling my nose.

Then I opened my eyes.

I realized it wasn't dandelion fuzz that was brushing against my face—it was my own hair. And the rustling sound wasn't the cornfields—it was the rattling of the old air conditioning unit by the window. The drab colors of the motel room came into focus as I blinked.

Rolling onto my back, I stared up at the popcorn-textured ceiling. The queen-size bed felt massive and cold. I knew waking up without Travis was going to hurt, but I didn't realize just how much.

As I trudged to the bathroom to get ready for the day, I felt like I actually had to remind myself to breathe because the tightness in my chest was so overwhelming.

I thought about the many mornings I'd be waking up alone in the future and I wondered if this was really worth it.

What was I even doing here?

I'd been so focused on the end goal—rebuilding a relationship with my mom—that I didn't realize what it would feel like to be here by myself.

It felt extremely lonely. Even lonelier than after Claire passed away. Because now I knew what it meant to feel like I belonged somewhere.

But that somewhere wasn't here.

Did I really want to be in California?

Immediately, I felt guilty. My mom was here, and this was my chance to have her back in my life. What if she regretted leaving me? What if she needed me?

Moving into the hot spray of the shower, I forced myself to think about visiting the prison later and I felt a hint of excitement.

I was going to see my mom. That was what I needed to focus on. I'd been waiting for this moment for the majority of my life.

As I did my best to push all thoughts of Travis and Tolson from my mind, I thought about what it would be like to be face to face with my mom for the first time in over ten years.

∽

Sitting at one of the visitor's tables, I nervously shuffled my feet on the linoleum floor while I waited for my mom. The visitor's room was large with gray walls and several tables throughout. A few vending machines sat at one end of the room. I took out the three dollars I had in my pocket and thought about getting a snack for us, but I had no idea what my mom liked. Deciding to wait for her so I could ask, I refolded the bills, then slipped them back into my pocket.

Wiping my sweaty palms on my dark wash jeans, I quietly

repeated Beverly's words. "Expectations are your friend. Don't sell yourself short."

As I finished my little pep talk, I noticed the people sitting at the table next to me giving me odd looks. I sent them an apologetic smile then clasped my hands in my lap to keep from fidgeting.

I caught sight of short blonde hair by the doorway, and even though she looked much different than I remembered, I instantly knew it was my mom. The bright fabric of the jumpsuit she was wearing didn't do her fair complexion any favors. I always did hate the color orange.

Standing up quickly, I braced myself for some kind of greeting as she came closer. I'm not sure what I was expecting. A hug maybe? Even a handshake would've been better than nothing.

I'd had more hugs in the past few weeks than I had in my whole life. Sad, but true.

Hugs were normal to me now, so I was disappointed when she just pulled her chair out and sat down.

Now that she was closer, I was able to tell how much she'd changed since the last time I saw her. The skin on her face was weathered and her hair was so thin in some places I could see her scalp. Her lips were pressed into a thin line and there was no warmth behind her gaze.

"Angel," she said, and I slowly sat back down across from her. "You're the last person I expected to see on my visitors list. You turned out real pretty. Even prettier than I was at your age." While her compliments were nice, her tone was distant. Cold. "How old are you now?"

"Eighteen." I tried not to feel hurt that she didn't know my age. Did she even remember my birthday?

"So, what brings you out this way? You're a long way from home."

The first response that came to mind was that I didn't have a home anymore, but I couldn't bring myself to say that out loud.

"Claire died," I stated quietly.

She nodded. "Yeah, they told me a while back. I'm sorry about that. Not much I could do about it in here."

"I understand," I said, wanting her to know I didn't hold a grudge. I wanted her to know I forgave her and we could start with a clean slate. "And, well, that's the thing. You're the only family I have left now—"

"You didn't come all the way out here for me, did you?" she interrupted me. "I can't be any help to you while I'm locked up."

"But you're getting out soon. I thought maybe I'd find a place for us. I can get a job. We could start over…" I trailed off from my rehearsed speech because she was slowly shaking her head.

"Angel, I can't be your mom. I wanted to love you. I tried for seven years to love you and I just couldn't," she said, completely emotionless.

I sat silently because I couldn't process what she was saying.

"I wanted to love you, but I couldn't," she repeated. "I wasn't meant to be a mother. Do you understand what I'm saying?"

"No," I whispered.

I really didn't understand. I *couldn't* understand. Weren't mothers supposed to love their children? It was simple biology. The laws of nature and whatnot.

This wasn't going how I pictured at all. Not even close. She wasn't happy to see me. She wasn't surprised or mad or confused.

She was completely *indifferent*.

That was worse than any worst-case scenario I'd thought of.

Pulling out the postcard, I set it on the table in front of me.

"You sent this to me." I tapped it with my finger twice before sliding it over to her before demanding, "Why?"

She studied it as if it was the first time she'd seen it, then flipped it over to see her name scrawled on the back.

"I was probably high as a kite. Most things I did back then didn't make any sense." She shrugged and slid it back towards me.

"But you remembered I liked the otters…"

She gave me a look of pity and it was the first emotion I'd seen from her during our meeting.

"Listen, honey," she started, but the term of endearment didn't sound affectionate. It sounded condescending. "Don't rearrange your life for me. I wouldn't do it for you."

And there it was. The cold, hard truth.

I felt so stupid. This whole idea had been so stupid. I was the fool who traveled over three thousand miles to see someone who left me and never looked back.

At least now I knew where I got my straightforwardness from. Heartbreak mixed with anger—mostly anger at myself—and I knew I needed to get out of here.

The chair I'd been sitting in made a terrible scraping sound against the floor as I pushed away from the table.

I pulled the three dollar bills out of my pocket and placed them on the table between us. "For the vending machines."

She picked up the money but didn't say anything. Not even a thank you.

I looked at the stranger still sitting across the table, and suddenly I knew that's what she was—a stranger.

"It's your loss," I said. "I know that's a clichéd thing to say, but I mean it. I could be one of the best people you've ever met and you don't even know it. You're missing out."

I walked a few steps before I turned back and said the last word I'd ever say to my mother. "'Bye."

~

As much as I tried to hold back, several tears and sniffles escaped on the bus ride back to the motel. No one seemed to notice. Either that, or they didn't care. Maybe it was common for people to cry while riding away from the prison.

Ten years of hopes and dreams were just... Gone.

The bus came to a stop and the tears fell steadily as I stepped off onto the curb in front of the motel. A wall of intense midday California heat hit me but I barely noticed.

I swiped at the wet tracks coating my cheeks but they were quickly replaced with more tears. I sat down on a nearby bench and took out the tissues I'd known I was going to need.

When I bought them, I'd imagined they would be used for happy tears. I'd come prepared for a heartfelt reunion. Obviously, that was just wishful thinking.

Letting out a shaky sob, I mentally beat myself up for being the way I was. Naïve. Trusting. Gullible. Unrealistically optimistic.

My mother's brutally honest words repeated over and over again in my mind.

Don't rearrange your life for me. I wouldn't do it for you.

I took out the old postcard and looked at it through blurry eyes. It was a lie. A silly dream I'd conjured up out of nothing. My mother didn't send this to me because she was thinking of me or missing me. It was the result of some drug binge she couldn't even remember.

She didn't abandon me because she loved drugs more than

me—she left because she didn't love me at all.

Suddenly angry, I ripped it up. I ripped and tore and shredded it until tiny unrecognizable pieces slipped through my fingers and blew away in the breeze.

Burying my face in my hands, I cried for the past relationship that had been lost and the future relationship that would never exist.

My motherless life flashed before my eyes.

I would never get to hear her say she was proud of me. I didn't realize until now how much I'd longed for those words. There would be no sewing lessons or piano duets. No cinnamon rolls on Christmas morning.

She wouldn't be there on my wedding day. She wouldn't help me pick out the perfect dress and she wouldn't cry in the front row because her baby girl was getting married.

When I had kids of my own, she wouldn't be there to answer pregnancy questions or give me motherly advice. Someday when my child was sick and I was scared and I needed someone to talk to, I wouldn't be able to call her.

She would miss my whole life and she was okay with that.

It was what she *wanted*.

I gave up everything to come here. To give her a chance. To make things right with her. I left the place that felt like home and the people who had quickly become like family.

I'd left the love of my life for this.

Maybe now I could give up on this silly California dream. I could go back to Illinois, back to Travis. Maybe I could build a life there.

But as comforting as those thoughts should've been, I couldn't get past the devastation I was feeling. My heart was too busy mourning the loss of my mother.

CHAPTER 52

Travis

When you're young and you've never been in love before, it's easy to live in the *now*. Because you have no
idea what's on the *other side* of now.

I wasn't prepared for the pain I was feeling. It actually hurt.

And now I knew why they called it heartbreak, because it
felt like my chest was splitting in two. I rubbed the area over
my sternum, trying to ease the ache I felt deep inside.

Before Angel came along, I was happy.

I had a good life. Great, even.

I thought I had everything I needed. Family and friends. A
job I loved.

At the risk of sounding like a complete sap, I'd say she was
the missing piece I never realized was missing in the first place.
Angel filled up a place in my heart that had never been touched
before.

And now, her absence left a void that felt enormous. So
empty.

My biggest regret was not telling Angel the depth of my
feelings for her.

That I loved her. I loved her so much it hurt.

I lost count of how many times I'd almost said the words.
But I'd been a complete pussy about it and kept my mouth
shut.

I told myself the reason was because I didn't want to scare her away. That it was too soon.

It was a pathetic excuse. The truth was, I'd been a coward. I was too afraid she wouldn't say it back.

Well, fuck that.

The regret ate away at me until I couldn't take it anymore.

I was half-way across Utah when I decided to turn around. This wasn't something I wanted to tell Angel over the phone. Even if she didn't say it back, I still needed to see her face when I said the words.

Unfortunately, it meant I'd be delayed by two days getting back home.

I fueled up at a truck stop outside Salt Lake City, then decided to call Hank.

"Yo," he answered on the third ring.

"Hey, ah, I'm not gonna make it back in time," I said, feeling guilty for putting him in a tight spot. "I'm sorry."

He let out an obnoxious laugh. "Can't say I'm surprised. I already had a rental truck on reserve, just in case."

"Seriously?" Sometimes he knew me better than I knew myself. "I'll pay for it. I'll pay back whatever it costs."

"Nah, don't worry about it. You just do what you need to do, son."

"Thanks, Hank. You're awesome."

"Ten-four," he laughed, then hung up.

Although I felt bad about it, there wasn't anything that could've kept me from going back to Angel. Lucky for me, my boss was a pretty understanding guy.

After setting my phone back down in the cup holder, I put the semi in gear and headed west. Motivated by the thought of seeing my girl, I drove straight through the night.

As I pulled into the motel parking lot, I wasn't sure if my excess of energy was coming from all the coffee I drank or the anticipation of being with Angel again. Maybe it was a little bit of both.

I hopped on the balls of my feet as I knocked on her motel room door.

No answer.

I checked the time on my phone and realized she was probably visiting her mom right now, so I decided to wait in my truck. After finding a good country radio station, I leaned back in the seat and stared out at the crappy motel.

I must've dozed off at some point. When I jolted awake, I realized I'd been in the parking lot for over an hour. Thinking I might have missed her, I knocked on Angel's door one more time.

Still no answer.

If she'd come back by now, she probably would've seen my truck. It was kind of hard to miss.

Still amped by the thought of seeing her, I hopped back into the semi. Finding a station with upbeat music, I raised the volume to a level that would ensure I didn't fall asleep again. Pharrell William's 'Happy' blasted through the cab and I tapped my fingers on my knee along with the beat.

About ten minutes later, I saw the bus pull up at the curb at the end of the parking lot and Angel stepped off. I sat up straighter and turned off the music, preparing to get out to meet her, but instead of heading to her room, she slumped down onto the bench by the motel office.

I sat back in the seat as I watched the scene unfold before me. Although she wasn't dressed up, I could tell she tried to look her best today because her hair was styled straight.

Her shoulders shook as she buried her face in her hands, but at first, I couldn't tell what kind of crying it was.

Was she emotional because the visit went well? Was she overwhelmed with happiness because she finally reconciled with her mom?

Or had it gone badly? Maybe she didn't get to see her mom and she was disappointed.

When I saw her remove the postcard from her back pocket and rip it up, I knew I had my answer. She treasured that scrap of paper. There was only one reason she would destroy it.

Getting out of the truck I walked towards her, but she was so wrapped up in her grief that she didn't even notice me.

I sat down next to her and wrapped my arm around her.

At first she flinched, probably thinking I was some random dude.

"Baby…" I whispered and her breathing hitched at the sound of my voice. "Angel, please don't cry. God, it kills me when you cry."

"Travis?" she squeaked as she buried her face in my chest.

"Shhh. It's okay. I'm right here."

Several minutes went by as she soaked the front of my shirt. I rubbed her back and placed random kisses on the top of her head, wishing there was something I could do to fix this.

Without lifting her face, she took a deep breath and I could tell she was ready to explain what happened.

"S-she doesn't love me." She hiccupped as she finally started to spill the details of the visit with her mom. "She said so herself. Like, she actually said those words. She told me she'd tried and she just couldn't."

Angel wiped her nose with a tissue and sat up to look me in the eye.

Her face was red and puffy, and I used my thumbs to wipe at the black mascara running down her cheeks. Even like this, she was still the most beautiful girl I'd ever seen.

"I'm so sorry, baby," I said, knowing it wasn't enough.

Knowing it wouldn't take away her pain.

"What does that say about me? My own mother couldn't love me."

Her conclusion that she was unlovable hit me deep. The one person in this world who was supposed to love her unconditionally made her feel like she was unworthy of love.

I hadn't exactly done anything to help in that department by withholding my true feelings.

Well, that was going to end right now.

"Angel, that doesn't say anything about the kind of person *you* are." My tone was serious. "It says everything about the kind of person *she* is."

She didn't look convinced. It was time to break out the big guns.

"I love you," I breathed out, and my voice shook. "I should've told you before I left. I've wanted to say it for a while now. And this is a pretty shitty time and place to say it." I glanced at our surroundings. "But I promise to make it up to you. I'll say it every day—"

"Travis?" Angel interrupted my rambling. If I'd been paying attention, I would've seen the transformation on her face. Minutes ago she'd been devastated, but now a radiant smile was shining back at me. "I love you, too."

Best words I'd ever heard.

"Thank fuck." I sighed.

She giggled, and I touched my forehead to hers. I kissed her and pushed my tongue past her lips. They tasted salty from her tears and I licked at them, wanting to take away any evidence of her sadness.

Before we could get too carried away, she pulled back, breaking the kiss.

"What are you doing here?" she asked, confused, as if she was now just realizing I was supposed to be halfway across the country.

"I had to tell you I love you."

"That's it? You came back just for that?" Her bright smile told me she was really happy about that, and I knew coming back had been the right decision.

I nodded. "You're kind of the most important thing to me. And I kind of love you a lot."

She launched herself at me, wrapping her arms around my neck. I pulled her onto my lap so she was straddling me, and I was reminded of our first kiss on my couch. My heart sped up at the thought of what this could mean for her—what this could mean for *us*.

"Come home? With me?" I pulled back so she could see my face. I wanted her to know how much I meant it.

"Hmm, maybe," she teased, scrunching her face up while she pretended to think it over. "I guess I don't have anywhere else to go." Then her face got serious. "I'll try to find a job and I can get my own place."

"No," I barked out a bit too forcefully, then I softened my tone. "No. I don't want you to find a place. I want you to live with me."

"But people will think we're crazy!" she exclaimed. "Don't you think it's too soon?"

I smiled because it was a ridiculous question. "Angel, nothing about our relationship has been conventional. But I don't care. This is us. This is how we started, and I want it with you. I want everything."

I took her beautiful face in my hands and rubbed my nose over hers.

She placed her hands over mine and said the second-best words I'd ever heard her say.

"Let's go home."

CHAPTER 53

Travis

On the way home, we stopped at a rest stop outside of Reno and we made love in the back of the semi.

I was sitting sideways on the bed with my back against the wall as she moved her hips on top of me. Her tits were level with my face and I took one into my mouth while I palmed the other.

I let her take control, let her grind down onto me. This position was a particular favorite of Angel's and I wasn't complaining. Also, I was tired as fuck, so letting her do the work was fine by me.

Well, most of the work. She gasped as I gripped her hips and thrusted up into her. Her body started to shake and I knew she was close. I slipped my hand between us and circled her clit with my thumb.

She threw her head back, pushing her tits into my face, and I gently bit down on her nipple.

"I love you," she whispered, right before she cried out and her pussy clamped down on my cock.

Her orgasm triggered my own and I spilled into her tight heat. I stayed inside her for a couple more minutes while we kissed. She didn't like it when I left her right away. I loved that.

After that, I needed a nap.

"Are you okay? Really okay?" I asked her, still concerned.

We were driving through the middle of Oklahoma and it was one of the most boring strips of highway in the country.

"Yeah. And no," she replied. "It just makes me…" She paused as she searched for the right word, and tears appeared in her eyes. She swallowed thickly before continuing. "…sad. I know that's not a very elaborate explanation. But it makes me sad."

She was right—it was a very simple way to describe how she was feeling, but it was enough. Even the simplest words could be powerful.

"When I was a kid, I thought I was so lucky," she went on. "Out of all the moms in the world, somehow I ended up with the best. I really believed that." She let out a humorless laugh and shook her head. "I actually felt sorry for the other kids because their moms weren't as good as mine. Even after she left, I held on to the idea that she cared. That she was somewhere, missing me, regretting the worst decision of her life."

With no idea what to say, I stayed silent. How could I tell her I was happy with the way things turned out? I was getting everything I wanted. She was here, in my truck, heading back home.

To *our* home. And it wasn't temporary this time.

"I don't want to hate her, Travis," Angel whispered.

"You don't have to hate her," I said. "But you don't have to love her either. You don't owe her anything. You've gone the last ten years without her. You don't need her. Not needing her and hating her are two separate things. She can just be someone you used to know."

She frowned. "Well if that isn't depressing, I don't know

what is. But you're right."

"I wish things had gone better for you." I hated that she was hurting. Her pain was my pain. "But am I a selfish bastard for being happy that you're with me now?"

"No." she smiled a little. "California isn't where I belong, anyway. Even if things had gone well... I'm not sure I would have decided to stay. My home is with you in the middle of a cornfield."

I chuckled. "Damn straight. And all those things you wanted with your mom... Someday when we have kids, you can still do those things with them."

Glancing over, I registered the shock I knew I'd see on her face. Mentioning the future this soon in the relationship could've been considered taboo, but I didn't care. I had already told her I loved her and I meant it.

"Our kids?" She raised her eyebrows at me.

I nodded. "Yep. I'm in this for the long haul, baby," I said cockily, making her laugh. "And you know how much I love long hauls."

CHAPTER 54

Travis

I threw a piece of popcorn at Angel's face and she tried to catch it with her mouth. Missing my intended target, it tapped her on the nose and she giggled.

A buttery kernel came flying at me and I caught it on my tongue. I crunched on it happily while Angel shoved an over-sized handful into her mouth.

We were sitting at opposite ends of the couch, facing each other, ignoring whatever was on the TV.

A week had passed since we left California, and we effortlessly fell back into our usual routine. It was just as good as it had been those first three weeks, only now we didn't have the feeling of impending doom looming over us.

Angel was here to stay.

This was the new normal for us. Easy. Fun. So fucking happy.

"So…" She chewed up the popcorn before continuing. "I think I know what I want to be when I grow up."

"Oh, yeah?" I tossed another piece her way and she caught it between her teeth. "What's that?"

"Beverly thinks I'd be a good in-home health aide for the elderly. There's a certification program at the community college. It only takes one semester."

"I think that's a great idea." Honestly, I couldn't think of a more perfect career for her.

"And my savings will cover the tuition. But I really do need to find a job in the meantime."

Angel had been asking around about job openings and even filled out a couple applications in Daywood, one of which was at her favorite thrift shop. She hadn't heard back from them yet, but I knew she had her hopes up.

"You could always get a job at Buck's," I suggested, already knowing what her response would be.

Her face screwed up like she smelled something bad. "Oh, yeah," she scoffed. "Kendra would love to have me working with her. I'm sure we'd end up being BFFs."

She pelted the next piece of popcorn at me with more force than necessary and it bounced off my forehead.

Using the back of my hand, I brushed the butter and salt off my skin before calmly setting my bowl off to the side on the coffee table. Then I started prowling towards her on the couch, closing the distance between us.

"Travis?" She held her container of popcorn between us, as if it was a shield. "What are you doing?"

"You wanna play, baby? We can play," I taunted with a hint of warning.

Prying the bowl from her fingers, I set it down on the floor before crawling over her body.

Bringing my hands up to the sides of her stomach, I started to wiggle my fingers along her ribs. I knew it was her most ticklish spot.

"Don't! Don't you dare, Travis," she said through giggles. "I'll pee! I'll pee my pants!"

She always made that threat, but I had yet to see her follow through on it.

"You two need to get a room," Colton said as he walked through the front door.

"I have absolutely no problem with that." I smirked.

Standing up from the couch, I picked Angel up and threw her over my shoulder. She laughed as I carried her down the hallway to the bedroom.

"You guys are a couple of lovesick fools!" Colton called after us.

I kicked the door shut with my foot and tossed Angel down onto the bed. Our bed.

Lovesick. Fool. Crazy. People could call us whatever they wanted. It didn't matter because it all added up to one thing.

Happiness.

EPILOGUE

Angel

The smell of cinnamon invaded my nose and I sighed as I rolled over in the bed. I was momentarily disappointed when I realized I was alone, but it quickly turned to excitement when I remembered what day it was.

Christmas.

And I knew that smell. No, it wasn't cinnamon rolls, but it was my favorite breakfast. The same breakfast Travis made for me on my birthday and almost every Sunday morning since I permanently moved in.

The snow fell steadily outside, piling up on the window sill. I almost didn't want to leave my warm cocoon in the bed, but my growling stomach urged me to get up.

When I found Travis at the stove in the kitchen, I didn't hesitate to come up behind him and wrap my arms around his stomach. I kissed the warm skin between his shoulder blades and he made a sound of contentment as he placed his hands over mine.

He turned to face me and tenderly brushed his nose over mine. "Merry Christmas, baby."

"Merry Christmas." I grinned.

It was our first Christmas together. The first of many.

The present sitting under the tree in the gold sparkly bag

was my gift to Travis. Deciding what to get for him had been difficult.

What did you give someone who already had everything they needed?

Since I sort of took over ownership of his favorite T-shirt (it was totally mine now), I decided to get him one for when he was on the road without me. The new shirt I bought him had a picture of two otters hugging and it said 'I miss my significant otter'. It wasn't an extravagant gift but it was so freaking cute.

Just in case he didn't like it, I also included a hand-made coupon for one naked FaceTime session. I knew for sure he'd love that.

I'd ended up getting a part-time job at the thrift store, and because of that and my classes I couldn't always go with Travis on his trips.

The days apart were hard for both of us, but my classes had ended and I was going to be getting an in-home health aide job after the new year. Planning the hauls around my schedule would be much easier once I had regular hours.

Travis set our plates down on the table and I eagerly dug in, moaning when the sweet icing hit my tongue.

While unattractively shoveling food into my face, I noticed Travis wasn't eating and he was much more quiet than usual. His lips were pressed into a thin line as he poked at the waffle, and his face was an ashen hue.

"Are you feeling okay?" I reached my hand up to feel his forehead and cheeks, noting that he didn't feel feverish. "You're looking a little green."

He shook his head. "No, I'm fine," he insisted with a tight smile before changing the subject. "So, what's on the agenda today?"

Travis

My stomach churned, and I was pretty sure there was a real possibility I might puke. The plate shook in my hands as I brought it over to the sink, dumping my unfinished breakfast into the garbage disposal.

Angel was still sitting at the table, talking about our plans for the day—something about presents here, then going to my mom's for lunch—but I wasn't able to concentrate on what she was saying.

Slipping my hand into the pocket of my pants, I wrapped my fingers around the cool metal that was burning a hole through my jeans.

I wanted today to be perfect. The ring had been sitting in the back of my sock drawer for over a month. A dozen different ideas had gone through my mind, and I still couldn't think of a way to ask Angel the most important question ever.

I knew people might say we were too young or that we hadn't known each other long enough. But I had zero fucks to give about that.

I'd known I wanted to marry her for a while now. She was it for me.

"Do you want coffee?" she asked, walking by me to the cupboard.

The T-shirt she was wearing—which was mine—rode up her backside when she reached for the mug on the second shelf, giving me a good view of her ass. Momentarily distracted, my nerves were pushed aside as I ogled the scrap of light blue lace stretched over her supple skin.

Suddenly, I couldn't wait a second longer. I took the ring out and held it in front of me in trembling fingers.

When Angel turned around, her gaze zeroed in on the

shiny object immediately and her eyes widened.

"Angel." My voice cracked, and I cleared my throat. "Will you—"

My question was cut off when she let out a squeal, snatched it from my hand, and shoved it onto her left ring finger. She turned her hand back and forth, looking at it in awe and admiring the way it sparkled in the light.

The ring was white gold with intricate designs etched into the band, giving it an antique look. The ¾-carat round-cut diamond in the center set me back a good amount, but it was worth it. This was something she would keep for the rest of her life. Hopefully.

"I was wondering when you were finally going to give me this thing!" she exclaimed.

"Wait," I said, taken aback. "You knew I had it?"

She shot me a look, unable to keep the smile off her face. "I'm the one who does your laundry, Travis. Your sock drawer? Really?"

Damn. I thought it was a good hiding place.

"I take it that's a yes, then?" I asked, relieved. Obviously, she liked it. And she put it on the correct finger, so that was a big plus.

"Oh! Sorry. So sorry," she quickly apologized as she pulled the ring off and handed it back to me. "You probably wanted to be the one to put it on me. Yes. That's a yes." She bounced excitedly as she held out her left hand.

I grinned as I looked at Angel.

Big blue eyes were shining at me with so much love, it took my breath away. There was a smudge of icing on her chin that begged me to lick it off. Her cheeks were flushed from excitement and her blonde hair was in total disarray from sleep. She brought a whole new meaning to the term 'bedhead'.

Fucking beautiful.

Picking up her hand in mine, I gave her finger a soft kiss.

"Thank you for being my forever," I said against her skin before sliding the ring home.

It was a perfect fit.

THE END

TRUCKER PLAYLIST

"Don't Worry Baby" by The Beach Boys

"On the Road Again" by Willie Nelson

"Highway 20 Ride" by Zac Brown Band

"Earth Angel" by The Penguins

"Must Be Doing Something Right" by Billy Currington

"Raining On Sunday" by Keith Urban

"Silver Wings" by Merle Haggard

"Wouldn't It Be Nice" by The Beach Boys

"From the Ground Up" by Dan + Shay

"Kiss me" by Ed Sheeran

"Another One Bites the Dust" by Queen

"Already Home" by A Great Big World

"Quit Your Life" by MxPx

"Happy" by Pharrell Williams

ANGEL'S SLOPPY JOES

1 lb. ground hamburger
¾ cup ketchup
1 teaspoon mustard
2 Tablespoons brown sugar
1 teaspoon white vinegar

Brown hamburger and drain extra grease. Add ketchup, mustard, brown sugar, and vinegar. Mix. Enjoy.

OTHER BOOKS

GOOD GUYS SERIES:

Trucker

Dancer

Dropout

Outcast

A Trucker's Christmas (Short Story)

Untamable

ACKNOWLEDGEMENTS

When I first decided to write a book, I had no idea I would need so many people to help me along the way. Thank you to my husband and kids for being so supportive of this new adventure. I couldn't have done this without your encouragement, especially on the days when I felt like giving up. And a special thanks to my hubby for volunteering to be my cover model. (That's right. The man on the cover is mine!)

Thank you to my betas Brittaney and Carole. You were the very first people to enthusiastically volunteer to read my book, and I appreciate you!

Thanks to my Newbs. Writing a book was incredibly lonely until you came along. Your support, knowledge, and encouragement has helped me so much.

Last, but certainly not least, thank you to my readers!

ABOUT THE AUTHOR

Jamie Schlosser grew up on a farm in Illinois, surrounded by cornfields. Although she no longer lives in the country, her dream is to return to rural living someday. As a stay-at-home mom, she spends most of her days running back and forth between her two wonderful kids and her laptop. She loves her family, iced coffee, and happily-ever-afters. You can find out more about Jamie and her books by visiting these links:

Facebook: www.facebook.com/authorjamieschlosser
Amazon: amzn.to/2mzCQkQ
Twitter: twitter.com/SchlosserJamie
Bookbub: www.bookbub.com/authors/jamie-schlosser
Newsletter: eepurl.com/cANmI9

Also, do you like being the first to get sneak peeks on upcoming books? Do you like exclusive giveaways? Most importantly, do you like otters?

If you answered yes to any of these questions, you should consider joining Jamie Schlosser's Significant Otters!
www.facebook.com/groups/1738944743038479

Made in the USA
Coppell, TX
19 November 2021

66064036R00177